Love Finds You ™

— I N —

NAZARETH

PENNSYLVANIA

Love Finds You™

— IN —

NAZARETH

PENNSYLVANIA

BY MELANIE DOBSON

summerside
PRESS™

Summerside Press™
Minneapolis 55438
summersidepress.com

Love Finds You in Nazareth, Pennsylvania
© 2011 by Melanie Dobson

ISBN 97-8-160936-194-5

All scripture quotations are taken from the King James Version
of the Bible.

The town depicted in this book is a real place, but all characters are
fictional. Any resemblances to actual people or events are purely
coincidental.

Cover design by Lookout Design | lookoutdesign.com

Interior design by Müllerhaus Publishing Group | mullerhaus.net

Back cover and interior photos of Nazareth, Pennsylvania, provided
by Melanie Dobson.

*Summerside Press™ is an inspirational publisher offering fresh,
irresistible books to uplift the heart and engage the mind.*

Printed in USA.

Dedication

....

In memory of my (fifth) great-grandparents,
Johann Beroth and Catharina Neumann,
who married by lot in Bethlehem, Pennsylvania (1758).
Two hundred and fifty years later, their legacy endures.

And to Lyn Beroth, whose passion for our
family's heritage inspired this story.
Thank you for encouraging me to research and write
about those who followed the Savior before us.

Nazareth, Pennsylvania

THE WINDOWS OF NAZARETH GLOW EVERY CHRISTMAS, EACH ONE lit with a solitary candle that beckons visitors inside, out of the snow. Pine wreaths wrapped in ribbons decorate painted doors, white stars adorn wooden and stone homes alike, and twinkling lights color the evergreen that towers on Center Square.

The citizens of Nazareth embrace the Christmas season with both cheer and quaint charm. And in the midst of the celebration, there is a constant reminder of the child who initiated this season, of the boy who lived an ocean away and almost two thousand years past in another village called Nazareth.

Pennsylvania's Nazareth is an eclectic mixture of old and new, colonial and contemporary. A gray stone hall, built in 1744 by the Moravians (Unity of the Brethren), anchors the east side of town, and sprinkled throughout the village are grand Victorian residences beside smaller clapboard homes.

The town is located in the Lehigh Valley, between the city of

Philadelphia and the Pocono Mountains. Bethlehem, another town founded by Moravians, is a short drive south.

In Nazareth, you can enjoy sandwiches for lunch at the local copy shop and have an assortment of all-you-can-eat grilled meat at the Brazilian Steakhouse for dinner. You can walk across the plaza below the grand manor built for Count Zinzendorf in the 1750s or up to the tower on a quiet hillside above the town, where the first Moravian brothers and sisters were buried. From the Indian Tower, you can see miles and miles of hills, farmland, and forest.

Six thousand people now make Nazareth their home. While there are a variety of different denominations and faiths represented among the residents, Moravian tradition is still embedded in the culture of Nazareth. And the history and heritage of the Moravian people is threaded through the heart of the town.

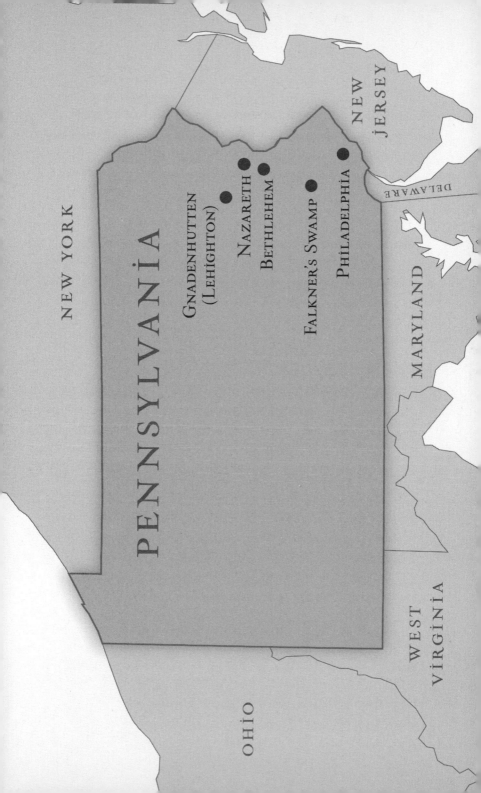

Prologue

....

May 1754

Susanna couldn't concentrate on the Count's eloquent words, not when her groom stood just four paces behind her. Everything within her wanted to glance over her shoulder to see the color of Christian Boehler's eyes. And to see if there was a hint of love within them.

But she couldn't turn around. Her curiosity would only embarrass her future husband, with so many brothers and sisters behind them watching the great wedding, solemnly attentive, while her mind danced around the possibilities of life with her new husband and the adventure before them.

Instead of turning, Susanna fiddled with the ribbon that zigzagged up her bodice while trying to listen to Count Nicholas Ludwig von Zinzendorf as he performed the ceremony from the front of the castle's great *Saal*. Even as she tried to cherish the significance of this day, the beginning of her marriage, and her journey as a messenger, she couldn't concentrate on what the Count was saying.

Her laboress had told her stories about Christian Boehler's dedication to their Savior and of his burden to share their Savior's love with the Indians in the Colonies. Her burden was the same, but she also wanted to love her husband and be loved by him.

Susanna rocked back on her heels. God had given her a man who

11

served Him, but would he love her as well, in their journey together, like a man should love his wife?

Eleven other brides were fanned out beside her in a giant horseshoe for the Great Wedding. Their grooms stood in a curved row a few steps behind them, and then at the back of the large hall were a hundred brothers and sisters on benches, witnesses to their matrimony.

Morning light stole through the lofty windows on both sides of the room, trailing like a veil down the ancient castle's hall. Outside the windows, rolling hills surrounded the German community and castle, blooming with the purples and yellows of spring color.

As Count Zinzendorf spoke to them about the blessed society of marriage and the beautiful mystery of it, Susanna's mind wandered far from the walls of Marienborn. For a moment, she longed to be roaming through the coolness of the hills this morning and talking to the Savior instead of marrying a man she'd never before spoken with.

If only she knew why Christian had selected her to be his wife.

Couples were divided into pairs for the wedding, and in front of each pair of couples stood an elder who would speak to them when the Count completed his sermon. She and Catharine Weicht and their grooms had been paired with Elder Seidner, a young minister who shifted the book of marriage vows back and forth in his hands as if the words burned his fingers.

Beyond the rows of grooms and brides and six elders—the leaders of their community—the regal Count Zinzendorf continued to speak. A large, imposing man, the Count had black hair and an aura that spoke of both power and love. Other members of the German royal court powdered their hair white, but the Count rarely powdered his. Even without the powder and robes, his demeanor could intimidate his subjects if necessary.

The Count was a man who pursued the heart of God, and as part of this pursuit, he had opened up his estate to those persecuted for their faith, those known as the Unity of the Brethren. During the past thirty years, he had been leading all of them into deep, fulfilling relationships with their Savior.

Each bride was simply dressed, with a white cape draped over her bodice and a petticoat dyed blue or green. They all wore white *haubes*—caps with delicate pink or white ribbons tied under their chins. Widows wore white ribbons while the single sisters wore pink.

Susanna's ribbon was pink.

She blinked in the sunlight, her hands brushing the smooth ribbon that would change within the hour. If only her mother could have been here for her wedding day. She could almost hear the soft but determined voice of her mother, calming her fears, reminding her of her dedication to the will of their Savior and not to herself, reminding her of their Savior's love.

Her mother knew firsthand of this love. Their Savior had taken her to Him eight years ago while she served alongside Susanna's father as a messenger of the Gospel to the African people.

As Susanna stood before the elder, she pretended that her parents were sitting on the benches behind them. Her mother to comfort her. Her father to tell Christian about the Fritsche family's past and to talk to him about the future.

But she stood today in the company of her sisters instead of her family.

When she glanced to her right, Catharine Weicht winked at her, and Susanna smiled at the boldness of her friend on this somber day. In spite of her plainness of dress, Catharine was anything but plain. The waves of her auburn hair were pinned up neatly under her cap. Her ivory skin was as pure and pretty as the edelweiss that bloomed wild in the hills around them. Instead of the humility borne by the other sisters, her friend's presence breathed the air of aristocracy that ran through her veins.

On Susanna's left side stood a young widow, a white ribbon tied under her chin. With her dappled skin and slightly crooked nose, Rebecca wasn't nearly as pretty as Catharine, but Susanna admired Rebecca for her devout relationship with the Savior. Even though she was just five years older than Susanna, Rebecca had already lost her husband on a mission to Greenland, and she'd made it clear she would never marry again. Yet here she stood, chosen like the rest of them. No one argued with the lot.

The Count had divided their community into groups and called them each a *choir* hoping, perhaps, that the many different personalities in each choir would learn to live in harmony. There were choirs for both married men and women as well as single choirs. Boys and girls choirs. The widows choir and the choir for widowers. Each choir was led by a laborer or laboress, and they lived, ate, and worshipped together like a family, separated from the other choirs.

Women remained with the Single Sisters Choir until one of the single brothers conferred with their laborer about the possibility of marriage to a certain woman. The elders prayed about their request and then put it before the lot, just as they did with every major decision in their community. Sometimes the chosen lot was a blank piece of parchment that simply meant to wait. Sometimes the elders picked the paper that said "no," and sometimes they selected the paper that confirmed the marriage. The requested woman was then given the option to decline or to accept the proposal.

Together, Catharine, Rebecca, and Susanna had faithfully served in the Single Sisters Choir in Marienborn for more than two years until the lot matched them with a man to wed. After the lot matched her with Christian Boehler, Susanna was given the opportunity to reject their marriage. But who was she to reject what God had so clearly ordained? Even though she'd never actually spoken with Christian, she had watched him from afar. He was a respected member of their community, but even more than that, her heart sparked with the possibility of going with him to the new colony. She could roam the wilderness with Christian Boehler and share Jesus's love with people who might never have heard of Him. She would befriend the Indian women and be the best possible companion to her husband.

Behind her, the congregation began to sing "Oh Creator of my Soul." As Susanna mouthed the words, she glanced over at Catharine again and saw the graceful smile on her friend's face.

Catharine was the daughter of an English noble, her father once a member of Parliament who had left his esteemed position to join the United Brethren. He and Catharine's fashionable mother now traveled around Europe, sometimes alongside Count Zinzendorf, to speak with leaders about their church.

Even though she lived in the common room with all the sisters, Catharine still treated her sisters like servants. Susanna didn't fault Catharine for her upbringing or for her demands—the Savior was transforming all of them—but she tried to gently remind Catharine that they all lived and served in humble circumstances.

No matter how or where they had been reared, all the sisters were clothed in modest apparel—though Susanna knew that Catharine wore maroon stockings under her long dress while the other women wore gray or blue. The sisters slept on the same straw mattresses and ate the same soups and breads at mealtime.

Susanna hadn't been educated like Catharine. There'd been no governess for her or years of training at an exclusive boarding school to teach her how to handle stress with dignity and grace. She often wrestled with the jealous feelings that conflicted with her devotion to both her Savior and her friend.

She wasn't jealous of the fine home where Catharine had been reared or the lofty manners that embarrassed the other girls. Susanna was jealous of Catharine's vast knowledge based on years of education in the finest schools for girls. Catharine could read and write and paint, and she knew about faraway peoples and places.

It was Catharine who had told Susanna about the town of Philadelphia and the wilds beyond in the tiny community of Nazareth, where Susanna and Christian would live when they weren't visiting the Indians. Catharine told her about the fierce warriors in the Colonies and the Indians who sought peace by sharing and even selling their land to the white men.

Susanna and Christian. Catharine and her betrothed, Elias Schmidt. They had all been selected to travel to the new colony of Pennsylvania after their wedding.

"Be content again my soul, for the Lord does good to you," the Count said when the singing ended, sharing the watchword for their wedding. "Do not forget it, oh my heart!"

Susanna's gaze wandered over the shoulder of Elder Seidner, out the wide window behind him to the hills. She knew she shouldn't wonder at Christian's feelings, not when she didn't even understand her own.

She wished her heart were filled with love for Christian, like what some of the other brides felt for their betrotheds, but fear filled the hollows of her heart instead. She admired the man behind her greatly, had admired him since the moment he'd marched through the gates of their castle five months earlier. Though she'd admitted it to no one, she thought him to be one of the most handsome men she'd ever seen, and she respected his strength and his passions and his desire to serve their Savior as a messenger in the Colonies.

But she didn't know why he'd chosen her.

The Count paused, and Elder Seidner motioned Christian and Elias forward. She felt Christian step up beside her, saw the outline of his shoulder beyond her own.

What would it feel like to have Christian Boehler take her in his arms and kiss her, as the laboress in their choir house described? What would it be like to lie next to him in the bedchamber? She trembled at the thought, not knowing whether it was from pleasure or from fear of the certainty that she would fail him.

She wasn't educated nor was she beautiful like Catharine. She didn't have the manners of politer society or even the knowledge of how to speak with a man. Her father had left for Africa a decade ago, and her memories of him were pleasant but few.

Every day in Marienborn, she saw both the married and single brothers—she sat across the aisle from them at the love feasts and the foot washings and the quarter-hour devotions—but she never spoke with them and certainly had never touched one of them. She didn't know how to be this man's—or any man's—wife.

Across the room, a minister began conducting the marriage vows to one of the other couples, and then all the ministers began to speak as they joined the men and women in front of them. Susanna listened as Elder Seidner joined Elias and Catharine in marriage. Then he turned to Christian.

"Brother Boehler, will you love Sister Susanna Fritsche as thy wedded wife, to live together in holy wedlock?"

As she turned, Susanna was close enough to see Christian's light brown eyes that were tinged with yellow in the sunlight. But she didn't see the hope in them that she desired. Or love. Instead, she saw regret.

Her gaze dropped to the hem of his black coat, and her entire body shook from disappointment. Already she had failed the man, before she even married him.

The vow hung between them, waiting for his response.

Was it too late for them to change their minds? Maybe Christian could ask for another spouse before he left for Pennsylvania and Susanna could travel as a single sister?

She clenched the seams of her dress as she waited for Christian's refusal, but instead of rejecting her, he vowed to love her as his wife. Her stomach twisted like the cotton in her fingers.

How could Christian agree to live with her, to marry her, when he didn't love her?

The elder nodded at Christian's words and then looked to her. "Sister Fritsche, will you love Brother Christian Boehler, honor him, and be subject unto him in the Lord?"

Susanna's gaze wandered back to the window as she pondered the words. She could honor this man and even be subject to him, but why did the elder ask her to love a man who didn't love her?

She scanned the hills in the distance and wished again that she were outside this hall so she could think, breathe. Just days ago, she'd been dreaming about marriage to a man like Christian Boehler, but she wanted her husband to look at her the way Elias Schmidt looked at Catharine—like a thirsty soul who'd discovered a desert spring. A spring he would drink from for the remainder of his life.

"Sister Fritsche?" the elder whispered.

She lifted her eyes, not to Christian but to Elder Seidner. How could the Savior require this of her?

The elder nodded at her again, urging her to answer. The other elders in the room were quiet, the vows of the other couples complete. Everyone in the room was waiting for her now. Watching.

Susanna took a deep breath. With God's help, she would learn to love this man. And maybe one day he could learn to love her as well.

She summoned up the strength within her to match the confidence in Christian's voice.

"I will," she finally said. And she meant it.

Elder Seidner smiled. "I now pronounce you Brother and Sister Boehler."

Sister Boehler. The name echoed in Susanna's ears.

She had a new name now, a new identity.

But what would this new name require of her?

The Count began to pray. "Lord our God, You who have Yourself established and blessed the holy marriage, You wanted these husbands and wives to be bound together through the band of holy marriage, in order to do Your work together."

Beside her, Elias took Catharine's hand as the Count prayed. When Christian didn't reach for her hand, Susanna rubbed her fingers together. Even if her husband didn't love her, their marriage was blessed as holy, to work together as a couple to fulfill the greatest commission of all—to take the Gospel into all the world.

"In the name of Jesus Christ, our Head, Bridegroom, and Elder," the Count announced. "And in the name of our dear Father in heaven, we bring you honorably together and commission you to the colony called Pennsylvania."

The bell tolled above them. Trumpets blared in the courtyard below. One of the married women stepped forward and placed a new haube over Susanna's hair, a white cap with blue ribbons, to set her apart as a married sister.

Catharine's parents gathered around Catharine and Elias to offer their congratulations. Another married sister kissed Susanna's cheeks, saying how blessed she was. And in the midst of the kissing cheeks and shaking hands, Susanna glanced across the room to search for her new husband. She found him near the doors, shaking the hand of one of the other newly married brothers, and she longed for a simple word from his lips. He didn't have to call her "beloved" or even "wife"; she would be content with just a kind word from a brother.

As she watched, Christian turned and searched until he found her face in the crowd. The clamor around her seemed to silence, and though he stood far from her, in that moment it seemed as if they were alone.

His hat against his chest, Christian slowly nodded to her. Then his broad frame disappeared out the door.

Chapter One

....

August 1754

Candlelight flickered in Bethlehem's windows to welcome the weary travelers to their new home. Even though Christian's legs were worn from the days of walking from the harbor in New York to Pennsylvania, the lights invigorated him as he hurried up the hill with five of his brothers. If it weren't almost midnight, he might bypass Bethlehem all together and continue onto Nazareth, but they must stop and rest before continuing their journey in the daylight.

Signs on the sprawling stone houses announced which choir resided inside. There was a stone house for sisters who made up the Single Sisters Choir and an identical building for the brothers who remained single. There was a house for widows and one for the boys and the girls and another for the married sisters.

Christian pounded on the iron knocker of the residence of the married brothers, and the man who answered it introduced himself as Abraham, the laborer of their choir.

"Come in." Abraham waved them out of the night air and into the dining room. The windows of the house were open, and a small fire burned in the hearth. "We've been up petitioning the Lord on your behalf."

Abraham swung a kettle away from the fire and ladled hot coffee into mugs to fight off the night's chill. Footsteps pounded above them, and moments later, their married brothers, clad in nightclothes, poured into the room to greet them.

David Kunz jogged toward Christian, his long brown hair draped over his shoulders without a ribbon to tie it. He slapped Christian on the back. "I never thought I'd see you out in the wilderness."

Christian laughed at his old friend. "I've only come because you have need of me."

"We have need of twenty men like you."

Christian took a sip of the bitter coffee. David was a blacksmith by trade, but he was much more talented at playing an organ than he was with a hammer and anvil. "I've never known you to need another."

"We all need each other in Pennsylvania." David glanced toward the door. "I heard you were bringing a bride with you."

Bride?

The word tumbled in Christian's mind. He'd been married for three months now, but he still felt like a single brother.

David cocked his head. "Where is this fine and perhaps slightly mad woman who agreed to marry you?"

"She—" He hesitated. "Susanna and the other women traveled through Philadelphia to rest for a few days."

"Ah…but you never rest, do you?"

Christian shrugged his shoulders. "We had plenty of time for rest on the ship."

"When we were on the ship, Marie and I counted the days until we could finally arrive in Bethlehem, just so we could be *alone*." David winked at Christian as he drew out the word "alone."

Christian didn't return his friend's grin. Instead, he held out his hands near the fire, even though he wasn't cold.

How he had wanted to be like David, anxious to be alone with his bride. He couldn't tell his old friend, though, that he dreaded the appointed time for him and Susanna to be alone. Nor could he tell his friend that he hadn't taken the opportunity to speak with Susanna on their long journey across the ocean.

He didn't know what to say to her, but he had watched her from afar to make sure she was safe. He couldn't tell her exact hair color under her haube, not without staring at her, but he thought it was a honey brown. And she had a gentle smile that seemed to calm the fire in Catharine's spirit and the other sisters around her.

None of the newly married couples had private quarters on the ship, and no cabin had been set aside for weekly visits. The married brothers stayed together in a large room, just as they had when they were single, and the married sisters ate and rested and worshipped together as well. Christian was married in the eyes of the church, but nothing else had changed.

Elias stepped up beside them. "Are you talking about Christian's wife?"

"I was trying to, but the man won't tell me a thing about her."

"Her name is Susanna Fritsche," Elias told David.

"Is she handsome?"

"Of course," Christian interrupted before Elias replied on his behalf.

Elias rolled his eyes. "I think he is a bit frightened of her."

"Plenty of things frighten me, my friend, but I am not afraid of my wife."

"Of course not." Elias slapped his back, and the other men joined in his laughter.

"I've been married nine years now," David told him. "And I'm still a bit afraid of Marie."

"You are a wise man," Abraham said.

"And what of your wife?" David asked Elias.

"Ahh," the man sighed—and then he began quoting Song of Solomon. "She is the 'fairest among women.'"

David elbowed the man. "And her faults?"

"Catharine has no faults."

Christian choked on his coffee, but with David's laughter, no one seemed to notice.

"Well, then, you are blessed above all of us," David said.

Elias took a long sip of his coffee. "Indeed."

Christian stepped back from the fire, away from the laughter of the men, as Elias told them about the day he asked the elders for Catharine's hand and how the lot had concurred with his choice. And how he had worried as he awaited her decision.

"And then she said she would marry me," Elias explained to the others. "The elders said it was what she desired as well."

Christian cringed at the man's words. Surely Catharine had to question the lot.

As the Brethren peppered Elias with questions, Christian moved to the other side of the room. Nailed onto the hewn logs of the wall was a large map of the colony. Christian examined it for a moment until he found Bethlehem, and then he traced his finger north to Nazareth.

Nazareth was only ten miles away, and beyond that was the wilderness of the Pennsylvania Colony. The Brethren's scouts had sent back long reports as they visited different Indian nations, trying to determine the needs of the Indian men and women and how the Brethren could share the good news about Jesus's love and forgiveness with them. Christian had read every report given to him, multiple times. Even though he'd never actually met an Indian, God had called him to tell the friendly and savage Indians alike about their Savior. The desire to answer this call had beckoned him forth for months, all the way to Pennsylvania.

David joined his side and clamped his hand on Christian's shoulder, glancing at the map. "Are you ready to go on another journey so soon?"

Christian nodded. "If the elders permit it, I will leave in the morning."

"After your wife arrives, of course."

Christian wanted to discuss his mission, not his wife. "Have you been out to visit the Indian villages?"

David shook his head. "The elders keep me quite busy here at the blacksmith shop and playing doctor when necessary."

"I've heard so many stories," Christian continued. "I wonder what the Indians are really like."

A long pause followed his words, and then a voice boomed behind him. "They are very much like you."

Christian spun and found himself looking up at the face of an Indian man a half foot above him. Unlike David, the man's coal-black hair was pulled back with a tie, but his nightdress was the same as the other men. Instead of the stark white skin of the others, his skin was the yellowish-brown color of sand. He seemed older than Christian's twenty-seven years, though Christian wasn't certain about the man's age.

"I don't know." David responded with another laugh. "Christian doesn't look a bit like you."

"He is probably very glad of that."

"Brother Christian, this is our dear brother Samuel. He comes to us from the Delaware nation." He waved his hand toward Samuel. "Christian comes to us from the ship *Irene*."

Christian studied the Indian with a bit of awe. In the weeks they'd spent on the ocean, he'd prepared himself to meet a native, but he hadn't expected to meet one tonight, nor had he anticipated meeting an Indian who spoke English so well.

The Indian man seemed amused by his trepidation. "Most white men can't stop talking."

"Oh, Christian has plenty to say." David looked over at him in expectation, but when Christian still didn't reply, David added, "The night air has captured his tongue."

Samuel's eyes narrowed a bit. "Or maybe someone gave him beer instead of coffee."

"I apologize—" Christian set his mug on a table. "This is unexpected."

"Samuel and several other Indians joined our community last winter," David explained. "They have honored us with their gifts and their presence."

Christian nodded. He had traveled many miles to share the good news with the Indians, but for a moment, he wondered if Samuel had ever been a warrior…if he had ever scalped a white man.

When Samuel turned to walk back up the stairs, Christian felt like he had failed the man. He reached for his mug of coffee on the table and took another long sip.

David gestured toward the stairs. "The Savior will teach you how to love our Indian friends."

"I am here to teach them the truth."

"You can't just tell them," David explained. "You have to show them God's grace before you share the truth of salvation."

Christian winced. "It is the truth that burns within me."

"I pray God will teach you how to love the Indians." David paused. "And I pray he will teach you how to love your bride as well."

"I don't know what you mean—" Christian started to protest, but David silenced him with a wave.

Christian leaned back against the table.

Even as he coveted David's prayers, he knew he could never love Susanna Fritsche Boehler. Not when his heart longed for another.

Chapter Two
....

Twelve sisters rested on the mats and blankets spread across the weathered floor of the log church halfway between Philadelphia and Bethlehem, at a marshy place named Falkner's Swamp. Cool rain stole through the cracks in the walls and roof, misting Susanna's blanket and nightdress. Even with the wool blanket covering her shift, she shivered in the darkness.

"They should have split us into groups," Catharine whispered into Susanna's ear, "so we could all sleep in someone's home."

"We wouldn't be in homes. We'd be sleeping outside."

"We might be drier if we were in tents."

Her eyes closed, Susanna pulled the damp blanket up to her neck. Her body ached, and even though she desperately wanted sleep, it eluded her. The trip to America had been an arduous one for all of them. After four weeks of travel across Europe, they embarked on a ship in Holland, and for the next two months, they'd weathered storms and treacherous waves across the Atlantic until they'd finally anchored in the New York Harbor.

While they were on the *Irene*, Susanna had battled fierce headaches and nausea, but she thought her sickness was from the rolling waves. Once she got off that boat and onto solid ground, she'd assumed both the pain and nausea would disappear—but three days had passed and her sickness still clung to her like her damp clothes, reminding her of her weakness when she so wanted to be strong.

On the ship, she'd dreamed of the comforts of a featherbed, of hills to roam, of sunny skies and warm fires and roasted meat. Instead of resting or wandering in New York, though, they'd been whisked away from the shipyard on a wagon and bumped along for a good day to Philadelphia. Then they'd spent two nights on the floor of an inn before they started to Bethlehem.

While Susanna had yet to sleep in a bed, the sisters ate roasted pheasant in the village tonight for dinner. But instead of being satisfied with the food, her stomach still rumbled.

Catharine inched closer to her. "They should have let us go with Christian and Elias to Bethlehem."

"The men walked the entire way."

Catharine sniffed. "I would have walked."

"I wish I could have walked." But even if Susanna had wanted to go, her body wouldn't have allowed her to walk that far, not yet. She needed a few days' rest and some ginger tea and she would feel better again.

In Philadelphia, members of the Lutheran church had given them bags full of tea, coffee, chocolate, and spices for the celebration her congregation called a love feast. Tomorrow night they would celebrate what the Lord had done for them. A new home. A new mission. And most of all, that their Savior had brought them safely across the seas and land. He had provided a safe journey for them and friends to welcome them when they arrived.

Catharine pushed her wet blanket away from her. "I'm going to freeze."

"It's August," Susanna said with a sigh. "None of us are going to freeze."

One of the older sisters called to them from across the building. "And none of us will sleep, either, if you two don't stop talking."

Catharine ignored the woman. "If Elias were here, he would find me a warm and much drier place to sleep."

"If your husband were here," the woman said, "he would be sleeping outside with the rest of our men."

Catharine was silent for a moment, and in the silence, Susanna wondered what it would be like to long for Christian like Catharine longed for Elias. The farther they traveled, the more Susanna dreaded being alone with Christian Boehler. Even though he'd talked at length with the brothers on their journey, he'd made no attempt to be with her.

How was it that her husband had no desire to know the woman he'd married? She hardly expected that he would want to know her in a biblical way on the ship, but she thought he would at least ask where her family had come from before they joined the other families at Hernnhut on the Count's estate. She hoped he would wonder what pleasured her heart and what made her sad.

Long ago, her father's eyes sparked with adoration and desire whenever her mother walked into the room. They would hold hands and whisper late at night when they thought Susanna was asleep. They never seemed to stop talking or debating, but even when their voices were raised, Susanna knew they loved each other.

While she'd always wanted a marriage like her parents, she could learn to be satisfied with a husband who admired her even in the smallest way. What troubled her heart the most was that Christian didn't care enough to ask basic questions.

Tears dampened Susanna's cheeks, and she wiped them on the wet blanket. Many of the sisters told her how blessed she was to be chosen for a man like Christian, but right now her marriage felt more like a curse than a blessing.

Catharine elbowed her. "When we get to Bethlehem, we'll be able to sleep with our husbands."

"Catharine"—she hissed—"don't talk about that."

"Well, we will." Catharine paused. "And you and Christian will be able to sleep together every night on your mission."

Susanna rolled over. None of the women were quite as bliss-ful about their match as Catharine. But her friend—and the other women—had to know that Christian had no desire to be with his new bride. After three months of traveling in such close quarters, it was no secret which husbands and wives had desired to marry and which had not.

The laboress at Marienborn had clearly explained that the women were marrying messengers of the Gospel and a messenger's first call-ing was to follow God, not please his wife. She assured Susanna and the other women, though, that what God had brought together, He would make complete.

Even as Catharine continued talking about her husband, Susanna hummed softly to herself until she drifted to sleep.

Instead of dreaming about Christian or their journey ahead to the wilderness, Susanna dreamed about sweet rolls and hot coffee and featherbeds. When they arrived in Bethlehem tomorrow night, she prayed she would be well enough to celebrate their homecoming with the others.

* * * * *

Gray mantled the summer sky as two wagons filled with sisters clat-tered through the forest. The brothers walked beside the horses or trailed behind them, and Susanna stared into the cloak of branches and vines that surrounded all of them.

She hadn't slept well in the wet garret of the church last night, and instead of a cool morning to travel, the temperature climbed higher by the minute until the heat sucked out the little energy that remained in her body. As they rode toward Bethlehem, she struggled to keep her eyes open.

The wooden wheels hit another rut and tossed her around like the ship had while on the waves. She clutched the side board, pain shooting through her nerves as her body shook.

The driver tugged the reins on the horses to slow them. "The road is a bit bumpy," he told the women.

In spite of her pain, she smiled at the understatement of his words. How could he call this overgrown path a road? There would be a lot of changes in this new country, but it was the small, unexpected things, like the rutted roads through the wilderness instead of gravel or smooth stone, that reminded her of how they were no longer in Europe.

Their friends in Philadelphia had said the village of Bethlehem rose above the forest like the stone turrets of a castle, so she tipped her head back and tried to look above the covering of leaves. Soon she would be in a place where she could rest. She only had to stay strong for a little longer.

Catharine pushed back her hood. "Do you see anything?"

"Not yet."

Her friend scanned the trees. "My mother told me there are wolves in the Colonies...and snakes."

Rebecca shifted beside her. "Don't forget the Indians."

"There aren't any Indians in Nazareth," Catharine said. "And I'm staying in Nazareth."

A chill raced through Susanna. She rubbed her arms to ward it away, closing her eyes. Catharine wouldn't be going into the wilderness like some of the others—Elias had been sent to help oversee the building of the Disciple's House in Nazareth for Count Zinzendorf and his family.

Susanna had no desire to stay in Bethlehem or Nazareth or any of the Brethren's villages. As soon as she was better, she wanted to go to the Indian women and tell them how much God loved them. She'd heard the stories of the darkness that shadowed so many of them, of the witchcraft that bound them. It was the light she wanted them to hear about, a light that chased away the shadows.

Susanna knew she would miss her friend when she and Christian left for the Indian settlements. She didn't know how often they would return to Nazareth, but she guessed it wouldn't be often, if the journey back to Nazareth was as grueling as their journey during the past five days.

The wagon splashed into a creek, and Susanna opened her eyes. Rocks glistened pink and orange, and the colors reminded her of jewels sparkling in the sunset.

Catharine shook her arm and pointed upward. "Look!"

Her gaze rose from the beauty of the rocks to the twinkling lights above them, and tears soaked her eyes and tumbled down her cheeks. After months of journeying, they had finally arrived.

Faint strains of music greeted them as they rode up the hill, and a crowd of men and women flocked around the wagons. Susanna wiped away her tears as she scanned the group, longing to see a smile on her husband's face, welcoming her...but she didn't see Christian among them.

Elias stepped forward and took Catharine's hand.

"He must have been detained," Catharine whispered.

Susanna pulled her hood over her head. "Of course."

Catharine descended into Bethlehem like a noblewoman stepping out of her carriage, but Susanna didn't move. Every muscle in her body ached and shook under her cloak.

Instead of leaving her in the wagon, Elias held out his arm. "May I help you, Sister Boehler?"

Her legs trembled as she tried to stand. Looking behind Elias, she searched for Christian. She found his face in a window above the street.

Her head bowed, she took Elias's arm and stepped off the wagon, glad for the help of Catharine's husband since her own husband didn't greet her.

When she released her grip on Elias, her legs wobbled on the firm ground. Catharine reached for her hand, and together they walked into the stone *Gemeinhaus*, or meetinghouse.

A man was playing the organ in the front, and while the Saal wasn't nearly as grand as the one in Marienborn, it was a welcome sight. White benches were lined up on both sides, and a candle glowed at the end of each. Catharine guided Susanna toward the rows for the married women, and when Susanna sat down, she pushed back her hood.

The women worshipped in song as the men unloaded the trunks and bags of food for the love feast. They praised their Savior for bringing them safely through this journey. They sang about the beauty of His faithfulness, the strength of His love.

Even in her sickness, Susanna knew her Savior loved her. Even when she didn't understand His direction, she trusted Him to use her life as He saw fit. Though it sometimes hurt terribly, she would follow His guidance, even if it felt like she must travel this path alone.

Closing her eyes, she rested her head on Catharine's shoulder. The rocking from the boat had stopped, but her legs were sore from the bruises wrought by the wagon. And her muscles continued to ache.

Catharine gently elbowed her side, and Susanna sat up as fifty or so men walked through the doors and sat on the benches across from them. She didn't know most of the men, but she found Christian's face among them. He was looking at the front of the Saal, and she glanced away, worried that he might see her watching him.

Women dieners filed into the room after the men. Dressed in white, the dieners passed baskets of sweet rolls down each row for the men and women to eat for their love feast. Cinnamon and brown sugar dusted the top of the bread in Susanna's hands, and melted butter pooled in the middle. Her stomach rumbled as she sniffed its sweet aroma.

An elder prayed for them, and she bit into the roll and relished the warmth of the dough, the sweetness and butter. She'd never tasted anything quite as good.

Male dieners passed by with a tray of coffee mugs, and Susanna sipped the black coffee as the others sang.

"Not Jerusalem, lowly Bethlehem 'twas that gave us Christ to save us."

A single trombone accompanied the song along with the organ, and in the dim light, Susanna found Christian's face again across the Saal as he sat among the brothers. This time he was looking her way.

She searched his face, and his eyes were intent, an expression of fascination filling them and something else. Desire, perhaps.

Her heart leaped. Perhaps her husband did love her after all.

A smile stole across her face, but when he didn't return her smile, she ducked her head. And the bench felt like it collapsed under her.

Something was happening inside Christian Boehler. Something she didn't understand.

Chapter Three
....

Faint light crept through the solitary window in the hallway on the third floor of the Sisters House, but the dawn of morning did nothing to calm Christian. Pausing before Susanna's door, he listened for sounds of life, a foot shuffling or a voice praying. At the silence, he began pacing the floor again.

God had given him Susanna Fritsche as a wife, and while he wanted to serve her, he didn't know what to do with such a delicate and gentle woman. She deserved a husband who adored her, a husband who knew how to care for her in her sickness, but he'd failed to protect her, and he didn't know how to care for her now. He wanted to love Susanna as Christ loved the church, but even in his desire to love her, his heart warred within him. And envy plagued his very soul.

Stopping, he banged his fist on the wooden wall. He was commanded to love his wife and yet he couldn't stop himself from thinking about the woman he should have married, the woman he'd loved before the lot rejected his request to marry her. He desperately wanted to break free of this longing that gripped him. He felt trapped within himself even as he wanted to do what was right and love the woman God had given him.

Outside the window, the men were loading two wagons bound for Nazareth this very morning. For the past two years he had felt God's strong calling on his life to travel on a mission to the New World, and finally he had been sent from Marienborn as a messenger to the Indians—he and Susanna had both been sent to deliver the good news. But now the others were leaving for Nazareth without him and Susanna. And he didn't know when they would join them.

What if the others were commissioned in Nazareth and sent to the Indian villages before Susanna was well again? Where would the elders assign him to work if he remained in Nazareth or even in Bethlehem? The Brethren in these villages either traveled to the Indians or labored as a community to support those who had been sent.

His eyes had been on Catharine across the Saal two nights ago when Susanna had collapsed an hour after their journey ended. Many of the women became sick from exhaustion after such a long journey—David said it sometimes it took the women weeks or even months to recover after arriving in Bethlehem. But what was he supposed to do for months, waiting for a woman he didn't know to regain her strength?

He worried about the fragile woman on the other side of the door, wanting her health to return to her quickly…but part of him, the darker part he would admit to no one, was frustrated. Not at Susanna but at himself, for agreeing to marry before he came on a journey that he knew would be riddled with suffering and hardship. God had ordained him to travel to the Indians, to take the Gospel across the swamps and bogs in this new colony. The elders had said he needed a wife to accompany him, and at the time he had agreed with enthusiasm. Glancing back out the window, he watched Elias Schmidt walk toward the wagons with the woman Christian was supposed to marry.

Catharine was intelligent, educated, a talented seamstress, and— Elias was right—she was very beautiful. The laboress of the Single Sister's Choir had confirmed what Christian already knew. If Catharine ever went on a mission, she would be able to learn the language of the Indians quickly, perhaps even faster than he could. And her charm would help him win over even the most hostile Indian.

Why had the lot matched Catharine with Elias, a godly man for certain, but one who wasn't destined for the mission field?

He stepped away from the window and leaned back against the wood. Elias didn't know that a week prior to his and Catharine's engagement, Christian had gone to the elders and they had agreed with his choice to marry Catharine Weicht. Elias didn't know that Catharine had almost been Christian's wife.

He'd never forget the day in the castle chamber when he'd joined with three other elders to pray and select the lot that would determine the future for Catharine and for him. He'd held his breath as the elders had drawn from the lot, waiting for God to approve the marriage that everything within him desired. Everything that Catharine once said she desired as well.

But on that summer evening, as the elder unfolded the paper, the answer stunned him.

Nein.

God didn't even give him the option to wait and see if he and Catharine were meant to marry later. Instead, God had taken her away from Christian and given her to Elias.

Surely Catharine had to question the lot like he had. Elias believed Catharine loved him, but Christian's poor friend didn't know the truth.

Christian had prayed in earnest for a strong wife who was devoted to their Lord, and he had desired a beautiful and smart woman who would be just as comfortable in the hut of an Indian as she was in the castle at Marienborn. The laborer at his choir house had told him that Susanna Fritsche was anxious to go on a mission to the Indians, but no matter how strong she was in spirit, how was Susanna going to endure the trials of their wilderness journeys, the dangers of being among the Indians, when she was so weak in body? And how was he supposed to care for this woman and do what the Lord commanded of him at the same time?

The door of the sick room squeaked as it cracked open, and Christian sprang forward.

"Come in," David's wife, Sister Marie, said as she greeted him.

He slipped through the doorway and glanced at the young woman, his wife, who was asleep on the narrow bed. "How is she?"

The sister closed the door. "She has the chills."

"Will she be all right?"

"I believe so, with much prayer and rest."

Relief filled him along with a revival of hope. "When will she be ready to travel?"

"A week, perhaps. Or two."

Christian turned so Marie wouldn't see the disappointment in his eyes. "What can I do to help you?"

"Pray for her health and her spirit."

Christian stepped toward the door, but before he could leave the room, the laborer of the Married Brothers Choir joined them. "The wagons are almost ready."

Christian nodded. "I watched them prepare for the journey."

"Sometimes as followers of Christ, we must do hard things." Abraham pinched his smooth chin as he spoke. "Sometimes we must leave the ones we love to pursue what He has for us."

Christian studied the man's stolid gaze. "What are you saying?"

"There is no reason for you to stay in Bethlehem—"

"My wife is here," he interrupted.

"Susanna will be well cared for by Marie and the other sisters, and you would be—" He glanced over at Marie. "Well, you would be in the way."

Christian weighed the man's words, wondering if he really might be able to leave without her. His spirit tugged within him. Should he stay with the wife the lot had given him to love or proceed with the mission ordained by God?

"There must be—" He paused. He may not love Susanna as a wife, but he wanted to do what the Savior required of him. "There must be some way I can help."

"The only thing you'll do here is worry, I'm afraid, and that will be good for no one. You can pray for her in Nazareth as earnestly as you pray for her here."

Could he really go on to Nazareth without his wife? Should he go?

Christian glanced at the darkened window beside Susanna's bed and then back to her face. Her eyes were closed, her face covered with sweat. She looked so helpless lying there. It was his duty to protect her, yet Abraham was right. Marie and the other sisters would care for Susanna much better than he could.

What did God require of him? Even if he knew his wife, even if he loved her as more than a sister, God might still want him to go on this mission while she recovered.

"If I go—" He drummed his fingers on his legs. "How would she get to Nazareth?"

"When she is well again, David or one of the other men can bring her." Abraham stepped toward the door. "I will tell the others to wait for you."

Christian rubbed his palms together as he moved toward the door to follow Abraham. But Marie stopped him and pointed back to Susanna. "You don't know when you'll see her again," she said softly.

Nodding, he turned again slowly, and when Marie shut the door, he moved toward the bed. It was the first time he'd ever been alone with his wife.

He'd watched Susanna on the ship, but he'd never studied her before, not like he had studied Catharine during the worship ceremonies and in the privacy of her English manor. Susanna's hair tangled around her face, like the vines that adorned the trees in the Black Forest. Her light skin was unblemished, her small nose tipped at the end, making her look more like a child than a woman. She was pretty in a simple way. Pure.

The elders said Susanna was a woman of faithful devotion, uneducated but smart in her own right. They said she was renowned for her compassion and strength. He was glad for her faithfulness, glad for the skills God had endowed her with, but he wasn't certain how she would fare in the hut of a drunken Indian or eating strange foods from a kettle. He'd heard the stories of hardship from the other messengers, and he wondered if Susanna had heard them as well.

Gently, he placed his hand over hers. It was so small compared to his, so fragile. He prayed quietly that the Lord would heal her sickness and give her strength—and he prayed even more quietly that God would give him strength as well.

A lock of hair fell over her eyes, and he reached out to push it aside. But just before he touched her, he yanked back his fingers.

He had no right to touch her face or her hair, no right to even be here, not when he couldn't stop thinking about Catharine.

Shaking, he stepped away from her.

"Good-bye, my wife," he whispered as he left the room.

* * * * *

Susanna stirred in the face of the daylight, and when her eyes crept open, she searched the strange room around her. It was a bedchamber of sorts. A washstand stood under a large dormer window, and there was a bureau next to the door. Sunlight waffled across the wooden floor beside her bed, and the simple coverlet on top of the bed was stitched with green and white.

The room wasn't rocking in rhythm with the waves on the Atlantic, like it had on their ship. But if she was no longer on the *Irene*, where was she?

Pushing against feathers and sheets, she tried to prop herself up with the pillows, but her strength collapsed under her and she couldn't manage to lift herself even a couple of inches. Falling back against the pillows, she glanced out the window beside her bed.

Across the street she could see the gray stone of a medieval-looking building. Her muscles ached and she was terribly cold, in spite of the blankets piled on top of her. She couldn't remember the last time she had awakened in a room by herself, without the beds of her sisters lined up along the walls beside her.

Why was she alone this morning?

She closed her eyes. Not long ago she had crossed the rough Atlantic on the *Irene*. They'd traveled through the dense forest, and then they had made it to Bethlehem.

Her eyes sprang open again. She was in Bethlehem; the people here had celebrated their arrival. Hours ago, or had it been days now, they had arrived. Her head had pounded, her whole body aching with each step, as she and Catharine had gone into the Gemeinhaus to worship with the others. There was the taste of the sweet rolls and coffee and the wonderful singing.

When she had looked across the room, when she had tried to meet Christian's eyes, she thought he had been looking at her, but then he didn't return her smile. She didn't remember anything else.

She blinked in the sunlight, struggling with her memories, wondering at the intensity of Christian's gaze in the Saal. Perhaps he hadn't been watching her at all. Perhaps he had been meditating in prayer, oblivious to anyone on the other side of the aisle. In her wistfulness, she had hoped he was looking at her, but his focus was on the Savior instead.

She wanted him to focus on their Savior, of course, but a part of her longed for his gaze to wander toward her as well. Even for a moment, to let her know that he was thinking about her too.

No matter how distant Christian seemed, he had chosen her to be his wife. If she weren't careful, her fears would destroy the thread of trust they needed to develop between them. Once they were alone, once they were able to talk, surely their love for one another would grow.

Where was Christian now? And where were Catharine and Elias and the others?

She heard footsteps outside and her heart leaped in her chest, thinking her husband had come—but instead of her husband, a man and woman walked into her chamber. She searched their faces and found familiarity in them, but not from Marienborn. She didn't know where she had seen them before.

"I'm Sister Marie," the woman introduced herself, her hands folded to her chest. "I'm the laboress for the Married Women's Choir in Bethlehem."

She recognized the woman's voice. "You've been praying for me, haven't you?"

Marie nodded and then introduced the man with her as her husband, David.

"I've seen you before," Susanna said as she turned back to the woman. "Were you at Hernnhut?"

"We lived on the Count's estate for a short season." Marie straightened the quilt on the bed. "David and I were married at the Great Wedding in 1745."

Susanna studied the couple again and wondered for a moment if they had known each other before their wedding. If not, were they still strangers after so many years?

David stepped forward. "I knew your husband before Marie and I married."

At his words, Susanna remembered hearing another voice in her dreams. A man. "Where is my husband?"

Instead of answering her question, David glanced at his wife. In their silence, panic filled her chest. "Did something happen to him?"

Marie shook her head. "Christian has gone ahead to Nazareth."

"He—he left me?"

"Oh no," she insisted. "Brother Abraham asked him to go with the others since there was nothing he could do to help you here."

Susanna closed her eyes, wishing for a moment that the darkness would welcome her again. Instead of becoming a helpmate to her husband, she had become a burden. She had to get out of this bed, had to get to Nazareth so she would be ready for their mission.

When she opened her eyes again, David and Marie were both watching her. "How long ago did they leave?" she asked.

"Three days."

She pushed herself up on her elbows this time, trying to force her legs over the side of the bed. "I need to go to Nazareth."

"Not quite yet." David's calm laugh quelled some of her frustration. "We have to get you well first."

She shook her head as she forced her legs to the edge of the bed. "I can recover in Nazareth."

"You can't travel yet, not with so much sickness still in you." He held up a bin in one hand. And then he held up a knife in the other. "I'm the town blacksmith, but sometimes they ask me to use my tools to help people get well."

Susanna cringed at the thought of him bleeding her and struggled again to get out of the bed, but her body refused to cooperate with her. She fell back against the pillows, hesitating for another moment before she reluctantly surrendered her arm to the blacksmith. She flinched as he began to drain the sickness out of her.

Chapter Four

....

Catharine Schmidt dabbed at the sweat masking her face as she scanned the partially built stone structure at the crest of the plaza, looking for her husband. But she didn't see Elias among the thirty brothers and a hundred laborers they'd hired to finish the work before winter. He was in the midst of the work, she was certain of it, but there were too many men plastering and setting stones into place for her to find the one her heart longed to see.

As she rocked in the chair on the porch, her mind wandered to the glorious hours on the ship when she and Elias had stolen away from the others and hidden in the depths of a storeroom to share the pleasures of their marriage. It wasn't how she had envisioned marriage, sharing their love among the steamer trunks and crates, but there was beauty in the darkness of that ship, two souls coming together as one.

The rocking of the ship hadn't bothered her like it had Susanna and so many others. Catharine wished she could be back on that ship, in that storeroom, if only she and Elias could be alone again.

Now that they were in Nazareth, Elias lived in the choir house for the married brothers and spent his days finishing the construction for the Disciple's House—a grand manor home for Count Zinzendorf and his family. Elias has been sent from Germany to oversee the building, but when they'd arrived, Catharine was surprised—and a bit dumbfounded—to discover the house almost built. In the months it took for word of the plan to build this summer home to reach Europe and then to commission Elias and travel to the Colonies, one of the elders from Bethlehem had been asked to oversee the massive project. The letter saying they no longer had need of Elias's services never arrived, or at least not before they'd left Europe.

So Elias had been assigned to help the others in the completion of the manor, and instead of spinning wool and stitching as she'd done in Marienborn, Catharine was assigned to clean the women's quarters. Her back ached from scrubbing floors and windows alike. Her schoolteachers had taught her how to read and entertain and sew, but they'd never taught her how to clean a home, nor had her parents groomed her for such menial tasks. At one time her parents were preparing to marry her to a nobleman, but those plans had changed three years ago when they chose to join Count Zinzendorf and his band of Moravians.

Catharine rocked back and forth on her chair, fanning her face with her hands. She was supposed to be inside working with the thirty or so other married sisters right now, but she couldn't scrub another inch of floor in that dreadfully hot house this morning.

Her gaze swept across the Disciple's House again, and then she looked across the plaza to the Brothers House, the small Gemeinhaus, and the orchards and trees beyond. Before arriving in Nazareth, she'd expected to find a village like Bethlehem, with its many houses and grand Gemeinhaus, with mills and a tannery and schools. The stone structures here were imposing, but there were so few of them that they reminded her more of mausoleums in a graveyard instead of a growing town. Everything around their settlement was wilderness, vast and dark.

She pushed her heels against the floor again, rocking back and forth. She missed the grand cathedrals and castles of Europe, the cobblestone streets and universities and busyness of the carts and animals as they scurried through the narrow streets. Even though she was working harder than she'd ever worked in her life, the world around her moved unbearably slow.

In Marienborn, they had women who worked as laundresses and women assigned to scrub chamber pots and floors and other menial tasks. They were the women who had once lived as servants and slaves, and they did this work quite well. Catharine had no talent for laundry and no stomach for chamber pots, yet here in Nazareth they expected all the married sisters to help accomplish these tasks. They had Negro and Indian women living among them in the house in Nazareth, but even they were assigned more pleasant tasks than she.

Before they traveled to the Colonies, Catharine had been respected as Lord Robert Weicht's daughter, but no one knew her father here. When she tried to tell the women about the aristocracy of her family, they didn't seem to care. Even the sisters who had come to Nazareth from Marienborn seemed to have forgotten Catharine's heritage.

Back in Europe, she had been ready to leave her parents and embark on this journey with her husband. She'd wanted to be known as Elias's wife instead of Lord Weicht's only child, but she wasn't prepared for the indifference of the women around her—it was irrelevant to them that her husband was a renowned builder and that Count Zinzendorf had personally sent him to build his house.

If the *Irene* hadn't already left for Europe, she would have tried to convince her husband to return to Marienborn…but she doubted Elias would return anyway. And she certainly wouldn't go without him. If only Susanna were here in Nazareth instead of back in Bethlehem; Susanna could help her cope.

She glanced down at the stains on her hands and felt the calluses hardening her fingertips. Her mother would be appalled if she felt her daughter's fingers, likely demanding a better position for her only child. Maybe Elias would fight for her as well.

They might not be able to go back to Marienborn, but they could easily go back to Bethlehem. When Elias finished the manor house, she would plead with him to return to the much larger and more industrialized town. Surely they could use him in some capacity there.

She glanced toward the house to her right again. She could see Christian Boehler working among the men, but she still couldn't see Elias. Annabel, the laboress, had told her that there was a chamber in the Sisters House for married couples and each couple was assigned an hour a week to be alone with their spouse. But they had been here for four days now, and she and Elias had yet to receive their assignment.

The laboress was a married woman—surely she must know that newly married couples needed their time alone. Here in Nazareth, though, building the manor and cleaning the houses seemed to be more important than a wife being with her husband.

Everything was scheduled and quite punctual here. The blast of trumpets and a trombone awakened them every morning. Mealtimes were the same every day. So was worship. And work. Quarterly hour teachings and intercession. When the men and women came together for worship, her husband always winked at her from afar, but she was never able to speak with him. It had been two whole weeks, back on the ship, since they'd even spoken more than a greeting.

One of the men separated from the rest of the group, and she watched the man's long strides as he crossed the courtyard. Then she caught her breath when she recognized him.

Elias was coming to her.

She smoothed her hair under her cap and glanced behind her, hoping that Annabel wouldn't see him.

Elias grinned as he jogged up the steps. If he wasn't a member of the Brethren, he could have been a member of Parliament like her father had been. His dark curly hair was tied at the base of his neck, and his white work shirt barely concealed the strength of his arms. He was steady and smart and handsome enough to make the worldliest of girls swoon.

He sat on a chair beside her. It was a stolen moment with her husband, a moment to cherish.

She teased him with her smile before she spoke. "Hello, Brother Schmidt."

He glanced at her face, then at her dress. Admiration flooded his eyes. "You are beautiful."

Hiding her callused hands in the folds of her petticoat, she wondered how beautiful he would think her if he saw her on her knees scrubbing floors or stripping sheets from beds.

She tilted her head toward him. "You are foolish."

"Call me whatever you want, as long as I can be with you."

He scooted closer to her and she thought he might kiss her, but he glanced toward the window instead.

Her gaze dropped to the floor. "We'll be together again soon, won't we?"

"Very soon, I think." He reached for her hand, hidden in her dress. As he rubbed his fingers over her skin, he didn't seem to notice, or at least he didn't mention, the hardened shells forming over her fingertips. "How is your new choir?"

"I miss Marienborn," she told him honestly, though she didn't mention that she missed London even more.

He nodded toward the Disciple's House, his grin dimming for a moment. "They have no real need of my skills here in Nazareth."

Her heart seemed to leap within her. "Could we go back to Bethlehem?"

"Not now." He hesitated. "Elder Graff spoke with me this morning. He said they are praying about sending us on a mission to the Indians."

"The Indians?" She swallowed hard, wondering if he'd lost his mind.

"The people who live in the wilderness around us." He was teasing her, but this time she didn't return his smile.

"I know who the Indians are," she huffed before forcing the lightness back into her voice. She didn't want to go on a mission, but it wouldn't pay to make him angry in the short time they had together. "But I was hoping we might be able to go back to Bethlehem if they have no need of you here."

"They have no need of my skills in Bethlehem either." He shrugged, seemingly oblivious to her dismay. "But they need help building a gristmill in Gnadenhutten, and I could assist them with that."

"I'm not supposed to go on a mission," she insisted. Not like Christian and the others who'd been called to go.

"It would just be for a few months." He continued like he hadn't heard her. "There are almost five hundred Christian Indians who live in and around Gnadenhutten, but they have no mill to grind their grain into flour. We could really help them, Catharine."

She rocked back in her chair again. When she'd accepted the assignment to come to Pennsylvania, to be with Elias, the laboress in Marienborn, along with the elders, had assured her she would stay in a town. She knew that assignments sometimes changed, depending on the needs of each community, but the elders had sent Elias specifically to use his building and planning skills in Nazareth. He would even do well building this mill for the Indians, but anyone who knew her—well, they would know she just didn't fit in an Indian village. She wanted the Indians to know their Savior, but she wouldn't do well living among them, even if it was temporary while Elias worked with them.

"God often works in ways we don't understand." He watched her face carefully as he spoke. "You will come with me, won't you?"

She looked into his pale blue eyes and saw a glimmer of excitement there. Her husband wanted to go to the wilderness. To the Indians. And he wanted to go with her.

"We'll have our own tent for the summer," he whispered. "No one in Gnadenhutten can separate us during the night."

She rocked again slowly as she considered his words, imagining herself wrapped up in Elias's arms for an entire night. Instead of one hour together each week, they'd be together hours upon hours, in the solitude of a tent.

He looked into her eyes, squeezing her hands. "I won't go without you."

Gnadenhutten couldn't be any worse than Nazareth. And perhaps there would be no floors to scrub or mounds of dishes to wash. She could care only for herself and her husband, and they would be alone for weeks, maybe even months.

"The elders have to take it before the lot first. If the lot concurs, we will go."

The door flew open beside them, but he didn't seem to notice the interruption as he embraced her with his smile. The porch groaned under the laboress's stomps.

Elias's eyes lingered on Catharine's face for a moment longer before he turned.

"What are you doing here?" the woman demanded, like he'd committed a crime.

"It is a delight to see you, Sister Annabel."

Catharine choked on her laughter, bowing her head to hide her grin.

"You are supposed to be working."

Elias stood up, but his hand remained entwined in Catharine's. "I took a break to visit my lovely wife."

"There are specific times for that, Brother Schmidt." She turned to Catharine. "Just as there are specific times for you to work and specific times for you to rest. Right now you both must work."

Elias winked at Catharine before releasing her hand. With a

quick tilt of his hat toward Sister Annabel, he hummed as he walked down the steps.

Catharine backed toward the opening of the door, her eyes on Elias as he strolled away. She wasn't sure if she could bear a mission into the wilderness, but if he were going, she certainly wouldn't stay here without him.

Chapter Five

....

September 1754

Brown puddles muddied the pathway toward Nazareth, but there were no clouds above them. Instead, the late summer sky was a piercing blue color so bright that Susanna had to shade her eyes with one of the blankets Marie Kunz had bundled her in for the journey. Her chills were gone, but Marie was worried that the morning air, no matter how warm, would sicken her again.

Beside her David Kunz drove the wagon, and an Indian man named Samuel rode in the back for propriety—and probably protection—though no one mentioned the latter to her. Samuel held a musket in his hands, and every time she turned around, he was scanning the trees.

The trees called to her as well. They implored her to explore the forest and the hills, to roam in the fresh air and the wilderness, but it would be a long time before she could explore again. It had taken all her strength this morning just to walk down the hallway of the Sisters House in Bethlehem to attend breakfast, to show all of them that she was strong enough to go to Nazareth.

The moment her feet touched the floor, she refused to get back into the sickbed, no matter how tired she felt. Christian and the others were preparing to go on a mission to the Indian villages, and she didn't want to be left behind.

"How much longer?"

David chuckled. "Are you excited, Sister Susanna?"

"Of course," she replied, though she was more nervous than excited.

"It won't be long now. Less than an hour."

She shifted under the covering of blankets, trying to prepare herself for the disappointment that Christian had already left on the mission.

Leaves hung from branches overhead, making a sort of canopy over their path until the ceiling grew so low that she ducked under them. Even so, the branches tugged off her hood and scraped her forehead. Her shoulders hunched over her lap, she rubbed her skin and then pulled the hood over her cap once again.

When they emerged into the sunshine, David asked, "Did Christian tell you that he and I used to travel together?"

She shook her head.

"Your husband is a modest fellow."

"He's also a man of few words."

David glanced back at Samuel behind them and then laughed. "Just give him a little time, Sister Susanna. The words will pour out all at once."

She didn't tell the man, but she longed for the day when he spoke a single word to her. "Where did you and Christian go on your travels?"

"The Count asked us to go to England, Prussia, Saxony. People everywhere were hungry to hear about the Savior, though there were always people who thought we were heretics. Those people often chased us away from their town."

She nodded. Her father had written about how some people on the African coast were hostile to the message of Jesus while others wanted to know more about Him. Until she'd received her call, she'd read every letter of his over and over, wondering what it would be like to one day be sent out herself.

"One time we were traveling along the Rhine, telling people they could know Jesus as a friend." There was no laughter in David's voice now. "A mob followed us along the river, and they intended to kill us for bringing the truth to the people. But instead of running in fear, Christian bowed his head and began to pray. Our enemies quieted to hear his words."

The horses splashed through a shallow creek and continued through the trees on the other side. A pinecone landed on Susanna's lap, and she savored its spicy sweetness. David seemed oblivious to the beauty around them, as if his memories consumed him.

"The Rhine was behind Christian and me, and I looked to both sides, trying to figure out how we could run away. When I looked back at the mob, I realized that the anger had drained out of their eyes. They were listening to Christian as he asked God to forgive them like He had forgiven those who crucified His son on the cross."

Susanna closed her eyes and imagined the angry crowd swarming Christian and David, bent on injuring them and worse. The truth of Christ's love threatened those who hated peace, and she wondered what she would do, faced with a mob wanting to hurt her. Would she flee at the threat of persecution, or would she stay and pray for them like Christian had?

She could see him standing tall among the mob, a strong man petitioning the Lord God for strength. No wonder the crowd had stopped. They were expecting him to run.

She opened her eyes. "What happened?"

"The men slowly backed away, so Christian and I continued sharing the Gospel with those who came to hear it."

Susanna shifted on the hard bench. There was so much she didn't know about her husband, so much she wanted to learn, though she wished she could hear the stories from him instead of from his friends. She wanted to ask him about his family and his life before he joined the Brethren. And she wanted to ask him why he had wanted to marry her.

Samuel was still behind them, though he had said nothing during their journey. When she glanced over her shoulder again, she recognized the longing in his eyes. He wanted to be in the wilderness even more than she did.

"Where is your family, Brother Samuel?"

He looked up at her quickly, like he was startled that she had spoken to him, and then he looked away. "Most of them are in a village about thirty miles north of here."

"Do you miss your town?"

"I miss the people in my town," he said. "They are kind and generous when sober, but when the white traders bring them a keg of rum, they don't stop drinking until it is gone. Their kindness turns into hostility for each other and the men who brought them the rum."

"Is that why you moved to Bethlehem?"

Samuel paused, seeming to contemplate her words or perhaps his answer before he spoke again. "I met Brother David when I came to trade corn and blankets in Bethlehem. He shared with me how God could redeem me from my past. I decided to trade the binges of drinking for the love and forgiveness of his God."

Susanna's heart lightened. That was what she wanted to do. She wanted to shine God's light on the evil that pervaded this new world.

"Have you always been called Samuel?"

He shook his head. "I found a new identity in the Savior, so I received a new name."

"It must be a bit strange, to have a new name replace the one you've known all your life."

"My old name and my old self passed away when I joined the Brethren."

"What was your Indian name?"

He glanced down at the musket in his lap. *"Paiachco."*

"Paiachco," she repeated slowly.

His eyebrows arched, and instead of avoiding her gaze this time, he looked right at her. She couldn't tell if he was pleased or irritated at her attempt to pronounce the name.

"Did I say it wrong?"

"No," he said with a shake of his dark head. "You said it quite well."

She smiled. "What does your name mean?"

He hesitated again, and David spoke beside her. "There's no harm in telling her, Samuel."

"It means 'to shoot with a gun.'"

She swallowed, wondering why parents would call a baby by this name. "Do you shoot well?"

He nodded slowly, his gaze moving away from her again as David spoke. "He was the best in his tribe."

Samuel shifted the musket to his other hand. "There is no need to speak of it any further."

As the day grew warmer, Susanna peeled back the blankets that enveloped her and leaned back against the bench, watching for animals or Indians or even traders among the trees…until she spotted a squirrel. The creature leaped across four branches before it shimmied up a tree, and she quietly applauded its performance.

The horses hauled them up a steep hill, and when they neared the top, she saw a stone building rising from the wilderness in front of them. The three stories of the gray building looked drab against the blueness of the sky, but the yard was full of life as dozens of young children played on the wide grassy area surrounding the structure. A tall Negress supervised their play. Some of the children barely toddled across the muddy grass while others ran races between the oak trees, but as the wagon drew closer, the children stopped and watched them.

David slowed the horses.

"Where did they come from?" Susanna asked, her voice low, as if she might startle the children by speaking too loudly.

"Their parents are in Bethlehem and Nazareth and away on various missions," he explained as he scanned the heads of the boys and girls. "We may not live together as married couples, but we sure know how to procreate."

Her expression must have reflected her horror at his words, because he quickly apologized. "I'm not used to keeping the company of women."

Nor was she used to keeping the company of men.

David circled the stone building slowly, the boys and girls alike keeping watch of them.

Mothers of the Brethren gave up their children after they were weaned so that they could devote their energy to working on their assigned trade or with their husbands as messengers. Children were raised by loving sisters in the Nursery, and when they grew older, they were moved into separate homes for boys and girls while their parents continued to pursue the call God had placed on their lives.

In Marienborn, parents were able to visit their children quite regularly, but she wondered how often the Bethlehem women were able to travel these three hours to visit their little ones. Her own parents didn't leave for Africa until she was thirteen, but after they left, she never saw them again.

David stopped the wagon and hopped out.

"Timothy!" David called to a group of young boys. A blond-haired boy probably about three years old looked up, but he didn't step forward.

David rushed toward the boy and ruffled his hair. "Don't you know your own papa?"

The boy searched his face.

David held out his arms, but the boy didn't walk into them.

Susanna's heart felt as if it were about to shatter for both father and son.

Timothy looked over his shoulder first, until he found a young woman who crossed the yard quickly to be at his side. The woman nudged Timothy forward. "Go say hello to your father."

Timothy shuffled a few steps. "Papa?"

Instead of hugging David, he stared up at his father in trepidation. Susanna could see the longing in David's eyes, wanting to pick up his son, perhaps, and twirl him around, but he patted the boy on the shoulder instead.

How sad, Susanna thought, *to be worried that you might frighten your own son.*

During the past weeks she had spent with Marie, her nurse hadn't mentioned once that she had a son in Nazareth. Had she grown used to the idea of living apart from her husband and even farther apart from her son, or did she long for her family?

If God blessed her with a child one day, taking the child to the Nursery would be one of the most difficult sacrifices of living in their community, even more difficult than marrying a man she didn't know. Susanna couldn't imagine giving her son or daughter to another woman to rear.

David spoke quietly with the children's guardian, and as Susanna watched, she remembered well her childhood in her family's home—the musty scent of her father's leather coat and the soft touch of her mother's fingers brushing through Susanna's long hair. Others had scorned her family for their faith, but when she was with her parents, she believed no one could harm her. But Timothy relied on his guardian instead of his parents to keep him safe.

David lifted the boy and put him on his shoulders before he brought him to the wagon. The man was smiling again. He looked at Samuel and then at Susanna. "You don't mind if we stow away this little boy, do you?"

"I don't mind at all." Susanna patted the seat beside her. "As long as the stowaway is named Timothy."

David set Timothy on the seat and the boy scooted toward Susanna, his eyes rounded in awe. "Are you my mama?"

"Oh—" She shifted again as she glanced over to David for help.

"Your mama has brown eyes," David said. "You remember her, don't you?"

Instead of answering, Timothy stuck up his fingers. "I'm almost three."

Susanna laughed softly, relieved that they had moved on to a much more comfortable subject. "I'm almost twenty-three."

He grinned at her as David picked up the reins and urged the horses around their audience of children. She thought Timothy might be afraid of the Indian man sitting behind him, but he didn't seem to notice the difference in the man's skin color. As she looked across the Nursery children, she realized that there was an array of color among the children—brown, saffron, and a color that reminded her of the burnt red of autumn leaves. She might not be used to different skin color and cultures, but it seemed that little Timothy was.

"Will you spend the night in Nazareth?" she asked David.

He shook his head. "They are expecting us back in Bethlehem before dark."

She glanced back in the wagon and realized that Samuel was gone. She scanned the grass and the trees beyond, but she didn't see him or his musket.

David's gaze trailed hers. "It's amazing how quietly he can slip away, isn't it?"

She nodded.

"He goes often into the forest to pray for his tribe." He put his arm around his son. "I believe he misses his family."

Susanna glanced down at Timothy. She didn't say anything,

but David seemed to know what she was thinking. "Marie and I—we brought him here almost two years ago but haven't been able to return."

Timothy stretched his hands in front of him like his father, pretending to hold the reins.

"Would you like me to visit with him when I'm able?"

David's eyes grew wide, just like his son's eyes moments before when he thought she might be his mother. "Would you do that?"

She elbowed Timothy. "Can I come visit you sometime?"

"Sure," he replied, though he didn't stop watching the horses.

She glanced back at his father. "Where is the choir house for the boys?"

David's smile returned. "Bethlehem."

He would be able to see much more of his son after Timothy turned five.

A muddy path linked the nursery with the rest of the community less than a half mile up the road. As they rode west, David pointed out the stone residence where the married sisters resided. The single sisters, he said, either worked in the Nursery or lived in Bethlehem.

The married brothers resided in a smaller home on the other side of the plaza. The Gemeinhaus stood next to the brothers' home, and at the top of the plaza was a massive stone structure not quite complete, but the building reminded her of the castle at Marienborn. It was much smaller than the actual castle, but it towered over the village.

She pointed at the building. "Who lives there?"

"It will be the summer home for the Count and Countess."

She'd heard the story before, of Count Zinzendorf and his daughter coming to Pennsylvania to celebrate the first Christmas in Bethlehem. They'd slept in a single log dwelling with the others. Susanna knew that Elias had been sent to work on this house, and she marveled that the Zinzendorfs would come to live among them in the wilderness again—but this house was almost as grand as some of the manor houses in Saxony. The Count certainly knew about the house; he had personally sent Elias to work on it. But did he know how enormous his house was?

David stopped the horses in front of the Married Sisters House, and when the door opened, a dozen or so women poured outside to welcome Susanna. She didn't recognize all the women, but she saw Rebecca and several of the other women from Marienborn. And then she saw Catharine.

Even as her friend hugged her, Susanna felt woozy. She would need to lie down soon.

Catharine let her go and looked at her. "I'm so glad you are here."

Susanna's gaze traveled over her friend's shoulder, to the men working on the house. "Where is Christian?"

Catharine nodded toward the house. Even as Susanna searched for her husband, as she watched David and Timothy walking hand in hand toward the workingmen, she realized that Christian was just like David's son...completely oblivious to the family God had given him.

In that moment Susanna was afraid for herself and for Christian, afraid that, like Marie, she might become calloused against the pain of losing someone she once loved. She wanted to love her husband, not guard her heart from him. And she wanted her husband to love her as well.

Chapter Six

....

Christian believed with his entire being that God answered prayer. During his travels across Europe, he'd spent hours praying that God would provide ears to hear the words he and the other messengers spoke, along with hearts to receive the words of truth. He prayed that in answer to these prayers, people would choose to forsake their sins to follow the Savior.

In the past week, God had also heard his earnest prayer for Susanna's health. Across the Saal, his wife sat among several dozen other married women, her head bowed and her hands folded over her light green petticoat, as they waited for the lot to decide whether they would be going to the Indians during the autumn and winter months. He and Susanna had yet to speak together about their assignment to the mission field—they'd yet to speak at all—but he hoped she was petitioning the Lord on their behalf this morning.

He sat back against the bench in the Saal. Not only did he believe that God answered prayer, he also believed God could answer the Brethren's prayers outside the lot. Why couldn't God speak directly to people today, just like He'd spoken to Jacob and Joseph and Mary and other men and women in the Bible?

In the Old Testament, people sometimes cast lots when they didn't know the answer to one of their prayers. Even in the book of Acts, the apostles drew lots to determine if Matthias or Justus would replace Judas as the twelfth apostle. But this morning, as Christian waited with the brothers and sisters who'd gathered to pray and listen to the findings of the lot, he wasn't certain that the lot was the most effective way to determine God's will in every decision. If the truth were told, he was a bit afraid of the lot.

Two couples would be selected this morning to serve the Indians at the settlement known as Gnadenhutten, while Christian and Susanna were to travel to the Indian villages around Gnadenhutten to share the good news. The elders remained convinced that the lot was the best way to determine God's direction as to who would go to the Indians.

He'd journeyed from Marienborn to Nazareth to go on this mission, and he'd married because the elders had wanted him to have a companion. But even with the recommendation of the Marienborn leadership, the elder in Nazareth believed they should go before the lot one more time to determine who should go. And Christian feared that his assignment, like Elias Schmidt's, might change.

He sat stoically on the bench, trying to calm the anxiety that boiled inside him. God had planted this burning desire in his heart to share Christ with the Indians—surely the lot would concur. All he'd been able to think about this past week was the mission and the health of his wife. And Susanna was well now.

If the messengers left him and Susanna behind, he wouldn't be able to focus on planting the fields or finishing the Disciple's House with Elias. The calling on his life was strong, and it was urgent. Only Christ's love and peace could subside the fighting that had begun among the Indians and the Europeans in this new world, and he had to deliver the message before it was too late.

As Christian waited for Elder Graff to arrive, his gaze wandered again to the married women across the aisle. Catharine's head was bowed beside Susanna, but he knew well the beauty hidden under her haube, the soft lines of her cheeks and the fiery color of her hair. Shaking his head, he tried to break free of her hold, but still he watched her, imprisoned by the haunting thought of what might have been.

The lot had to send him on this mission. If he and Susanna remained here, he would continue to be confronted every day by the temptation of Catharine's beauty and the constant frustration of his inability to resist this temptation.

He blinked and then forced himself to look down at his hands. Perhaps among the Indians God would purge his desires, even change his heart. If God didn't turn his heart toward Susanna, he would pray that he could break free of the chains that seemed to bind him to Catharine.

Closing his eyes, Christian focused his mind on his prayer until their elder, Francis Graff, arrived along with Brother Edward, the laborer from the Married Brothers Choir, and Sister Annabel, who oversaw the married sisters. Elder Graff pushed his spectacles up his nose, and with Edward and Annabel on each side of him, he called for Joseph and Rebecca Wittke to come forward.

Joseph lumbered to the front of the room. His clumsy hands and feet often distracted from a heart willing to work and serve, but Christian hoped this man would join them on their journey. In the months Christian had known him, he had never heard Joseph complain about their work or their travels or what God required of him.

As Rebecca joined Joseph at the front, Elder Graff unscrewed the red leather cap of the glass tube and slipped three pieces of parchment inside. When he held out the tube, Joseph pulled out a paper. He showed it to Rebecca first, and when he held it out to the elder, the man announced the answer to be a yes. Joseph gave a short nod before they walked back to the benches.

A second couple from Marienborn went forward. This brother had told Christian that his new wife didn't want to go and, unlike Christian, he preferred to build for their community instead of ministering outside it. When the lot rejected their travels to Gnadenhutten, the man smiled in relief as he returned to the bench.

Next Elder Graff called Christian and Susanna's names. His wife joined him at the front of the Saal, but he couldn't bring himself to look at her or even at Brother Edward. He was ashamed of his feelings for another, embarrassed at his neglect of his wife. Instead of meeting her eyes, he bowed his head as Elder Graff prayed. Then the man held out the tube.

Christian reached into the glass, the crisp edges of the paper teasing his fingers. In that moment, he stopped praying for God to allow them to go to Gnadenhutten and begged Him silently as he selected a paper.

He slowly pulled out the paper and opened it.

Then his hand dropped to his side and he bit back the curse that had frequented his lips often before he'd come to know the Savior.

Once again, the lot told him no.

He twisted the paper in his hands. How could God put such a passion, such an overwhelming desire in his heart, and then deny him the opportunity to go? And how could God require him to stay here in this small settlement with Catharine when he was fighting so hard to flee temptation?

The other men had stepped back toward the long bench after they received their answers, but Christian stood like a statue as he opened his hand and stared down at the paper, as if the word might somehow transform into a yes.

"What does it say?" Susanna whispered.

He handed the paper to her, and she turned it over. Then she gave it to the elder.

Christian's fists tightened as he eyed the glass tube in the elder's hand, the other two pieces of paper taunting him. What would the elder do if he threw the tube onto the ground and watched it shatter? What would the others do if he refused the will of the lot and demanded to go on this mission?

But even as he wanted to smash the glass and tear into tiny shreds the papers that determined the course of one's life, he stepped back to the bench. If they wouldn't send him this fall, he wanted to be chosen on the next mission, in the spring, perhaps. His fury would only ban him from the Brethren and from ever journeying to the Indians.

He turned and took a long stride back toward the bench, but Susanna stopped him, whispering for him to wait.

Stopping, he turned toward her. In his own frustration, it hadn't occurred to him that she might be angry as well. For the first time since they married, Christian looked directly into the light blue of Susanna's eyes, but instead of anger, he saw compassion in them. And kindness.

"What is it?" the elder asked.

Everyone was looking at Susanna, and he stepped closer to her.

"Is something wrong?" he asked quietly so that none except the elder could hear.

She cleared her throat and lifted her head. Instead of answering him, she turned to the elder, her voice strong. "Perhaps the problem isn't with the answer. Perhaps it is with the question."

Elder Graff cocked his head. "There's no problem."

Her voice quieted. "I wonder if this answer is for me alone and not for my husband."

When she looked back at him, Christian studied the gentle strength in her eyes, trying to understand what she was saying. The lot's answer was for both of them, wasn't it?

The elder twisted the tube in his hands. "You think he should go without you?"

"I—I don't know for certain," she said softly. "But I've been ill, and I wonder if the Savior means for me to recover more before our next mission."

The elder pushed his spectacles up on his nose and focused his eyes on the tube. Then he closed his eyes and began to pray for wisdom in sending Christian alone, but Christian couldn't concentrate on the man's words. If the lot concurred, was it possible that their leadership would let him go to the wilderness without his wife?

As he finished his prayer, Susanna slipped back to her bench, and Christian watched her retreat in awe. In spite of her desire to travel to the Indians, she was letting him go without her.

But was he abandoning his wife by leaving her behind? This wasn't like going to Nazareth when she was sick; they'd only been separated for a few days and he could have visited her whenever necessary. If he went on this mission, he would be gone for months. Once they left, there would be no visits back to Nazareth until their journey was complete.

Susanna's head bowed when she sat down, and he wished he knew what she was thinking. Did she really want him to go on this mission without her? If he wasn't abandoning her, if he wasn't forsaking what God meant for him to do, he would be fleeing the temptation that plagued him. Perhaps God did will him to go—time for both of them to heal what ailed them.

Elder Graff folded three fresh pieces of parchment and slid them into the tube before he prayed again that God speak through this lot, that God show them whether Christian should go ahead without his wife or stay in Nazareth.

Christian held his breath as he reached into the tube to pull out a paper and then hesitated as he wrapped his fingers around it. The answer crinkled against his palm—the answer that would change their lives. The lot had seemed to mock him in past months. He couldn't allow himself to hope that this time would be different.

Brother Edward prodded him. "What does it say?"

Christian cracked open the edge of the paper and then handed it to the elder before he looked at it.

Elder Graff reached for the paper and showed it to Edward and Annabel before he spoke. "Brother Christian will be joining the others on this mission."

Joining the others.

He stared at the man in disbelief.

This time the lot had given him what he wanted. He was going with the Wittkes to Gnadenhutten, to share the love of Christ with the Indians. He wanted to shout with the joy that bubbled up in him, but when he glanced over at Susanna, he saw tears in her eyes.

She had given him a gift. A gift he would never forget.

He turned away from her, returning to his seat in the silence.

How could he ever be the husband he should be to a woman so selfless? In her love, his guilt ballooned. The lot had been wrong in Marienborn—she should have been married to one of the other brothers, one that was much more devout than he. It made a mockery out of her faith.

He looked over at her, but her head was bowed again and he wondered if tears still filled her eyes. And if she was crying because she wanted to go. Or because she didn't want him to leave.

He bowed his head and prayed silently that he would make good use of Susanna's gift to him, that the Indians would accept a gift as well—the gift of Christ's love for them.

And perhaps when he came back, he would be free of his feelings for Catharine. Perhaps he could begin to love the wife God had given him.

Elder Graff cleared his throat and then called for Elias and Catharine.

Christian's head jerked up. They were supposed to send a third couple to the mission field, but he never imagined that the elder would ask the Schmidts to go. The Count had personally sent Elias to serve in the building of Nazareth, not to go on a mission.

In spite of his determination to flee, in spite of his desire to break free of her hold, Christian watched Catharine stand and, with her air of elegance, saunter toward the front of the room to join Elias.

Perhaps, since the Disciple's House was almost finished, the elder wanted the Schmidts to go back to Bethlehem. Or maybe they were being sent someplace else. He didn't care where they went, as long as Catharine wasn't going to Gnadenhutten.

But then Elder Graff began to pray about sending the Schmidts out to the Indian village, and Christian fell back against the seat. Elias was one of the best builders in their community—he wasn't a missionary.

Even as the elder prayed for wisdom and direction, Christian prayed that the lot would keep Elias and Catharine in Nazareth. Or send them someplace else. Anywhere except Gnadenhutten.

Elder Graff held out the tube to Elias, and after Elias drew the lot, a smile spread across his face. It was the elder who made the announcement. "The Schmidts will be joining the others."

Christian leaped to his feet. In that moment, he didn't care what the others thought about him. He wanted to protest the decision of the lot but quickly realized he would have to explain why, and the truth would ruin all of them.

His head spun as he rushed toward the door. Five months in the wilderness. Five months of seeing Catharine for hours without the protocol and schedules of this community. He could avoid her in a place like Nazareth, but it would be impossible to do so on a mission trip. The entire time, he wouldn't be able to stop himself from thinking about Catharine instead of about his wife.

And he really wanted to start thinking about his wife.

He opened the large door and stepped outside.

When the ceremony was over, the women would hug Catharine and Rebecca and tell them how blessed they were that God was sending them. The men would congratulate Elias and Joseph and tell them the lot had chosen well.

Christian loved God with his entire being, but he was beginning to hate the lot.

Chapter Seven
. . . .

Wind rattled the dormitory windows as Annabel extolled the virtues of marriage with an enthusiasm that would have made the finest preachers in Europe proud. Susanna picked at the lint on her petticoat as the woman marched up and down the aisle, her audience both newly married women and seasoned wives sitting on neatly made beds. The longer the woman preached, the further Susanna drew into herself.

Standing in the Saal, she had seen the sorrow in Christian's eyes at the lot's initial rejection of their journey. He wanted to go on this mission even more than she did, and when she'd looked at him this morning, she knew she had to let the lot make a decision for him alone.

It wasn't Christian's fault she was so weak. Even though she desperately wanted to be well enough to journey with him, her body must not be ready. He may never love her, but she didn't want him to resent her. She couldn't allow her health to hold him back from his calling.

"Therefore shall a man leave his father and his mother, and shall cleave unto his wife…" Annabel tapped on the black Bible in her hands, but she didn't open it to quote the Scripture. Clearly she was an expert on the subject. "…and they shall be one flesh."

Catharine sat on a narrow mattress beside Susanna, and Annabel stopped her march directly in front of them, towering over them.

"The man and his wife were naked in the garden, and they were not ashamed," Annabel preached. "Nor do you have to be ashamed with your husbands."

Catharine elbowed Susanna, and Susanna flinched. The part

about leaving her parents didn't frighten her—they'd left her a long time ago—but how was she supposed to be with a man she didn't know and be unashamed?

She squirmed on the edge of the straw mattress.

"Hold still," Catharine whispered, and Susanna squeezed her hands together in her lap, trying not to think about being alone with Christian.

"In Nazareth we schedule an hour each week for a woman to be with her husband," Annabel explained.

Susanna secured her hands under her legs as Annabel proceeded to describe their wifely duties in even more detail than the laboress had in Marienborn.

The laboress back at the castle had stumbled over her words as she tried to explain how a man and his wife became one flesh, seemingly as embarrassed as most of the single sisters. But Annabel wasn't embarrassed in the least. She'd been married for two decades now and obviously enjoyed her role as educator.

As Annabel moved back down the aisle, Susanna edged back on her pillow.

When she was a girl, she used to dream about marrying one of the boys in their small village. There was one boy in particular, by the name of Jonathan Bauer, who used to follow her home from grammar school and try to impress her with his talent of skipping rocks across the pond. He'd never stirred her heart like she had imagined of the man she would marry, but he'd made her smile.

She'd known so much about Jonathan Bauer. She'd known what made him angry and what filled him with joy. She'd known about his little sister's illness and the older brother who often provoked Jonathan to wrath. Even as a girl she'd wanted to join the Brethren with her parents, but some days she wondered what it would have been like to stay in their village and marry someone like Jonathan. Someone she knew.

The Brethren did things so differently than the people in the world, but in their differences, they had been able to leave the world and cling to their faith without the persecution that threatened many of Christ's followers across Europe. When her father began to be persecuted for his faith, her family fled Moravia and joined Brethren from across the German states at the small village on Count Zinzendorf's estate called Herrnhut—*Watch of the Lord*—so they could serve God freely together. It was worth the sacrifice of leaving their country and home and even Jonathan Bauer to worship and serve their Savior without persecution or scorn.

Like Catharine, Susanna wasn't certain that the Brethren's way of separating husbands and wives, parents and children, was the best way to live, but they did avoid many temptations by separating the sexes. Men and women alike were able to devote their lives solely to God without the burden of parenting or marital conflict.

Susanna had dedicated her life to serving God, no matter how difficult. She wanted her faith to be alive and strong and real, unlike the faith of so many they'd left behind in Europe. Still, some aspects of this faith scared her.

She wanted to please both God and her husband, but it didn't matter what Annabel said, nor did it matter how handsome or respected Christian was. She wasn't ready to join him in the marital bed.

Catharine groaned beside her. "That woman makes it sound so—prosaic."

"How do you know what it's supposed to be like?"

Her friend giggled. "Oh, I know plenty."

"If you find pleasure in your husband," Annabel said behind them, "he will find pleasure in you."

Susanna squeezed her eyes closed, wishing she could block out the sound of Annabel's voice as well as the sight of her. This wasn't what she'd dreamed about when she thought about marriage—a rushed appointment of two strangers coming together as one. At one time she'd wanted her husband to court her, even for a small season, and ask her parents for her hand. And then she'd wanted her husband to take her far from her little village so together they could see parts of the world she'd only dreamed of visiting.

What would Annabel think this afternoon if Susanna stuck her fingers into her ears and started singing? If the woman didn't stop talking about wifely duties, she just might do it.

Catharine sighed. "What's the point of being married if all we do is talk about what to do with our husbands instead of actually doing it?"

"Hush."

"What is wrong with you?"

Susanna hesitated. She couldn't tell her friend about her fears; no wife should be afraid to be alone with her husband. "I'm still not feeling very well," she whispered.

"You'll feel much better after your hour with Christian."

She was certain that she would not.

Annabel was beside them then, her hand on Catharine's shoulder. "Did you have something you wanted to say, Sister Catharine?"

Catharine straightened her back, as poised as she always was. "I was wondering when I could cleave to my husband."

A few of the women snickered.

"The couples leaving on the mission will visit first."

Susanna's stomach fluttered again.

"So I can see Elias tomorrow?" Catharine persisted.

Annabel stepped around them and slid a piece of paper out of her Bible. "Catharine, you are scheduled for Friday."

"But that's two days away—"

Annabel ignored her.

"And Susanna." Susanna held her breath as Annabel scanned her paper. "You are scheduled for tomorrow morning."

"Lucky," Catharine whispered.

Susanna didn't feel lucky at all.

* * * * *

In the candlelight, Catharine pulled the thread through the white cotton to monogram her pillowcase with her new initials. All she really needed was a stitch of red to separate her linens and underclothing from the others, since the rest of the women used black or blue thread to monogram their things, but she liked sewing her married initials on everything she owned.

The candle flickered beside her and women rustled in their beds around her. Some of them were reading, others stitching. Two women were nursing their babies before they put them down in wooden cradles beside their beds. Susanna had left to bathe for her meeting with Christian in the morning.

Catharine slid her needle through the linen one last time. In a few days, she would leave behind Annabel's strict hand and the menial tasks she kept assigning Catharine, as if instilling Catharine with humility was the laboress's sole responsibility.

After she tied a red knot, Catharine tucked her stitching under her bed and, leaning back against her thin pillow, lost herself to favorite memories of London. Not too many years ago, Catharine had servants to do menial tasks for her so she could spend her days painting and entertaining and attending lovely parties across the city. She used to wear silk dresses and ride in carriages and attend the London balls. But when Christian convinced her parents to change their religion, she had no choice but to follow.

She reached for the small bag she kept hidden around her waist. Her father had given most of their personal wealth to the Brethren when they joined the community, but before she left for the New World, he'd given her this bag full of gold coins in case she ever needed money to support herself. No one—not even Elias—would ever know about her treasure unless it was necessary. The coins reminded her of her years in London. And they reminded her that she wasn't trapped in Nazareth like some of the women. If necessary, there was always a way for her to get out.

She blew out the candle on her nightstand and untied the bag from under her shift, hiding it beneath her pillow like she did every night, but she didn't close her eyes. Usually she tried to fall asleep before Agnes—the old woman two beds down from her—because Agnes snored so loud that it rocked the posts of the beds around her. But tonight she would wait to sleep until Susanna returned.

Anyone would think that Susanna would be elated with the anticipation of her time with Christian tomorrow, but her friend had spent the evening sulking instead. God had blessed her with one of the most handsome brothers, but she acted as if she'd been cursed. Perhaps she was upset because Christian was leaving on this journey without her.

Catharine shifted on her bed, trying to understand why the elders would send Christian to Gnadenhutten without his wife. And why Susanna would request that he go alone.

Going on a mission was all Susanna had talked about since the Count announced they were sending a new congregation to the Colonies. God had created Susanna for an adventure exactly like this, just like He'd put a longing inside Catharine to make a home with her husband. She'd wanted to marry Elias, though she didn't realize how challenging it would be to steal time away with him. Her parents traveled together often since they'd been married; they'd never been separated into the choirs.

At least she and Elias could be together soon, even if they lived in a small Indian settlement. She would create a home for Elias and herself in Gnadenhutten, and they would thrive.

She didn't have to wait long in the darkness for her friend. Minutes later Susanna slipped by in her shift, looking more like a ghostly child than a grown woman, and slid quietly under her covers.

"What took you so long?" Catharine whispered.

"I was praying."

"Praying about what?"

"That—" She scooted to the edge of the pillow, her voice low so none of the other women would hear. "That my husband would come to love me, like Elias loves you."

Even though Susanna whispered the words, they seemed to echo around the dormitory.

"How did you make Elias love you?" she whispered.

Catharine swallowed hard. "Elias loved me before we married."

"Christian doesn't love me." Susanna sighed. "He doesn't even seem to like me."

Catharine looked out the window across from them. The candlelight from several sisters still danced across the panes. No man in London had captured Catharine's attention until she met Christian Boehler. After he left for Saxony, she'd actually pined for him for a season, but she'd stopped pining a long time ago, around the time she met Elias Schmidt— a man more intriguing than any man she'd ever known. A man who ignored her until she carefully made her presence known to him.

Back in Marienborn, she had dreaded the day the laboress came to her with Christian's proposal. She had rehearsed exactly what she would say in response, but the laboress presented Elias's name instead. And Catharine had accepted with pleasure.

Nothing had happened between her and Christian in Marien- born. She'd caught Christian's gaze upon her at times, but she had disregarded it—many of the brothers over the years had looked at her with longing in their eyes. She used to revel in their admiration for a moment and then put it behind her, but she no longer enjoyed Christian's attentions, even if it was from afar.

If Elias knew that Christian cared for her, and that she had once cared for him, it would destroy everything she was working so hard to build. Years from now, perhaps, when she and Elias had grown roots together as husband and wife, she might tell her husband the truth, but disclosing it in the infancy of a relationship could kill the first blossoms of their love.

She cleared her throat. "Has Christian talked to you about your marriage?"

"He doesn't talk to me at all."

"Your husband loves you," Catharine insisted even as she inwardly chided Christian for his foolishness. While she would never tell Susanna for fear that she'd become vain, her friend was plenty pretty. Even though the trip had weakened her body, Susanna was the strongest of all of them when it came to her faith. She didn't waver in the face of danger, nor did the wilderness scare her like it did most of the women.

Catharine never would have done what Susanna had done this morning, suggesting her husband go on a mission without her. Too many temptations accosted a lonely man. Susanna seemed to be more concerned about winning Christian's love than losing what little they had.

With her friend's silence, Catharine repeated her words. "Christian loves you."

From the bed off to the left, Agnes shushed her. Instead of saying anything in response, Catharine made a noise that sounded more like a snort of a hog than a snore. Agnes pulled her blanket over her head and rolled over.

"Why did you ask for Christian to go to Gnadenhutten without you?"

There was a long pause before Susanna answered. "I didn't have a choice."

But that isn't true, Catharine thought as she clutched her fingers around the bag. They always had a choice.

Chapter Eight

....

At a quarter till nine, Annabel escorted Susanna out of the dormitory. A few of the women smiled and winked at Susanna as she passed between the beds. She nudged up her chin even as she wished that she could crawl someplace and hide. This was supposed to be her private hour with Christian, but there was nothing private about a procession. The sisters would be watching her, as well, when she returned, but she wouldn't tell a soul about her moments alone with her husband.

They climbed up the steps to the bedchamber on the third floor. A few doors from the bedchamber, a dozen women sat behind wheels spinning cloth for the residents and laborers in Nazareth. The door to the spinning room was open, but the door at the end of the hallway was not.

Susanna shuddered at the sight of the closed door. And at the empty bench in the alcove outside the room.

Her heart volleyed between relief and irritation at the sight of the empty bench. Every one of her sisters would find out if her husband missed their appointed time together. Even so, even in the face of the certain humiliation, part of her didn't want him to show up.

Annabel was silent beside her, but the many instructions spoken yesterday seemed to trail them down the hallway. Was she the only one who hadn't been with her husband yet? How many of the newly married women, like Catharine, had gotten their first taste of marital relations on the *Irene*?

And why hadn't her husband come looking for her?

She knew she wasn't pretty, but her heart grayed at the thought that she repulsed Christian. Would her husband ever love her, desire her even, or was it too late for her to dream?

"We're a bit early," Annabel said when she saw the empty alcove.

Susanna stepped toward a window as Annabel picked up the timepiece by the doorway. The white sand was piled up at the bottom. Annabel twisted the doorknob to the bedchamber, and when she found it locked, she knocked.

"It's been over an hour," she called to whoever was in the room.

Footsteps scurried across the floor, and seconds later, the door opened as one of the married sisters rushed outside. The woman blushed when she saw Susanna, though her face glowed with a smile.

The woman hurried down the hallway, but her husband didn't rush out of the room behind her. When he passed, Susanna didn't dare look up at him. Their time as husband and wife might have been biblical, but she was still embarrassed at the knowledge of their togetherness on the other side of the wall.

"Wait for him here," Annabel said before she stepped in to prepare the room.

Susanna looked outside the window. The sun was hidden behind rain clouds this morning, its rays trying to streak through the gray, but they couldn't seem to break free.

Why had God brought her here, married her to this man who didn't care about her, if He wasn't going to use the passions He'd placed in her heart? She felt as trapped as the sunlight this morning, not free to say or do as she pleased.

Now she was expected to become one with a man she didn't know.

She'd been up most of the night, rehearsing what she wanted to say to Christian, but she could hardly remember any of the words now. She needed him to care for her before she could submit her body to him, but she didn't know how to communicate that without making him angry. If he even had a temper.

Footsteps pounded down the hallway toward her, and she caught her breath. Slowly she turned, her heart racing as she prepared herself for another disappointment.

But she wasn't disappointed this time. Christian Boehler had come to her.

He took off his black hat, and his eyes locked on her like a hunter watching a bird or a deer, as if she might run away.

She glanced out the window again and tried to blink back tears, but anger and relief and fear erupted in her at once, flowing down her cheeks. She wiped them away with her sleeve.

When she looked at Christian, he was still studying her. Finally she was meeting her husband alone and she greeted him with tears. What must he think of her? A homely invalid who couldn't control her crying. A woman who now belonged to him.

Perhaps he could still change his mind and marry someone else.

"The room is ready for you," Annabel announced, and Susanna jumped at the woman's voice.

Her arms filled with sheets, the laboress bumped open the door for them with her hip. Christian waved Susanna before him.

The door clanged when Annabel shut it, and the sound of Christian bolting the lock reverberated around them.

They were alone.

Instead of focusing on her husband, Susanna absorbed the details of the small chamber. Wooden blinds were drawn over a narrow window on the left side of the room, and on the far wall was a double bed with a quilt that matched the curtains. A plain stool stood beside the bed, and under the window was a stand with a washbasin and towel.

As Christian hung his hat on a wooden peg, she eyed the freshly made bed, and her fingers twitched against her skirt. What exactly did Christian expect of her?

Christian gave her a wary smile and then held out his hand. "My name is Christian. Christian Boehler."

The burden of their morning together lightened at his words, and she offered her hand to him.

"I'm Susanna," she replied as she shook his hand. "Susanna Fritsche...Boehler."

His smile grew. "It's a pleasure to meet you, Susanna."

He sat down on the bed and patted the mattress beside him, but she sat down on the stool next to bed instead. She didn't care what Annabel said; she wasn't ready to be with this man.

He studied her for a moment, and she wished she had something witty to say, something at all to say to dissolve the tension.

"Thank you for what you did at the Saal."

Her heart fluttered in spite of her attempt to calm herself. "This passion you have is from God."

"And my wife is from God too."

"I cannot stop you from your calling."

He studied her again, his eyes looking a darker brown in the dim light. "I do not want to leave you behind."

"You must go to the Indians even if you don't have a companion."

There was more curiosity in his eyes this morning than regret. "I have to tell you, Sister Susanna, that I'm not exactly sure how to be a husband to you."

"I—I have no idea how to be a wife to you either."

He smiled again. "Then I suppose we have some common ground, don't we?"

She nodded as she fidgeted again with her hands in her lap, her mind wandering in the silence. What would it be like to feel the strength of Christian's arms around her, far away from the pressure of this marital bed?

He leaned forward, inches from her now, with his elbows on his knees, and he rubbed his hands together. "What is it that you would like to do in our hour together?"

"I—I—" she stuttered again. She'd come prepared to tell him what she wouldn't do, but she hadn't expected him to ask her how she'd like to spend their time. "I suppose I would like to talk."

Relief filled his eyes as he patted the bed again. She started to shake her head, but he reached out and cradled her chin. The shock of his touch electrified her. "I believe you'd be more comfortable sitting on the straw for an hour than on that stool."

When she hesitated, he stood up. "I will sit on the stool."

"No," she said softly. "I will join you."

Nodding, he sat back down and leaned against the wall, his legs sprawled the length of the bed. She moved to the other side of the bed, her petticoat rippling across the quilt.

"What would you like to talk about?" he asked.

"I—" She took a deep breath. "I would like to know why you chose me to be your wife."

"Chose you? But I didn't—"

His words faded away as he seemed to realize how callous his answer must sound to her. He floundered through his next words. "I mean, the laborer in Marienborn, he recommended that we marry."

She looked down at her lap, feeling foolish. That explained why he hadn't sought her out, why he hadn't spoken with her. He had never wanted her. "I thought you asked for me."

"I would have, I suppose, if I had known you."

"You agreed to marry me because you couldn't come to the Colonies without a wife."

He seemed surprised that she would question him. "Didn't you marry me to come to Nazareth?"

"Of course," she replied, too quickly. She couldn't explain how she had admired him for months before they married, not when she was only a means to an end for him.

"Where is your family?" he asked.

"My parents traveled to the African coast on a mission a long time ago."

"You didn't go with them?"

"No. I was too young when they left."

"The missions are hardest on the children, aren't they?"

She nodded. "Did your parents go on a mission?"

"I'm the only one in my family to join the Brethren." He looked toward the window. "My mother died when I was eight, and I left the rest of my family when I was seventeen."

"My mother caught a fever and died not long after they arrived in Africa."

His eyes swept to her, and she wished she could take back the words she'd spoken. If he thought she might die of her illness like her mother, he and the elders might never let her go on a mission.

She leaned forward a few inches, wanting to reassure him. "I've spent the last year preparing to go on a mission."

"If something happened to you—," he started, and her heart warmed at his words.

"My life is in God's hands."

He nodded. "What do you know of the Delaware?"

"Only a little," she said.

His gaze drifted toward the curtains before it returned to her. "Have you studied their language?"

"No, but I want to learn." She eyed him. "Perhaps you could teach me."

"I am still trying to learn it myself," he said. "But when I do, I will teach you."

An uncomfortable silence drifted between them. Even though they sat inches apart on the bed, it seemed like they were fathoms apart in spirit. Next to her husband, Susanna felt terribly alone.

Christian stood and reached for her hand. As he helped her stand, she caught her breath. He studied her face again and she thought he might kiss her, but he released her hand and stepped away.

"When will you return?" she asked.

He paused. "Sometime in the spring."

"For Easter?"

"Perhaps."

"This Easter is my birthday," she said, though her words were so quiet that she thought for a moment he didn't hear.

"I will try to be home by Easter, then." He hesitated. "I wish you could go with me."

She bowed her head. "Thank you."

"Next time perhaps we will go together."

He studied her for a moment longer and then he turned away from her. The door shook when he slid the bolt across, and he opened it wide for her. When she walked into the hallway, Annabel was reading a book on the bench.

The laboress looked at them and then at the hourglass beside her. The top glass was partially filled with sand. "You still have at least a half hour left."

Susanna expected to feel anger or humiliation at their short visit, but when she looked over at her husband, she felt sympathy for him instead. Neither of them knew what to do in—or about—this marriage.

"Yes," Susanna whispered to her laboress. "But we are finished for today."

Annabel eyed them both warily and then shut her book.

* * * * *

Christian wanted to bang his fist against the walls of the Sisters House as he hurried away from the eyes of the women. Of his wife. He had failed Susanna terribly.

He didn't know much about being a husband, but he knew he was supposed to comfort his wife with his love and concern. When he'd looked into her eyes this morning, though, reason seemed to escape him. He wanted to learn about her family, to learn all about her, but the pressure of forcing their conversation overwhelmed him. They had precious few minutes together and he'd botched it, not knowing what to say.

Upon his return to the manor, the laborer would pull him aside and ask about his time with his wife. Christian couldn't lie to him, but he couldn't tell him the truth either. He was a coward, perhaps, but he would tell the man that his silence was to protect his wife's virtue. He was protecting himself from embarrassment as well—none of the other married men would spend their hour talking with their wives, nor would they leave the room long before their time was finished.

What must Susanna think of him?

He'd seen the hurt in her eyes when she asked why he'd requested her hand. Most of the messengers married so they would have a companion in their work, but Susanna had every right to question his motivations. After all, he had asked to marry another woman before her. The only reason he'd married Susanna was because it was required of him and, at the time, he thought he had been doing the right thing—getting married as the laborer suggested.

However, after the lot rejected his marriage to Catharine, he hadn't given the elders any other input to this selection. In his mind, no other woman could compare. He relied on the advice of the laborer, like most of the men did, since he wasn't matched with the woman he desired.

Like Catharine, he had been raised on a manor located outside London. His grandfather and father had been respected businessmen who served the god of money, and they were quite devout in the worship of what mastered them. Christian had grown up in the clutches of this wealth, but even as their fortune and affluence grew, no one in his household seemed to think it was enough. He had to make a choice with his life—to pursue God or pursue money—and he'd chosen to serve God.

He didn't have blinders about Catharine like Elias did. He knew she had been pampered as a child and was a free spirit who didn't do well with rules. But her independence and her confidence had intrigued him along with her beauty. He'd given his heart to her when he was twenty-three and hadn't been able to break free of it.

Back in London, when he used to visit Catharine and her family, he had never felt nervous around her or her lifestyle. But this morning, in her simplicity and kindness, Susanna Fritsche had intimidated him.

Christian raced down the steps, and when he pushed it, the front door thudded against the stone. Heat accosted him as he stepped outside, and the sound of hammers pounding against wood rolled across the grassy plaza.

He stepped onto the grass, his mind on Susanna. He should have asked her more questions about her family and her education, as he'd done with the women he'd once danced with back in London. He should have asked Susanna why her parents joined the Unity of the Brethren and why she wanted to go on a mission.

But instead he'd sat on the bed like an idiot, unsure of what to say.

He wasn't fit to be a husband, certainly not one to Susanna and probably not even to Catharine. He was driven and awkward and completely obsessed with this mission. Susanna was a devout woman, while he struggled every day with the sins of his flesh. She deserved a devout husband who had conquered the sin in his life…and a husband who adored her.

Chapter Nine
....

The sun climbed above the trees, sprinkling rays of pink and orange across the dewed grass. Susanna stood on the top step of the stairs that led to the Gemeinhaus, most of the community below her as they watched the five messengers hike toward the forest. Each of the men wore a pack on his back, and a mule accompanied them with their remaining supplies. Christian hiked behind Samuel, who had joined their small party as guide and interpreter.

In that moment, Susanna felt more lonely than she'd ever felt in her life. Her husband and her two dearest friends were leaving on this journey without her. Even though she'd wanted them to go, she couldn't help feeling like they had all left her behind.

During the commissioning service, the elders had prayed for the messengers and then she had given Christian a cloth filled with gooseberries and slices of venison jerky. The travelers already had food in their packs, but still she had wanted to give him something else for his journey, something from her.

Before the travelers and their solitary pack mule disappeared into the forest, Christian turned back. She couldn't search his eyes this time like she had on their wedding day, but as he tipped his hat toward the crowd, she pretended he was saying good-bye just to her.

She waved one last time, and then her husband was gone.

The voices around her trailed away as the brothers and sisters returned to work, but she remained on the top step, her eyes still on the forest.

At the commissioning service, the elders had read the Count's familiar words to the messengers. "Remember, you must never use your position to lord it over the heathen. Instead you must humble yourself and earn their respect through your own quiet faith and the power of the Holy Spirit.

"The messenger must seek nothing for himself, no seat of honor or hope of fame. Like the cab horse in London, each of you must wear blinkers that blind you to every danger and to every snare and conceit. You must be content to suffer, to die, and to be forgotten."

To suffer, to die, and to be forgotten.

The words echoed in her mind now, and in the stillness of the morning, she prayed for the group's safety. No matter what happened, she knew she would never forget Christian, and she prayed that God would keep him from suffering as well.

A sister wandered up the steps, humming a lovely melody Susanna had never heard, and sat down beside her. Susanna knew this Indian girl from their dormitory, but she had never spoken with her. She was sixteen or seventeen years old, and while she wore a cap like the other sisters, her hair trailed down her back. The striking black color of her hair shone in the morning sunlight, and her eyes matched her hair as the light danced within them. Her face was as beautiful as her song.

Wrapped in the girl's arms was a baby. Susanna held out her hand to the baby, and he grasped her finger.

The Indian girl stopped humming and pointed toward the trees. "Your man leaves you?"

Susanna's gaze wandered back to the forest that had seemed to swallow Christian and the others. "He is going on a mission."

"Why do you not join him?"

"I wasn't chosen for this trip."

The girl studied her face and then lifted Susanna's free hand from her lap. She looked at both sides of her hand before placing it back on Susanna's lap. "Are you sick?"

"I am recovering."

The girl nodded. "I was very sick once, before I had my son. My husband brought me here to recover."

"Did he come back?"

"Not yet, but he will come for us soon. He is a great chief with our nation and has many important things to do."

The baby kicked, and Susanna gently squeezed one of his bare toes. "What is your child's name?"

"Nathan," she replied. "Among my people my name is *Wingan*, but here they call me Lily."

"I'm Susanna."

Lily's eyes went back to the forest.

"Do you miss your village?" Susanna asked.

"I miss the dancing and the singing. We sing here in Nazareth too, but it is not as lively as the songs of our people." She paused. "And I miss my husband."

"One day I would like to go see your village."

Lily smiled again. "Maybe one day I can take you."

The baby squirmed in Lily's lap.

"How old is he?"

"Eleven months," Lily said as Nathan reached for her fingers and pulled one to his mouth. She laughed as she removed her finger from his grasp. "Almost old enough to go to the Nursery."

Susanna's heart saddened at the thought, but Lily didn't stop smiling.

"Annabel said I could go visit him every Sunday if I like, and we will play and play." She brushed her slender hand over his head and then tickled him. "You and I, we like to play, don't we?"

The little boy giggled and laughed with his mother who was still a child. Lily said something to him in a language Susanna didn't understand.

Susanna leaned toward her. "I want to speak the language of the Indians."

"The Indians are made of many nations like the white man," Lily replied. "We have many languages."

"Which language do you speak?"

"The language of the Delaware."

Susanna's mind raced; that was the language that Christian wanted to speak as well. "That is what I would like to learn."

The woman studied her intently before she spoke. "*Gaja leu?*"

Susanna tried to repeat the words. "What does that mean?"

Lily brushed her hands over the boy's dark cropping of hair. "Do you really want to learn?"

"Very much."

The girl's eyes shone again. "I will not teach you how to speak our language."

As Susanna's shoulders fell, one of Lily's hands lifted to the sky and floated down like her fingers were sprinkles of rain. Under the sleeve of her plain dress, Susanna heard the clinking of bracelets as Lily waved in the air. "I will not teach you how to speak the language. I will teach you how to sing it."

Susanna watched Lily's arms dance as she hummed.

"You do know how to sing, don't you?" Lily asked.

"I love to sing."

Lily smiled at her again and sang a few words. Susanna repeated her song and then spoke one of the words. "*Kitschi.*"

"What does it mean?" she asked.

"It means that if you are determined, all things are possible."

Susanna shook her head. "Neither of us can do anything without our Savior."

"You really think the Christ Child is concerned about us?"

"I know He is."

Lily watched her closely as she asked the next question. "Then why did He keep you here while your husband went away?"

"I don't know the reason," Susanna said. "I may never know until the next life."

The baby began to fuss, and Lily lifted him to her chest and gently began to bounce him. "Your people talk a lot about the next life."

"We long for the life to come, to be with our Savior."

The two women stood and walked down the five steps.

"How do you sing 'With Christ all things are possible'?" Susanna asked.

Lily thought for a moment and then sang the words. When Susanna repeated the song, Lily's baby clapped his hands. A small piece of Susanna's loneliness began to subside as she laughed at his joy.

"I believe he likes to sing as much as you do," Susanna said as they crossed the plaza and moved toward the Sisters House.

"He has been singing since the day he was born."

"How do you know English so well?"

"My people trade with many British people. My father learned from them, and I learn from him."

"Your father is a good teacher."

Lily repeated Susanna's words and then she sang them in the language of the Delaware. Susanna laughed and sang with her.

Before she went into the house, she looked back toward the trees and then up at the clouds tinted with indigo in the distance. The messengers would be walking for at least two days to reach their destination. She would pray for safe travels for their feet and peace for their minds.

When Lily began singing again, Susanna didn't feel alone anymore.

* * * * *

The straps on Catharine's backpack chafed on her shoulders, and her shoes sank farther into the dreadful mud with every step. They'd been walking for almost two days now, up and down the mountains and through the rain. Her wet bodice clung to her breasts and her little bag of coins chafed her skin. Mud coated her hem and swept across her light blue petticoat like waves on a canvas.

"Only an hour now," Samuel called from the front of their group.

An hour?

She didn't know if her blistered feet could hike another ten minutes.

When Elias had suggested they go to Gnadenhutten, he'd neglected to mention that they would be climbing over mountains taller than she'd ever seen in her life. The way was treacherous in the best of weather, but the rain had turned the mountainside into a giant mudslide. She clung to the rocks and roots to avoid taking a trip down the crevices and cliffs that dipped on both sides of her.

Lightning flashed in the distance and thunder cracked overhead. Pieces of rock crumbled under her feet, and she clung to the bramble and rocks with her hands.

In front of her, a felled log lay like a fallen soldier across their path, and Elias reached for her hand to help her over it. With a glance back down the hillside at the piles of rocks and trees below, she pulled up on Elias's arm. Her stomach ached, but she wouldn't stop. If he thought she was ill like Susanna, Elias would send her back for certain.

Greasy kettles and grimy floors paraded through her mind. The drudgery of her days in Nazareth was even worse than walking up and down these mountains. There her feet had longed to dance and her fingers longed for a needle and thread to stitch more than just her initials on a pillowcase. Her brain had felt as if it were becoming as stale as the bread she carried in her pack, about to crumble into a thousand pieces.

She didn't want to go back to Nazareth, with or without Elias. She wanted to go back to Marienborn.

"Are you feeling all right?" Elias whispered.

"I will be much better when we arrive in the village."

He squeezed her hand. "So will we all."

In that moment, she realized her husband probably missed the comforts of Marienborn as much as she did. Elias was born to be an organizer. A decision maker. He'd been so excited about the challenge of building the grand Disciple's House before his assignment was taken from him. And she wondered if he, too, had regrets about coming to the New World.

The pack mule peaked the mountain in front of them, and Elias helped her climb over the last boulders to the top. From the mountaintop, she could see the wide valley they had just crossed. Clouds hung low over the hills and trees carpeted the earth for miles and miles. Warm rain drizzled down her head and her skirt, and her clothes felt almost as heavy as her backpack.

Rebecca and Joseph huddled together on a log across from Christian and their Indian guide. She and Elias joined them, sitting on another wet log. Christian rubbed his hands together, and she saw the passion in his eyes. In spite of the miserable weather, this man was enjoying himself.

"The village is on the other side of this mountain." Samuel looked at the lightning that flashed to the west of them. She'd seen lightning only on a rare occasion in London and never in Marienborn. "We shouldn't linger here any longer."

Christian glanced around their small group, but his eyes rested on her a moment longer than the others. At one time she would have felt some sort of pride at his loyalty, but she no longer wanted Christian's admiration or his affections. Elias couldn't find out what had transpired between her and Christian back in London. It would break all they had, his confidence in her. Christian must remain loyal to his wife, as she would to Elias.

"Is everyone ready to continue?" Christian asked, his eyes still on her.

She returned his question with a quick nod and then stood up. Lightning fired the sky to their west again, and the crash of thunder made her jump. If she were here, Susanna would enjoy this display of God's might, but Catharine longed for a dry place to rest for the night.

Elias reached for her hand again, and they trailed the rest of the group along a pathway that wound down toward another valley. Vines cascaded down the trees, and their gnarled tentacles looked eerie in the shadows.

Rain fell harder now, in heavy sheets that soaked Catharine's clothes. A sharp wind rustled the leaves, tangled her wet skirt around her legs. It felt as if the storm were chasing them their last mile or so to Gnadenhutten.

What else did the dark clouds contain in this new world?

"Hurry!" Samuel called back to them.

He didn't need to shout his command twice. She hitched up the weight of her skirt and rushed down the hillside with Elias.

"We're almost there," Elias said as he urged her forward.

Even though sunset was still hours away, the sky had turned black. Thunder cracked again and shook the ground under their feet. Catharine no longer cared about the mud or the rain or even the painful blisters rubbing against her shoes. She didn't know what the powerful display of lights could do to her, but she was certain she didn't want to find out.

As they rushed down into the valley, she saw a circle of log buildings above the tumbling rocks of the Lehigh River. The wind swirled her skirt around her legs again, and she tugged it away from her skin, trying not to trip over the material as they dashed toward the largest of the buildings.

Samuel opened the door, and when she rushed inside, Catharine stripped off her drenched cloak and flung it over a knob. Then she collapsed on a chair. Rain continued to pelt the windows, but it no longer seemed as threatening under the bark-slabbed roof.

Samuel greeted someone in a language she didn't understand, and when she turned, she gasped at the sight of seven Indians lined up by a long table, watching them. She hadn't realized there was anyone else in the room.

Samuel reached out his hand and embraced the first man with his arm. She watched the Indians for several moments, wondering what they would do, when one of them smiled.

"You are hungry after your travels?" he asked in English, looking at her.

Her stomach growled.

"Very much hungry," she replied for all of them. "I would eat just about anything."

"Good," he said, directing them toward the next room. When she walked through, she saw wooden trenchers filled with corn, bread, and some sort of meat.

"What is that?" she asked Samuel.

"Boiled eel."

She gasped, and when she turned to meet Elias's eyes, he shook his head ever so slightly at her insolence. She patted her hands on her wet bonnet. She was soaked, exhausted, and terribly hungry. How was she supposed to eat eel?

But their hosts didn't give them another option.

Her dress soggy, her body sore, Catharine sat down and began to eat the boiled meat with her fellow messengers and their new Indian friends.

Chapter Ten
....

Susanna sang one of Lily's songs as she skipped along the pathway to the Nursery. The lyrics challenged her, inspired her even, and threaded through each new song was the beautiful language of the Delaware. More important than the songs, her budding friendship with Lily helped soothe her loneliness. Even with the women living around her, she still often felt like she was alone, but not with Lily. The young woman was filled with song and life, singing as she carried her son in a woven cradleboard that rested on her back.

All morning Susanna and Lily hummed their songs as they dipped wicks into melted beef tallow to make candles. The long summer days were being replaced by long nights, and Susanna wondered if the winter gray would enshroud them like it had in Europe. She didn't yet know if she would be able to roam outside during the winter snow or if it would be too cold.

And when the snow began to melt, would her husband return?

Ahead of her was the Nursery, the stone as gray as Saxony's winter sky. She'd told Annabel about her promise to visit Timothy, and the laboress had finally allowed her to go to the Nursery before the supper meal.

This afternoon the children crowded around the Negro governess, and Susanna watched her toss a canvas ball into the air. The children raced after it until one of them brought it back. She turned and tossed it toward Susanna this time. Susanna reached up and caught the ball, and the children gathered around her.

Then she saw little Timothy, smiling up at her.

She reached down and picked him up. "I told you I would come for a visit."

She handed Timothy the ball and he tried to throw it, but it dropped just a few feet away. The children didn't seem to care. A little girl picked it up and ran toward their chaperone.

"Where's my papa?" Timothy asked.

"I believe he's back in Bethlehem, with your mother."

"Do you want to play with me?"

She set him on the ground and rubbed her hands together, looking back at the governess, but the woman was watching the other children. It had been a very long time since she'd played with a child, back when she was still a child herself. She'd never had any siblings, so as she grew older, there was never a brother or sister for her to play with—but perhaps she could remember how.

"Can you please play?" Timothy asked, his face beginning to fall from worry. He tugged on her sleeve.

"I would love to play with you," she said. "But you will have to teach me how."

He took her hand, guiding her away from the other children to a small hut made of sticks and leaves.

"Let's play…" He paused and then let out a shriek. "Indians!"

She stepped back. "I don't know how to play Indians."

"It's easy." He pounded his chest and twirled. "You run, and I'll chase you."

"Indians don't chase you."

He stopped the pounding and looked up at her like his small head held all the wisdom in the world. "Sister Greta says they will if we go outside at night."

She glanced behind him, at the windows of the Nursery. "Who is Sister Greta?"

"She makes our food."

"I've met several Indians, Timothy, and not one of them chased me."

His eyes were weighted with concern. "You best be careful. Greta says—"

She stopped him, about to point out the reddish and yellow shades of skin in the children around them, but perhaps Timothy didn't know his friends were Indians. "Why don't we play another game?" she asked instead.

He thought for a moment and then took off running. "Come and find me!" he shouted before he hid behind a tree.

Susanna smiled. She may not be the best playmate, but she remembered well the game of hiding and seeking. She looked in the hut and behind one of the trees and called out his name as she walked through the grass, searching the trees.

He laughed when she found him and then told her to hide. It took only seconds to find her.

"Timothy," one of the children yelled, "we're gonna race."

Susanna waved him toward their game, and after a quick hug, he rushed toward his playmates. His family.

The dark-skinned chaperone shouted for them to start, and the entire horde took off around the building. Then the woman walked toward Susanna and introduced herself as Mariana, one of five Nursery workers. Several of Mariana's teeth were missing, and her arms were so thin that they resembled two broomsticks. But there was an intrinsic beauty about her, like gold that had been refined by fire.

"How did you come to Nazareth?' Mariana asked.

"My husband and I were sent here from Europe as messengers to the Indians," Susanna explained. "Are you from the Colonies?"

Mariana shook her head. "I was born on a plantation in St. Thomas."

"You are far from home as well."

Mariana's gaze traveled to the children as they rounded the side of the house. "Not so far anymore."

Maybe one day this would feel like home to her as well.

"How long have you been in Nazareth?"

"Six years now," Mariana said. "One of the messengers bought me in St. Thomas and brought me here."

Susanna searched the woman's face. "You are a servant?"

"I was purchased as a slave, but here I serve the Savior alongside the rest of the women."

Susanna thought for a moment about her words. She'd met indentured servants in Saxony, some who had run away from their masters, but she'd never met a slave before. "Did you decide to follow our Savior in St. Thomas?"

She nodded her head slowly. "I made the decision to follow Him there, but my master despised the Christian faith because he wanted to be our only master. He punished my sister for her choice, and she wasn't strong enough to survive his strong hand."

Susanna shuddered. She'd heard stories of the Brethren messengers in St. Thomas and the other islands, about the thousands of slaves who'd come to know Christ as these men and women lived among them. Some of the messengers had been persecuted, horribly so, but they never stopped sharing the love of Christ.

The children shouted as they came near.

"What happened to you?" Susanna asked.

"After my sister died, one of the missionaries arranged for my purchase. I think my master was glad to be rid of me."

"Do you miss your island?"

Mariana leaned back against a tree. "The plantation was my prison. Here I live and work among all the other women as a sister instead of as a slave."

Timothy and a few of his friends gathered around the women and began circling them as they sang. Susanna wasn't sure what to do, but Mariana began clapping, so she joined in the clapping until the children raced away again.

"They like you," Mariana said.

She watched them. "Really?"

"Do you like working with children?" Mariana asked.

She turned toward the woman. "I don't know."

"Perhaps one day you can join us here in the Nursery."

Susanna thought for a moment of the children's games and smiles. She would never be lonely, surrounded by all of them. "I'm supposed to be going on a mission to the Indians soon, but if I weren't going...if I don't go, I would enjoy working with the children."

When the sun began to fade behind the trees, another woman opened the door of the house and the ringing of a bell echoed across the yard. Timothy hugged her leg and then rushed toward the house with the other children. Mariana took a step toward the door and then turned. "Please come visit us again."

"I will." Susanna was still standing in the yard when the door shut. Quiet drifted over the yard, replacing the children's lively shouts and laughter. Loneliness settled over her again, stifling her like a woolen cloak on this cool autumn day.

Turning, Susanna walked back toward the hill where she lived, but she didn't hurry home. Instead, she savored her minutes in the fresh evening air and the view of fields surrounding their tiny town. Trees stood like fortress walls beyond the field and beyond that, though she couldn't see them, were the blue mountains where Lily once lived, the wilderness where her husband now traveled.

No one was walking the path with her, but still she felt a strange sensation, as if someone were watching her. She scanned the trees and the earth in front of her, but she didn't see anyone in the golden forest or the fields or on the pathway. She hadn't seen a bear or a wolf since their arrival, but Lily had told her stories of those animals. And told her she wouldn't want to meet one alone.

She picked up her skirt and hurried along the dirt path, watching the fields and trees for an animal. And then she saw something looking back at her.

At first she thought it was an animal, but a man stepped out of the forest…followed by a second man. She almost screamed, but she swallowed the sound. No one would hear her yell except the men, and she guessed that they wouldn't respond well to hysterics.

She stopped on the pathway, watching them as they stared back at her. Both men were bare-chested and wore their black hair long over their shoulders. One of the men had something painted across his chest, but she didn't stare at his skin or at the tomahawks at their sides.

If she ran, would these men chase her, like Timothy in his games? Perhaps even worse, what would they do if she didn't run?

The men didn't approach her nor did they retreat into the den of trees. She lifted her hand in a wave, but neither man responded to her gesture of friendliness. With her eyes on them, she began walking along the path again, her pace steady. She wouldn't run, but she also wouldn't stand still like an animal they'd down with a musket or arrow.

As she hurried away, she wondered exactly what Sister Greta knew about the Indians in the woods.

Chapter Eleven
....

A great fire glowed in the middle of Tanochtahe, an Indian village fifty miles north of Gnadenhutten. The beat of drums echoed through the forest as Christian watched the Indians leap and dance around the blaze. The unearthly sounds of their yells sent tremors through his skin. Dogs barked beyond the fire, and the frenzy of the noise and drumbeats decimated the peace of the wilderness.

Those who weren't dancing filled hollowed gourds from a large oak barrel on the back of a wagon. He could only guess what evils the barrel contained. The Indians in Gnadenhutten had left this life to follow Christ with their minds and their bodies, but here in this village, Indians seemed to worship the god of darkness with their entire beings.

Another woman shrieked, and as the men drew closer, Christian heard the shaking of rattles on their legs, an erratic pulse against the drums. He was afraid, but he didn't fear the enchanting power of their wickedness. What he feared most, as the first missionaries to this village, was that they would fail to communicate the power of their Savior, of a God so great that He could remove this darkness from their hearts. He and Joseph had to make them understand.

Samuel motioned Christian and Joseph ahead, toward the frenzy of both body and soul, and when they walked into the center of the village, the drums stopped playing. An eerie silence replaced the yelling and drums until a fire log crashed into the inferno and erupted in a cloud of sparks flashing in the night. The men wore breechcloths around their hips, and the stiff hair that rose from their headdresses were dyed bright reds, blues, and yellows. Most of the women wore dresses made of buckskin and headbands decorated with beads and feathers, though some of them were as bare-chested as the men.

Christian lowered his eyes as Samuel guided them past the fire. He felt a bit like what the biblical David must have felt as a shepherd boy, being mocked by Goliath and the other giants. These warriors didn't mock Joseph and him with their words—or if they did, he couldn't understand what they were saying. But when Christian looked back up, he saw the Indians taunting the messengers with their eyes.

He was grateful that Elias had remained in Gnadenhutten with the women tonight. If these men and their drink turned angry, only the warriors from on high could fight them off.

Samuel motioned them into a large dwelling covered with bark and dried mud, and the moment they disappeared through the open door, the drums in the village center resumed their erratic beat. Hanging lanterns lit the smoky room as eight Indians sat in a circle, passing around a pipe. It was as if they didn't hear the hell being raised outside their door.

On a low bench was an old man, his weathered skin streaked with wrinkles. Even though his skin was tinted a tan color, he was dressed like an English gentleman, with linen stockings, breeches, and an embroidered waistcoat over his shirt. His dark hair was pulled back with a ribbon, and when Samuel spoke to him, there was no smile in his brusque reply. Christian couldn't tell if he was angered or honored by the presence of white men.

Samuel looked back at Christian and Joseph. "Chief Langoma requests that you sit."

Christian sat cross-legged on one of the rugs, and Joseph sat beside him as the chief continued speaking.

Samuel interpreted his words. "He wants to know why you have interrupted their celebration."

Christian leaned forward, speaking to the chief as if the man could understand his words. "We come to offer something that will give you much more joy than drinking and dancing."

Samuel spoke the words in their language, and then sadness laced the foreign words of the chief's reply.

"Many white traders come visit us." Samuel interpreted. "They want us to buy from them. They want us to give them our ancestors' land. We do not want to buy. We do not want to sell. We don't want to give up our drink or our dance."

Christian's gaze wandered toward the open doorway, at the dozens of Indians lined up to drink out of the barrel. He wondered whether it was the French or the British who had given them the drink and at what cost.

"We are not here to buy or sell any supplies," Christian replied. "We come to share the love of God and His Son with you."

The chief took a long draw from the pipe and slowly exhaled the smoke as he seemed to consider the words.

How many white men had come through their village, making promises and gifting them with rum? Both the French and the British were trying to win over the native people so they could rule the Colonies; sometimes they won through bribery and promises, and sometimes they tried to conquer them through force. Christian had no use for the political maneuvering and uprising. Christ could bring them all together, no matter where they had been born or what language they spoke or even what their ancestors believed.

When Chief Langoma didn't reply, Christian spoke again. "We are not traders or soldiers. We come to you only as servants of God."

Joseph reached into the pouch at his side and removed a piece of tobacco, one of the many small gifts they'd transported from

Nazareth. He set the tobacco in the center of their circle, and at a nod from the chief, the Indians divided it into small pieces. One of the Indians broke his piece into flakes for the pipe.

"We already have gods." Samuel translated the chief's words. "They are many and they are powerful."

The drumbeats outside increased along with the wild shouts. The drink must have been powerful to fuel this kind of frenzy. Christian feared what would happen when the fuel was gone.

"Are any of your gods powerful enough to forgive sin?"

Samuel translated the words, and the chief rested back on the bench, watching Christian.

"We want to come back and visit you and your people when they are sober." Christian leaned forward. "To tell the stories of our great God and of His power."

A young woman came into the room and set a bowl in front of each man. In each bowl was a white powder, and the woman spooned hot water from a kettle over each dish.

"*Cittamum*," she said simply and backed away to another room.

Christian glanced at Samuel.

"It is roasted corn," Samuel said. "They pound it into a flour."

"Cittamum." Christian repeated the woman's name for the mixture and then scraped the bowl with his fingers like the other men, licking the paste from it. The mixture tasted more like ashes than corn.

The chief nodded his approval.

"I want to tell you about our God and the Son He lost."

The chief paused for a moment. "I don't know your god, but I know what it is like to lose a child."

Christian opened his pack and retrieved a belt of polished shells.

"It is our covenant to you," Christian said as he held out the wampum. "We are here to help, not to hurt you. We would like to return to tell you more about this Son."

All the men began to speak, and as the minutes passed, Samuel didn't bother to translate what seemed to be an argument. As they debated, Christian prayed that they would accept the offer, that they could return to this clan when the Indians were sober and their ears ready to listen.

The chief motioned for the men around him to quiet. He eyed each of the white strangers before he reached for the wampum. Christian held his breath as he began to speak.

"We will accept your covenant of peace," Chief Langoma said, surprising Christian with his ability to speak English, and then he motioned toward the door. The Indians were jumping around the fire and wailing like they were mourning a great loss. "If you return after the drink is gone, we will listen to your story."

Christian's breath rushed out of him with relief at the chief's offer to return, but not all the men in the circle were pleased with the invitation. Their eyes blazed at him like the fire.

The chief pointed at the benches that surrounded the room, built against the log walls. "It is too dangerous for you to go back outside. You must sleep here for the night."

"We won't be able to sleep in here," Joseph said, and Christian agreed. Between the men raging outside and the council rustling within, they wouldn't be able to rest. It would be better to camp outside the settlement, in the quiet of the trees.

"If we leave—" Samuel's words were quieter now, and they were his own. "Not even the chief can stop them if they decide they want to kill you."

Christian weaved his fingers through this hair as he met Joseph's eyes. "We must stay."

A naked Indian raced by the doorway with a tomahawk in his hand, and when Joseph saw him, he concurred.

Christian took a blanket from his pack, even though the air was warm, and he pulled the blanket over him on the hard bench. Somehow it offered him a bit of security in this unfamiliar world. Beside him, the council continued their discussion as if the white men had already left, in a language he wanted to understand.

The words of Psalm 23 rolled through his mind. His life was not his own, even in the darkest of the valleys. Outside, the warriors continued to shriek and chant, but the chief remained in the room without a sip of the drink. Even more important than the protection of the chief, Christian knew his life was God's, to take home when his death would serve God in more ways than his life. If necessary, he was willing to give up his life for the sake of the good news.

As he closed his eyes, he thought of his wife back in Nazareth, grateful that she was sleeping in a safe place tonight. Catharine's face flooded his mind, and he opened his eyes. As he watched the chief and the council pass the pipe around again, he prayed that God would take away the sin of his flesh.

But even with his prayers, he dreamed of Catharine. He could fight the thoughts during the day, but in the darkness, in his time of rest, she tormented him.

Hours later Samuel shook his arm, and Christian blinked at the faint strain of moonlight that crept through the doorway. The night was quiet—almost too quiet.

"Christian," Samuel whispered, "You must get up."

He looked toward the dark frame of the door. "What is it?"

"They passed out after they finished the rum," Samuel said. "But when they wake, they will be in a terrible mood."

"Now that the drink is gone," Christian whispered, "perhaps we can share the Gospel with them."

Samuel shook his head. "They will be angry and looking for trouble."

A flame flickered in the doorway and Christian recognized the young woman who'd fed them the roasted corn the night before. She held a torch in one hand and a small burlap bag in the other. Her words were soft but sounded urgent.

"She baked corn bread for our travels," Samuel explained. "She says we must hurry."

Christian thanked her as he took the gift.

As Samuel woke Joseph, Christian quickly rolled his blanket and tied it to his pack. The three men slipped out the door, into the dark village. The quiet village. Not even a dog barked as they crept past the huts and cabins and back into the forest.

Christian imagined a host of angels silencing the dogs and deafening ears as the men moved toward the woods. It wasn't until they were hidden in the trees that they heard the dogs bark.

His legs shaking, he climbed into the canoe they'd hidden along the river and quietly began to paddle with the others toward their refuge on the Lehigh.

* * * * *

Annabel bustled around the kitchen in the basement of the Sisters House, seemingly more concerned about her kettle of lamb stew than the presence of Indians around Nazareth. The floor was packed dirt and the benches and tables were crudely hewn from trees felled in the surrounding forest. An assortment of iron kettles, pails, and utensils hung on pegs around the fireplace and brick oven, and on the wall to the left of the fireplace was the door to a pantry stocked full for the winter.

"Not long ago, this was Indian land," Annabel explained to Susanna as she added fresh thyme and carrots to the stew. "They pass around our town every few weeks and sometimes through it as they travel between settlements."

Susanna rolled the dough on the table. Even as she listened to Annabel, something didn't feel right. The men she'd seen hadn't been passing through their settlement. They had stopped outside Nazareth and tried to intimidate her with their presence.

She realized that there was nothing safe about living in the Colonies with so many dangers in the wilderness and people from around the world trying to abide together. Nor was there anything safe about going on a mission to the Indians. But she still wanted to be wise to the warnings inside her head.

"They were so close to the Nursery." The women and children who stayed there seemed very far away from the rest of their community.

"I will speak to Elder Graff," Annabel concurred.

Susanna sighed as she shaped the dough, guilt escalating from her fears. She was here to befriend the Indians, not fan rumors about them.

She sprinkled flour on a wooden peel and placed the dough on it, trying to chase away her fears by humming one of Lily's songs. Her assignment changed almost daily, but the kitchen was one of her favorite places to work.

She opened the metal door on the brick oven beside the fireplace and slid the peel inside. Shaking it gently, she left the bread to bake and began setting plates on the table.

That evening, as Susanna sat beside Lily during supper, she told her friend about the two Indian men she had seen the day before. Lily's eyes grew wide. "Were they dressed as English or as natives?'

"As natives," she replied. "Both of them had black hair as long as yours."

Lily set her spoon on the table. "Did one of them have a tattoo on his chest? A gray wolf with yellow eyes?"

Susanna looked away, trying to hide her blush at the thought of looking at the man's bare chest. "There was some sort of picture on his chest, but I don't know if it was of a wolf."

Lily reached down and unwrapped her son from the cradleboard. He cooed softly as she rocked him in her arms. When she looked up at Susanna again, her eyes filled with trepidation. "You will tell me if you see them again?"

"I will."

"Some Indians are good friends to us, but not all of them are friendly." Lily spooned lamb stew into her mouth and swallowed. "They kill both the English and those Indians who befriend them."

"Why do they want to kill us?"

"Some because white men stole from them and they think all white men are bad. Others because they want white men to leave this land." Lily looked down at Nathan again. "We must hide if they return."

Susanna thought of the few buildings in Nazareth and the hundred and fifty brothers and sisters who lived inside them. There wouldn't be many places for all of them to hide.

Lily began to sing softly to Nathan, a song about a mother bear who loved her cub, loved him so much that she had to leave him to chase the hunter away.

Chapter Twelve
....

Catharine fanned herself on her straw mattress with the turkey feathers Elias had gathered on the outskirts of Gnadenhutten. In spite of the complaints about the chilly air, she'd opened the shutters in their second-story room because it was too hot for her to sleep. None of her roommates complained any longer. Rebecca and the others slept while Catharine continued to fan herself.

Rebecca seemed to be satisfied with the sleeping arrangements in Gnadenhutten, but Catharine was not. Elias had promised her that they would stay together in a tent or a separate room on this mission. Some of the married Indians slept as families on a cliff above the main village, but after they'd arrived, Elias explained that he'd learned that, as messengers, they didn't want to separate themselves into a different house. They would live in community with their brothers and sisters as they had done in Nazareth.

She'd traveled all this way to be with her husband, and she wanted to feel Elias's arms around her at night, all night, like she had in their tent along the trail. Sometimes she even wanted him to sweep her all the way back to London, to the safety and comfort of the manor her father had abandoned when he joined the Brethren. They could live there together as husband and wife.

Coming to the New World had been a mistake. She'd known it the moment they arrived in Nazareth, but she had hoped that as the days passed, as she stole time away with Elias, she would forget her days in London. But she hadn't forgotten.

She could dream about the possibilities, but the truth was, even if she traveled back to Europe, she couldn't return to London. Her parents had sold the manor house along with most of their belongings so they could travel with the Count. Elias was her stability, her center, and she loved him with her entire being. She just didn't love the wilds of Pennsylvania.

Perhaps, if they couldn't return to London, Elias would take her to Philadelphia. Or New York. With his many talents, he could easily acquire a position as an architect or a builder, and they could live as a married couple in one of those brownstone homes she'd seen during their journey. She could send their children to the Brethren's school in Bethlehem, and she and Elias could attend the Lutheran church in the city.

She twisted on her mattress, but she couldn't rid herself of the aching in her lower back or her bladder. Her abdomen swelled, and she knew she had to use the privy yet again. The longer she waited, the less sleep she would get, and she refused to use that chamber pot they kept in the corner.

Standing to her feet, she tied her bag of coins around the outside of her cotton shift and wrapped her cloak over her shoulders before she crept toward the door. A small room divided the loft into sleeping rooms for the men and women, and moonlight trailed shadows across the floor, cascading down the staircase in front of her.

With a glance toward the closed door of the men's room, she wished she could sneak inside and nudge Elias to join her. The thought made her smile in the light. She could imagine him following her outside into the cool autumn night.

Of course, he would be mortified if the other men awoke and found her in their room. One day she would tell him what she suspected—that he would be a father in the spring—but she didn't want him or anyone else to guess her condition yet. They would want her to return to Nazareth right away.

Tiptoeing down the steps, she nudged open the front door and snuck out into the darkness. The privy wasn't far from the lodge, close to the hillside that separated their home from a cluster of Indian huts on the other side.

Before Samuel and the others left for their journey to Tanochtahe, she and Elias had met on the mossy bank of the river. Her pulse raced as she remembered the stolen moments they'd had in the starlight, hidden by the bramble. And in those moments together, she and Elias had made love. They'd made love and then they had fought.

She hated to fight with him, hated that there was no time for them to resolve their differences. Back in Marienborn she'd vowed to cleave to her husband but, as she told him on the riverbank, the opportunity to do so was a rarity, whether it was back in that ridiculous chamber in Nazareth or here among the Indians.

He'd chastised her for her selfishness, for her seemingly not caring whether the Indians heard the news about their Savior. She wanted the Brethren to share the good news with the Indians, but in her heart, she also wanted a home and a husband who could be with her every day. She wanted to bathe herself in the lights of the city and waltz across a dance floor.

Her very life seemed to be shriveling out here, and some moments she felt as if she could hardly breathe, as if she were a mouse trapped in a hole collapsing around her. She wanted to embrace life like she once had instead of being smothered by the bitterness that seemed to steal joy. She didn't have to live in a manor to do it, but she longed for privacy along with the companionship of the man she loved. She wanted to worship God every day, but she didn't want it to be required of her.

The next time she and Elias met, under the moonlight, perhaps, she wanted him to know how much she loved him. And she wanted to talk about their future. She needed to hear him say that they weren't going to be trapped in Gnadenhutten or Nazareth forever.

A pack of coyotes howled on the hill as she rushed toward the privy and then hurried back toward the lodge. Before she reached the door, though, something moved by the trees. Her heart lurched, not knowing if it was an animal or a person watching her.

* * * * *

Christian felt foolish for being outside, for stalking Catharine from the shadows, and yet he wanted to speak with her. After all these months, he'd never had the opportunity to ask what happened to their promises, and it tormented him every time he was near her.

Now that he was back from his travels and all the other Brethren were asleep, he could finally ask her about their past. And in their speaking, he hoped he could finally be relieved from the uncertainty of what had occurred between them. In her answers, he prayed he would find some relief.

"Catharine," he whispered as he stepped into the moonlight.

She opened her mouth, and he knew what would follow.

"Don't scream," he commanded, a little louder now, and he could see the powerful beauty of her eyes wavering between fear and relief. Her fear rapidly faded away as she pulled her cloak close to her chest.

"What are you doing out here?" she hissed.

"I heard someone on the steps," he began, and then he felt ridiculous at the words.

Initially he hadn't known that the footsteps were hers, but he knew it was Catharine when she returned to the lodge. Instead of staying in the shadows where he should have, hidden until she was safely in the lodge again, he had made himself known.

"So you followed me?"

"It's not safe for you to be out here alone."

She stepped away from him. "Elias would be furious if he found us

out here together."

Her skin glowed in the moonlight, and in that moment, he wished he had never heard her steps, never followed her down the stairs.

She picked up her skirt. "I'm going inside."

"Catharine—" If only he knew the truth of what had happened back in Marienborn, maybe he could stop the torment.

When she scooted around him, he reached for her arm. "Please, wait."

She yanked it away. "Elias doesn't know what happened between us, and he cannot find out."

"What did happen between us?" he demanded, still clutching her cloak. "I came to Marienborn to marry you, but you married another."

She stopped pulling away from him. "Why didn't you ask for me at Marienborn?"

"I did ask for you," he said quietly. "The lot rejected my request."

"The lot was right."

Her response rattled him; he couldn't seem to comprehend what she was saying. The lot wasn't right. It had kept them apart when they were supposed to marry.

"I couldn't marry you, Christian."

Her words scalded him, and he could do nothing but listen to her explain.

"I knew it the moment you were chosen to go on a mission to the Indians that we couldn't marry."

"You would have rejected the will of the lot?" he asked slowly, not knowing what else to say. Better to have her reject the lot than to reject him.

"I would have."

"You said you wanted to marry me."

Her voice softened. "I once cared for you, Christian, but I never loved you, not like I love Elias."

"You would have said no…." His voice trailed off in disbelief.

He remembered well their days together in London, the day he proposed the idea of marrying Catharine to her father. Robert Weicht had already decided that they would join the Unity of the Brethren, and he approved of their marriage. Christian and Catharine were walking in the gardens behind the Weicht home the afternoon he shared his heart with her, and she'd said she wanted to marry him as well.

He relocated from London to Marienborn the moment the Count requested he come. He'd been passionate about receiving his assignment to the Colonies and even more passionate about his marriage to Catharine.

"We never had an opportunity to speak at Marienborn," Catharine said, her voice soft again. "I'm sorry if you thought I was waiting for you."

"Of course I thought you were waiting, Catharine. We talked of marriage."

"That was before you decided to go on a mission."

His hand swept in front of him. "And yet here you are, on a mission."

"It's only temporary."

"The laboress in Marienborn…she said you would make a good companion for a missionary."

Catharine clucked her tongue as she took a step back toward him. "No woman wants to marry because she would make a good companion, Christian. She wants to marry because she believes in a man and his mission. She marries because she desires to love and respect him."

His mind flickered back to his talk with Susanna and how the light had faded from her face when he said he'd married her because it was required of him to marry. He shook his head in the darkness. He didn't know anything about women, not about what they wanted or what they needed.

He rubbed his hands together. "But you once desired to be with me—and I desired to be with you."

"Stop talking, Christian."

The sound of Elias's harsh voice made him jump, and Christian turned, tasting the words that had just left his mouth. The words about desiring Elias's wife.

Elias was a steady calm, his eyes on his wife. "What are you doing?"

"I was using the privy," Catharine said before she glared at Christian. "I'm not sure what Christian is doing out here."

When Elias turned his head, Christian saw fury in the bitter calm of his eyes.

I wanted to see your wife.

He didn't say the words, couldn't seem to say anything, but the truth ricocheted inside him. A truth too despicable to speak. He may not have known Catharine was out here when he stepped into the darkness, but once he knew, he should have run back into the lodge.

"You were saying you desired my wife," Elias said.

"Once." He stumbled on the word. "A long time ago."

Elias turned back to his wife, hurt laced through his demand. "What happened, Catharine?"

"Christian and I met in London, before my family joined the Brethren," she tried to explain. "We spent time together, Elias, but I never promised him anything."

"Did you flirt with him?"

How could Catharine deny her feelings for him? It had been there when she'd touched his arm, kissed his cheek. It had been there when they talked of marriage. It shouldn't matter—Catharine had chosen Elias over him—but it did matter.

"She didn't do anything wrong," Christian interjected. "It was all in my head."

Elias ignored him. "You didn't even tell me you knew of him before Marienborn."

"Nothing happened between us."

Elias twisted his hands together. "If nothing happened, then one of you would have told me."

The truth in his words hushed Christian's retort. Elias was right.

"Does Susanna know?" Elias asked.

"No, she doesn't," he started, but Catharine stopped him.

"She probably suspects. It would be hard not to, Christian, when you won't stop watching me."

Elias flinched. "You've been watching my wife?"

Christian couldn't look Elias in the eye. "I'm sorry."

"And what have you been doing, Catharine?" Elias asked

"Nothing," she insisted. "I swear."

Christian reached out, taking Elias's elbow. "She hasn't done anything to encourage me."

Elias shook his arm away. "Don't tell me about my wife."

"I'm sorry," he murmured again.

Elias moved away from them, toward the darkness of the trees. "Sort it out," he said. "And then decide who you will have, Catharine."

Catharine was seething when she turned again to Christian. "I asked you to leave me alone, Christian, and now you—"

He watched as she stomped away, back into the lodge. It didn't matter how sorry he was. They needed to bond as a community to spread the good news, but his selfishness, his weakness, was destroying it for all of them.

He walked slowly back up the stairs and lay down on his mattress. From now on, he would leave Catharine Schmidt alone.

Chapter Thirteen

....

March 1755

A trombone blasted from the plaza below to awaken the Brethren, but Susanna was already awake. She stood at the window like she had every morning since Christian left, praying that the messengers would be safe, praying that Christian and the others would return this spring. She was anxious to see Christian again, to see if something had changed within him in the six months he'd been gone, to see if he missed her as much as she had missed him.

Snow clustered around the edges of the glass panes and iced Nazareth's trees beyond the plaza. She shouldn't worry about Christian and Catharine and the other messengers out in the spring snow, but she couldn't seem to help herself. Rumors had poured into their community the past few weeks about hostile Indians scalping both white men and enemies from other Indian nations. There had even been stories of these Indians making alliances with the French and attacking the British forts near Canada as well as British settlers across the Colonies.

None of this should concern her—the Brethren embraced peace instead of war, refusing to take sides in any skirmish between the French and the British soldiers in the Colonies or among the Indians. But still she worried. The warring Indians and soldiers didn't know that their community aligned with God instead of man.

As she ran her fingers over the cold glass, she prayed that God would keep their people safe from those who were fighting each other.

Lily stepped up to the window beside her, her arms empty. She had taken Nathan to the Nursery in December, and while her friend had said she was ready for him to go, she continued to mourn the loss of him.

But she didn't speak of her son this morning. "Your husband must miss you as well."

Susanna slid her fingers over the glass, hoping again that Christian did miss her. "I'd hoped he would return by my birthday."

"When is your birthday?"

"The second of April."

"I'm sure he will do everything he can to return." Lily tapped at the pane and the snow fell away. "When you look out at the snow, thinking of him, he is probably thinking of you too."

Susanna twisted her hair and pinned it back before she placed her haube over it.

The great manor house was finally complete. The men had finished the inside two weeks ago, and a dozen women had scrubbed the interior before the laborers carried furniture into the house and hung the drapery. The appointed women had told Susanna and the others about the interior of the house, fit for the most royal of families, but Susanna had yet to see it.

Annabel's inspection had found a trail of footprints and dust the laborers had left behind as they removed the furnishings from the barn and arranged them inside the grand house. Susanna and Lily had been assigned to clean the interior one more time, in preparation for the arrival of Count Zinzendorf and his family.

While they were expecting the Zinzendorfs to live in the manor, she knew of no plans for the family to arrive. However, the Count often kept his travel plans secret so he wouldn't have to endure the fanfare that came with his visits. It terrified Annabel to think that the Count might arrive in Nazareth at any moment and find the manor their community had worked so hard to build for him and his family sullied with dust and dirt.

Even if the manor were spotless, if the Zinzendorfs did arrive this spring, there was still a problem of feeding their family. The workers the elders had hired to help build the manor had eaten through most of Nazareth's winter supply. Annabel would insist on the finest of their limited food supply for the Count's family, and while Susanna wasn't privy to the conversations of their leadership, she knew well the shrinking supply in their pantries and root cellar. Until the snow cleared away and the spring gardens began to provide for them, they would be pressing hard to feed the adults and children currently living in their community.

But Annabel was resourceful, as was the laborer named Edward. Susanna had no doubt that the two of them, along with Elder Graff, would find a way to supply food for Nazareth until summer.

After breakfast, Susanna wrapped her cloak across her shoulders and picked up a wooden bucket filled with water and vinegar for the floors. Flinging several rags over her arm, she joined Lily and two other sisters as they crossed the plaza.

They walked up the steps to the imposing front door on the manor, and Susanna's mouth dropped with they entered the great room.

"*Auwulsu*," Lily whispered.

Susanna nodded first before realizing she understood the word. *Beautiful.*

Lily stepped into the center of the great room and began to twirl, her dark braids whirling behind her. Like Catharine, Lily was too pretty to be wearing the simple haube and dress of their community. And too wild. She reminded Susanna of a great cat no one could tame.

Drapes flowered with greens and reds covered the windows in the great room, and woven carpets decorated the floors. The furniture and tables were covered with white sheets, and a mirror reflected the sunlight. The splendor inside was probably subdued compared to the castles and manors in Europe, but after living in the utilitarian rooms of the Sisters House for so long, Susanna was mesmerized by the beauty of it all.

As she passed by the mirror, she caught an image of herself. She stared for a moment at the strands of pale hair that circled the hem of her cap and eyes that were dulled by the gray light. Then she pressed her hands over her ginger-colored bodice and straightened her skirt before she looked away. Her health had recovered, but she still wished she were as beautiful as Catharine. Perhaps then she would see a reflection of this beauty in her husband's eyes.

She turned to the other women. "Where should we begin?"

"Usually we start up in the bedrooms," Ruth replied. "We work our way down."

Lily stepped toward the door.

"It is too much to clean," she said, but Susanna waved her forward. "Not if we work together."

A wide staircase led them up to the top floor and light flooded through the dormer windows in each room. For as far as she could see, snow covered the hills and trees beyond Nazareth.

She and Lily stepped into the room at the end of the hallway while their sisters began cleaning across the hall. There were no pictures on the wall of the chamber where they began, but the men had furnished it with a poster bed, a washstand with a ceramic bowl and pitcher, and a plain chair by the window.

Water sloshed out of the bucket when Lily dropped it onto the floor. "Who will sleep in all these rooms?"

"The Zinzendorfs will probably travel with their children."

"A whole family could sleep in one of these rooms."

Lily opened a window, shaking the rugs outside, as she began to sing a new song in her language.

"What does that mean?" Susanna asked.

"Too much work will steal your life away."

Susanna laughed as she dusted the posters of the bed. "That's not true."

Lily didn't return her laughter. "We will grow old cleaning this house and still your Count will not come."

"We don't know that," Susanna said. "There are more people arriving from Marienborn this month. The Count and his wife might accompany them."

Lily set the rug on the floor and looked back out the window. "If only we could go play in the snow."

Susanna followed Lily's gaze, wishing as well that she could be outside. "Perhaps Annabel will let us go to the Nursery later today and play with the children."

Lily clapped. "We could throw balls of the snow."

Susanna smiled. Sometimes she forgot that even though Lily had a baby, she was still more child than adult.

In broad strokes, Lily washed the footprints off the floor. Susanna didn't point out all the dirt she missed in her rushed work. Lily was made to be outside, playing and leaping like a panther, instead of being cooped up inside a house. On days like this, Susanna wondered why Lily continued to stay with the Brethren instead of going back to her tribe, but Lily refused to speak of her life before she came to Nazareth, except on those rare days when she mentioned that her husband would one day return for her. Susanna wondered why the man hadn't yet come.

Kneeling down, Susanna helped Lily finish the floor, and then they moved into the next chamber. This one was much bigger.

Curtains were drawn over the large bed, and glass vases were on the long dresser. Two pictures hung on the wall. One was of a staunch man in a dark cloak; the other, a woman wearing a haube with wide blue ribbons tied under her chin.

Lily's gaze remained on the pictures. "Who are they?"

"That's Count Zinzendorf," Susanna said. "And the woman is Countess Erdmuth, his wife."

Erdmuth wasn't a very pretty woman, but her ability to handle business matters was renowned among the Brethren. She was as capable as any man and certainly more capable than her husband when it came to financial matters. While the Count remained busy preaching and governing over the Brethren, the Countess ran their estates.

"Tell me about this Count Zinzendorf," Lily said.

Susanna thought for a moment. How could she describe this larger-than-life man who had sacrificed his position and much of his wealth for the Brethren?

"He was a Count with the royal court, but he felt a strong calling to begin a community called Hernnhut to harbor Christians escaping religious persecution in Moravia and across Europe and Russia," she explained. "He lay down his prestige and position in the empire to lead our people and become a Lutheran minister. Most of his family refuses to forgive him for it, but his wife supports him, as do the rest of the Brethren."

Susanna scrubbed the floor even harder, grateful at all the Zinzendorfs had done for them. The fact that the Count and his family would even consider staying here for a season, living among them, was remarkable.

"The Count always tries to do what is right for our community," she continued to explain. "He calms strife and helps people from many different countries and religious backgrounds to live and seek God together."

"He reminds me of my father," Lily said. "Or at least the part about calming strife in your community. My clan has yet to seek God together."

"Some day, perhaps, they will seek God."

While Susanna often watched the window for Christian's return, Lily never seemed to watch for Nathan's father. Or if she did, Lily never told her. She sang instead, of flowers and dance, and she played with Nathan in the Nursery whenever possible.

Susanna picked up one of the vases and slowly wiped it. It would take days for them to dust the stored furniture and wash the floors, but she wouldn't complain. It was a welcome relief from the monotony in the Sisters House. Still, she longed to go on a mission to the Indians.

Before she put the vase down, she heard footsteps racing up the hallway, and one of her fellow workers rushed into the room.

Ruth took a long breath. "The messengers are back."

Susanna dropped the vase.

Ruth jump backward as pieces shattered on the floor. The woman looked down at the blue shards and then back up. Susanna stared at the shards as well, unable to speak. How could she have been so foolish?

Lily scooted her out the door. "Go see him," she insisted. "I will clean up the glass."

But Susanna stood frozen in her place. After all these months of waiting and wondering, her husband had finally come home. She brushed her hands over her work dress. If only she'd known when he was returning, she would have chosen a different dress. The blue one from their wedding.

"Go," Lily commanded, nudging her again.

This time she listened, hurrying down the long hallway and steps. Would he ignore her like he had after their journey from Marienborn, or would he greet her with a kiss on her cheek? Surely he wouldn't ignore her, not after the moments they shared in the chamber. He may not love her, but they had connected in a small way as brother and sister. She prayed he would want to see her again.

Stopping on the staircase, she wiped her sleeve across her face and wished again she could change into better attire, but there was no time now. She wanted to be one of the first to greet him.

Her petticoat lifted above her knees, she ran across the plaza toward the Gemeinhaus. Dozens had already gathered inside to welcome their brothers and sisters home, and she scooted around them with no thought for protocol. She wanted to see her husband.

Rebecca was the first person she saw, standing beside Joseph. Her face was thinner than when she left, her haube replaced by a single braid that trailed down her back. Instead of looking excited when she saw Susanna, her smile faded a bit, and in the fading of her friend's smile, Susanna's heart began to plunge.

She greeted her friend with a kiss on each of her cheeks, and then she scanned the heads of the crowd. "Where is Christian?"

Rebecca shook her head. "He's not here."

"But—" She couldn't allow herself to consider what might have happened to him. "Where did he go?"

"There you are!" she heard Catharine exclaim. When she turned, Catharine engulfed her in her arms. And then she stepped back. Her friend's stomach had grown large in the months she was gone.

"Catharine?"

"The Schmidt baby will arrive very soon."

Her mind seemed to whirl. When had her friend gotten pregnant?

Catharine leaned in, whispering to her. "Elias and I snuck away together in Bethlehem."

Susanna studied her friend's face, but there was no glow like she'd seen among some of the other married women. Something was wrong.

"Where is Christian?" she asked again, this time more reluctantly than the first. She searched her friend's face, confused. "Where did he go?"

"He and Samuel left in January to visit the Indians."

"Why didn't you wait for them to return?" Susanna asked.

"Our baby is coming soon." Catharine rolled her hands over her belly. "Elias thought it would be too dangerous to have our baby in Gnadenhutten."

"Your husband is a wise man."

"No." Catharine shook her head. "He is a foolish one."

Susanna didn't know what to say for a moment. Catharine had never spoken an ill word about Elias. "The baby will be born in a safe place here."

"This has nothing to do with the baby."

"Come, Catharine." Elias stepped beside them, taking her arm. "You must rest."

As Susanna watched them leave the Saal, she wondered what had happened between them. Had the months Catharine and Elias spent together sapped the sweetness out of their relationship? This was the precise reason most of the married Brethren lived separate. The conflict from marital life was taxing on the spirit and the mind. But too much time apart was taxing on the soul.

She slipped back through the crowd, toward the Sisters House. Disappointment hung like a dark cloud over her as she shuffled into the house and collapsed on a leather chair in the common room. She'd wanted Christian to return for her birthday, but she never should have expected it. Of course he had stayed with the Indians. It was his passion to live among them.

As the others celebrated in the Gemeinhaus, her tears fell freely in the quiet space.

Her prayers would continue, that Indians would listen to the good news, that they would follow the Savior. And that Christian and Samuel would be safe in the midst of the turmoil.

And when God allowed it, she prayed He would lead Christian safely home to her.

Chapter Fourteen

....

Indian children gathered on bear rugs around Christian's feet in the warm lodge, their parents standing behind the circle. Many of the warriors' arms were crossed, their eyes and hearts hardened against any news white men might bring, but they waited in silence for Chief Langoma's nod to begin.

Christian ate from the platter of boiled trout Chief Langoma served him. Skepticism seemed to bleed through most of the villages they had visited this winter. Some chiefs allowed him to share the story of the Christ Child, while others commanded Samuel and him to leave when they began to speak about their God.

In all the villages they visited, only one Indian had inquired in private about following their Savior—a woman with the English name of Mary. He had wanted to baptize her, but she feared her clan might kill her if she rejected the many gods of their people to follow the Savior. Every day he prayed for her, that she would decide to follow Christ in the face of persecution. Even if her tribe stole away her body, God would protect her soul.

Joseph remained in Gnadenhutten to help Elias complete the gristmill, but as Christian and Samuel wandered from village to village this winter, seeing little fruit from their labor, his mind wandered back to Chief Langoma and his people. The last time he had seen the tribe, they were dancing and chanting around their barrel of rum, but now they stood like statues with the adults glowering at him in the firelight.

He wasn't sure which was worse, the Indians' animosity or their unruliness, but he refused to be intimidated. Samuel told him he had to do more than tell a story to the Indians; he had to demonstrate God's love through humility and grace. He wasn't sure how, exactly, to demonstrate these when they were so angry. But Chief Langoma had said he had lost a child. Perhaps his clan would understand what it was like for God to sacrifice His son.

Christian sat down on a rug in front of the children and folded his hands. At least the children were eager to hear his words.

When Chief Langoma nodded at him, he took a deep breath. And then, as Samuel translated his words, he began to share the grandest story of them all. He told of a little baby born in a cave, of the animals that crowded around the baby and his mother. He told how this boy, birthed in the hay, was sent from the God above all gods as a sacrifice.

And with those words, he watched the shift in their eyes. They understood sacrifice.

Talking faster now, he told of the boy in a faraway land who grew up to be a carpenter. Of a man who could turn water into wine and even make the eyes of a blind man see. Of a man who was accused of doing wrong when He'd sought nothing but truth and righteousness.

As many times as Christian had told the story of God's Son, it never grew old for him. So many had never heard that God loved them, that God could forgive their sins. They didn't know that Christ had died for them.

"And then," he said, scooting closer to the children, "the soldiers beat this innocent man with a whip and put a cross on His back. They forced Him to walk through the streets while people laughed at Him. Spat at Him. They didn't know it, but they were mocking the one person who could help them. The one person who could rescue them from the bad things they had done."

Even as he spoke, Christian felt the weight of his own words. The story breathed power through him, no matter how many times he told it.

Christian flung out his arm and pretended to pound a nail into his wrist. He told how the soldiers pounded nails through the arms and feet of the one man who had never sinned. He told them how the Lamb of God had to die so that each of them could be saved.

"The sky turned black when Jesus died, and the earth shook."

One of the Indian children spoke, and Christian turned to Samuel for interpretation.

"He said the gods must have been angry."

"It wasn't the gods you know," Christian said with a shake his head. "Our God is love and justice and mercy, and His heart broke as He watched His only Son die. He loved Him, you see, as only a Father can love His child."

Behind the children, several of the warriors had dropped their arms to their sides while listening to the story. The animosity drained from their eyes and changed into expectation. Perhaps a bit of their hearts tore as well at the thought of losing a son.

"Christ didn't stay on the cross." Christian's voice dropped to a whisper. "Nor did He stay in the grave."

He paused as his audience leaned forward, letting them wonder about the man who didn't stay in His grave.

"Three days after His death, the ground rumbled yet again, but this time the land brought forth the Christ Child instead of stealing Him away. This time Jesus unwrapped the clothes that bound His body and walked out of the tomb.

"Can you imagine it?" Christian asked and then waited for Samuel's interpretation.

"Can you see the faces of those who had seen Jesus die?" he asked. "They knew He was gone—they had wrapped and buried Him in a tomb three days before. But now, now He was here among them again. The scars were still in His wrists and his feet, but He was alive again. Alive and willing to forgive anyone who asked.

"God already made the sacrifice. You and I must only accept this gift of forgiveness. Of freedom. We are no longer bound to the evil in this world."

He reached for another piece of the white trout meat as the Indians around him peppered Samuel with questions. Samuel answered them on his own.

One of the women brought Christian a wooden bowl steaming with hot liquid and a large spoon. He dipped the spoon into the bowl and tasted blackberry and chicory as he sipped it.

We are no longer bound....

The words filtered through his mind as the Indians continued to speak around him. He'd traveled for months now, sharing the forgiveness of Christ with different Indian nations and clans, but even as he spoke about God's forgiveness, he realized suddenly that he had yet to allow Christ to forgive him of his sins. He still clung to the sin that tormented him.

Why could he not let it go?

Nothing had been the same since that night he had followed Catharine out into the darkness back in October, but after they had talked, when she finally told him the truth, some of the bitterness he'd harbored against the elders, against the lot, began to melt away.

But his search for the truth had caused harm, irreparable perhaps. After that night in Gnadenhutten, Elias's love for Catharine seemed to crumble, and it was Christian's fault. His sin remained in him even though what he thought was love wasn't love at all. It was lust. He had wanted her to fulfill his needs as a wife and a companion; he hadn't wanted to care for her. Not like Elias, who cared very much for her, so much that Christian's secret had crushed him.

He worried about Elias even as Christian tried to transform his own mind with the promise of the Gospel. God clearly hadn't wanted him married to Catharine, but what *did* God want of him?

Back in Marienborn, he'd thought God wanted him to share the truth with the Indians. He thought hundreds of them would decide to follow Christ once he shared the Gospel. He'd come to Pennsylvania to be used of God, but perhaps God didn't need him as much as Christian wanted Him to.

His dreams of Catharine persisted, but instead of relishing them, he fought against them.

"If we confess our sins, he is faithful and just to forgive us our sins, and to cleanse us from all unrighteousness."

The Scripture blazed through his mind, and in that moment, he knew exactly what he had to do. A long time ago, he had asked God to forgive his sins and God had done that. But even as he traveled around now, sharing the good news of this forgiveness, he hadn't allowed Christ to forgive him of his sin against Catharine or against himself. Or his sin against Susanna. He clung to the pleasures of his sin even as it tormented him.

He glanced around the crowded room, at Samuel as he continued answering questions. God was using Samuel to share his love with the native people; why did he need Christian to come as well? He started to stand—Samuel had told him before that the white men often hindered an Indian's decision to follow Christ. Tonight he would leave and let this clan decide as a tribe what they wanted to do.

Instead of sending him away, though, Samuel pressed on his shoulder. "Sit," he whispered. "This time you must wait."

Christian sat back on the rug and listened to banter he didn't understand. Samuel had been so patient with him, trying to help him understand the language, but he struggled with the pronunciation and the accents, straining to remember even the basic words. He thought he could remember the words if only he could read them, but the Delaware language was spoken, not written. So he kept trying—and failing—to learn it.

So as the Indians discussed the story, he watched the snow fall outside the window until darkness covered the white. And he wondered what Susanna was doing in Nazareth tonight. Very soon, the community would be celebrating the story of Christ's resurrection with song and a special love feast of coffee and sweet rolls. When he and Samuel were done here, they would return to Gnadenhutten so they could travel back with the Wittkes and Schmidts for Easter. For Susanna's birthday.

An hour or two passed, the talk growing more animated as the folded arms transformed into gestures, wide and strong. Then Chief Langoma lifted his arms, and the murmuring ceased. He spoke in the language of the Delaware for the benefit of his people.

Samuel interpreted the chief's question. "How do we get this forgiveness of our sins?"

Christian leaned forward. In the few words he'd learned from their language, he said simply, "You must ask God for it."

The chief paused a moment, everyone looking at him. "We will ask."

Stunned, the reply froze on Christian's lips. In all the places they had traveled during the past few months, all the stories he had told, this was the first time an Indian wanted this gift.

Finally he nodded. "We will ask together."

Christian bowed his head, Samuel interpreting his prayer beside him. He asked God to forgive the people around him, His children, of their sins. He asked the almighty God to empower each of them with His spirit to avoid the temptations of the world and follow Him into the light.

When he finished his prayer, the chief clasped his hand and shook it. "You promised us peace," the chief said. "And you have abided by your promise."

"It is God's promise," Christian said. "He desires each of us to be peacemakers."

It was what God desired, but he had failed miserably with the Schmidt family.

Christian spent hours reading the New Testament to the tribe over the next two days, and Samuel interpreted the words. The questions poured out of the Indians. What is a neighbor and how do you love them as yourself? How will a meek person inherit the earth? Where could they get the salt that never loses its savor?

He and Samuel wrestled and prayed through each question, for wisdom from the Lord. He didn't want to lead them astray nor did he want to leave, but the others were waiting for them in Gnadenhutten to return to Nazareth for the spring.

Before they left, the chief presented Christian with a gift of leather leggings to wear over his breeches. Then he held up the belt of wampum that Christian had delivered on their first meeting.

"It is my covenant to you," Chief Langoma said as he handed the belt back to him. "We will serve this Child of the High God with you."

Christian took the belt and strung the beads through his fingers. It was a testimony of all their Savior had done in this village, and he would be faithful to return to his new brothers and sisters to encourage and teach them about the ways of God.

"It is our covenant," he promised the chief. "For me to pray for your people and serve you in whatever way I am able."

* * * * *

With a square piece of wax, Catharine drew a cross on one side of the egg and rose petals on the other. She placed the egg in a basket, and across from her, Susanna dipped it into a ceramic pot of water boiled with rose hips to dye the egg a deep red color. This was a new tradition for her and the other sisters who'd yet to celebrate Easter in Pennsylvania, but those who had lived here for several seasons said the children enjoyed finding the colorful eggs hidden in the yard that surrounded the Nursery.

Catharine picked up another egg and started to draw again. It was hardly the artwork that she'd once created with her needle and thread, but it gave her mind and hands something pleasant to do this evening. Something to help her stop thinking about Elias and their baby.

She and Elias had spent more than six months together in the wilderness. Months that were supposed to be filled with marital bliss. But Christian Boehler, in his selfishness, had destroyed their delight in being together. Everyone in Nazareth would soon learn of her husband's disdain for her. And Christian would return any day now. What else would he destroy for her?

It didn't matter what happened so long ago. She and Elias were married now and she, for one, had been happy in her marriage. It wasn't her fault that Christian couldn't let go of what he'd imagined and embrace the wife God had given him. Neither she nor the lot had agreed to their marriage.

His foolishness had cost both of them. Or at least it cost her the trust and admiration of the man she loved. Elias had avoided speaking with her after he confronted Christian, and it wasn't like there was a bedchamber in Gnadenhutten for the married couples to meet or a laboress to coordinate their times together. It was assumed that they would steal time together on their own. Before it turned cold, Rebecca and Joseph had often snuck out together, but after that fateful night with Christian, Elias no longer whispered invitations to her.

She pushed so hard on the wax, the boiled egg cracked in her hand. She placed the egg in a separate basket. They wouldn't color it, but the Brethren would still eat it.

"Are you okay?" Susanna asked.

"As well as I can be."

Elias's trust had faded with Christian's words, but when she could no longer hide the baby within her, when he stopped to question her, she answered his questions. And she had to tell him the truth—that she had suspected she was expecting a child soon after they arrived in Gnadenhutten.

He was furious at her for keeping this secret from him, but when he asked if the child was his, she'd almost slapped him.

The baby was his, but Elias never spoke of it. Her deception had cost her—had cost both of them—and she spent hours trying to figure out a way to win him back. She couldn't imagine continuing on here in the shadow of Elias's hatred. It would break her.

Another egg cracked, and Susanna reached over and took it from her hands.

"Sit down," she said.

"I'm fine."

Susanna shook her head. "You need to rest, Catharine."

The baby kicked her, and she backed away from the table of eggs and dyes. She didn't need to rest, but perhaps her anger was aggravating their child.

She put her head in her hands. She never should have left Marienborn. She'd sought freedom and received it, but she didn't want to be here. Nor did she want to go back to Marienborn. She wanted to return to her home in London, to her servants and her painting and to a nanny who would help her care for the life within her.

She didn't know how to care for a baby, not even for the first year like they did among the Brethren. When she was a child, she'd been cared for by nursemaids who changed her clothing and fed her and sung her to sleep. Her mother was more of an apparition, floating in and out at mealtimes and between social events. She'd often dreamed of the day when she would become an apparition like her mother.

How was she supposed to care for this child with no husband and no nursemaid?

The thought terrified her.

She'd lost Elias's trust already, and she couldn't imagine what he would say if she told him she was unable to care for a child. He was too good a man to divorce her, with or without the commands of the Scripture, but if she told him this final revelation, the love they once knew, the fragile thread that might remain, would be lost forever.

Susanna slipped away from the table of eggs and sat down on the bench beside her. She slipped her arm around Catharine's shoulders and hugged her.

"What is wrong?"

The baby kicked Catharine again, and she rubbed her side. She didn't know the exact date that she conceived, nor did she know the signs of when a baby was supposed to arrive, but it seemed to her that this child was ready to enter into the world.

When she didn't answer, Susanna asked again. "Are you all right?"

Catharine looked into the light eyes of her friend, already mourning the loss of their friendship. Once Susanna found out about her and Christian, she would hate her too.

"Nothing is right anymore."

"Did something happen between you and Elias?"

She hesitated. How was she supposed to tell Susanna the truth?

"Gnadenhutten wasn't what I expected," she said. "But you would have liked it there. The Indians are all striving to serve the Savior and work together as a community. And most of them live as families so they can raise their children in their homes."

"Catharine—" Her friend's voice was gentle but strong. "That doesn't answer my question."

Catharine rested her hand on her belly, and then she conceded. "Elias and I quarreled."

"On your way home?'

"No," she said. "Not long after we arrived in Gnadenhutten. And then when he found out about the baby…"

"He was angry about the baby?"

She shook her head. "He was angry that I didn't tell him sooner about our child."

"You must have known he would be upset."

She glanced down at her hands. "But I didn't know he would find out about Christian."

Her head jerked up, and as she watched Susanna's eyes widen, she wished she could swallow her words, make them disappear, but it was too late.

Susanna set down her spoon, and her voice trembled when she spoke again. "What about Christian?"

Chapter Fifteen
....

Instead of sneaking through the darkness this time, Christian and Samuel hiked out of the village in the brilliant morning light. They had baptized eighteen Indians in the frigid river, and he wished they could stay behind and join Chief Langoma and the others in the initial months of joy that come when someone decides to follow the Savior. And journey with them through the months of trials that would surely come as well.

Their Indian friends waved to them as they walked to the edge of the settlement, and then the chief accompanied them down to the river. On the trees of the riverbank were red-painted pictures of bears and birds and turtles, and Christian noted the images as he promised the chief he would visit again when the harvest was done.

The chief shook his head at his promise, Samuel interpreting the warning that hostile Indians had been seen nearby. These Indians wouldn't be pleased to know that white men were sharing freedom with the Indian people. But Christian wasn't frightened or intimidated. God had brought them to Chief Langoma and his people, and if it was His will for them to return safely home, their Savior would guard them on their journey.

He climbed into the front of the canoe, and when Samuel began to paddle, Christian joined him. It was a four-hour canoe ride downstream to Gnadenhutten, and if the weather didn't hinder them, they should be back before dark.

As the bright red pictures disappeared behind them, Christian prayed that the new converts would stay strong in the next months, that they would pray together as he and Samuel had explained and hold fast in their new faith. It would be hard for them to remain strong without someone to read them God's Word and answer their questions.

Samuel guided them around a large rock in the middle of the water. "You did well back there."

"I did nothing," he said with a shake of his head. "It was God's story that inspired them."

"His story, yes. His story along with your love."

In that moment, Christian realized that he had begun to love these people. Their travels had started as a mission to share the hope and truth of Christ, a truth that continued to propel him forward, but now it was a mission of caring as well. He didn't want the Indians to simply make a decision. He desperately wanted them to know the heart of their Savior.

No matter what anyone had done, no matter how foul, God desired to remove the sin.

No matter what they had done...

"Samuel." He hesitated, wondering if this was the right thing for him to do. He put his oar on his lap and turned toward the back of the boat. "The Bible says we need to confess our sins."

Samuel questioned him with his look. "Yes, it does."

A clump of snow fell from a pine branch onto Christian's hat, and he shook it off. "I've been confessing my sins to God, but the Bible also tells us that we should confess them to each other."

Samuel nodded. "Satan can only control us if we hold onto our sin. He has no control over us if we tell our brothers."

Christian stared at Samuel, dumbfounded, even as he knew the man was right. Samuel didn't need another member of the Brethren to go on a mission to the Indians. God had infused him with wisdom and truth…and love for his people.

"You are my brother, Samuel."

Samuel lifted his oar out of the water, and they glided in the slow current. "I thought you were scared of me."

"Not anymore." Christian dipped his oar into the river. "For months I've been sharing the story of forgiveness for sins and yet I wrestle every day within myself."

"You wrestle to forgive?"

"I wrestle to rid myself of my sins."

Samuel waited a moment before he spoke again. "Elias's wife is a pretty woman."

Christian stared at him, shocked at his words. "How did you know about Catharine?"

"It is quite obvious, my friend. You watch her constantly, like she is a bear and you are the hunter."

The elation inside him from their time with Chief Langoma seemed to collapse. Samuel knew the truth now as well as Elias. Catharine had even hinted that Susanna might have guessed his affection for her friend.

Who else knew about what he tried so hard to keep secret?

Samuel began paddling again. "You must stop watching her."

"All day long, I try to force myself not to think about her—not to look at her—but then she haunts my dreams. Her heart belongs to Elias, but I can't seem to control my heart." Emotion poured out of him. Desperation. "I don't want to long for her any more. I want to love Susanna."

Samuel reached up and grabbed a branch overhead, stopping the canoe. Without saying another word, he bowed his head and began to pray. He prayed that God would deliver Christian from the devil's attempts to sidetrack him from his work in sharing the Gospel. He prayed that the demons would stop tormenting Christian when he slept. And he prayed that the message of forgiveness would transform Christian as well as all who heard it from his lips.

When Samuel finished his prayer, Christian felt like the stronghold of his sin had begun to crumble. Samuel released the branch and they began to paddle in sync again. And as they paddled, the mysterious power of God began to renew Christian's spirit and his mind.

Samuel's voice was low when he spoke again. "There is one other person you must confess to."

"Elias already knows."

"Not Elias," Samuel said. "You must tell Susanna."

Susanna?

His heart dipped again. It was hard enough to tell Samuel about his dreams, but to tell his wife? In the purity of her spirit, what could she possibly think of him in his sin? He had already failed her in their marriage. With his confession, she would think even less of him.

"I can't."

"You must tell her," Samuel insisted. "It is the only way for both of you to break free."

* * * * *

Susanna rolled over on her bed. Catharine had insisted that her words last night meant nothing, that she'd misspoken about Christian being the reason she and Elias quarreled. And yet the thought continued to niggle at Susanna. Why would Catharine and Elias fight about her husband?

Even though Susanna longed to hear more about Christian and his travels to the Indians, Catharine answered few of her questions, saying she would have to speak with Christian when he returned. But she didn't know when her husband would return or even if he would ever come back. She shuddered. If he were injured in the wilderness or taken away by another Indian, she would never know what happened. He would simply be gone. Lily assured her that no one with Samuel would get lost in the wilderness, but what if Christian, in his stubbornness, decided to go somewhere without his guide? Sometimes a man's determination could get him into trouble.

She'd gone over the possibilities so many times in her head, Christian lying wounded alone or wounded by an Indian. The worry never helped except when it inspired her to pray. And so she prayed yet again.

When she opened her eyes, she gazed at the starlight in the window as the snores of sisters on both sides of her harmonized with softer breathing. Easter was upon them now, and Lily and the other women assured her that the weather in the New World would turn calm in weeks if not days. They said wind and rain would replace the snow for a season and then the sun would warm the earth.

In a few days now, on Easter, Susanna would be twenty-three. Her mother used to celebrate the day of Susanna's birth with a picnic lunch and special cakes made of caraway seeds, sugar, and milk. They would spread a cloth in a grassy field, among the wildflowers that blossomed every spring. Perhaps this year Annabel would let her and Lily celebrate her day by roaming the hills outside the village after they hid the eggs for the children.

She closed her eyes, allowing herself to dream again.

The best birthday gift, of course, would be for her husband to return home on Easter day.

Chapter Sixteen

....

Smoke from the fireplace coiled above the white rooftop of Gnaden-hutten's Gemeinhaus, as water poured over the wheel of Elias's grist-mill and splashed into the river. Christian and Samuel had pulled the canoe out of the water about a half mile downstream and hiked toward the settlement. Christian's fingers were numb from the cold of the evening, his throat dry.

The sun had already set as the two men rushed into the warm lodge. Samuel greeted the Christian Indians who shuffled through the door to welcome them home. Christian tried to greet them with enthusiasm as well, but his body wanted to fold over itself and sleep by the fireplace. He sat on a cane chair by the table, and when he reached out in front of the fire to rub the numbness out of his hands, his fingers stung. He pulled them away from the flames.

An Indian named Benjamin ladled hot tea from a kettle over the fire and handed each of them a gourd filled with the drink to fight off their chill. Christian cradled the cup in his hands, his fingers awak-ened by the fire, and drank the mixture of peppermint and ginger. The pain began to subside, but even the peppermint couldn't warm the chill that tangled itself around his core.

With his last sips, he felt as if he had awakened from a stupor, and he glanced from the table to the stairs on the other side of the room. For the first time since they walked in the door, he realized that neither the Schmidts nor the Wittkes were among those gathered to greet them.

"Where is Elias?" he asked.

Benjamin turned slowly from the fire. "He already left for Nazareth."

"Nazareth…" Christian repeated the word. "What about Joseph?"

"He and his wife left as well."

"But we were all supposed to leave together on the last day of March."

Instead of responding, Benjamin turned to Samuel, speaking in the language of the Delaware. Christian understood very little of their conversation.

Samuel motioned him away from the table, and they stood by the doorway.

"They all returned to Nazareth four days ago," Samuel whispered. "Elias finished his work on the mill, and they needed to go back before Catharine's child was born."

"Catharine's child?"

Samuel watched him, and Christian thought his own reaction to the news might be one of anger, but oddly enough, he felt nothing.

"They were concerned she might deliver soon."

He quickly calculated the months in his mind, wondering for a brief moment when she had conceived this child, but the thought dissolved under the intensity of Samuel's gaze. The man knew what he was thinking, and that knowledge forced him to push the thought away.

"Benjamin guided them and the Wittkes back to Nazareth."

Christian rubbed his hands together. He wasn't anxious to confront the cold again, but it was time to go home. "We must follow them."

Samuel nodded. "At first light."

Benjamin looked at Samuel. "Howling Wolf and several of his men were spotted near here yesterday."

Samuel glanced at Christian, and Christian saw the slightest hint of fear in his eyes before he looked back at Benjamin. Christian had begun to believe that Samuel wasn't afraid of anything. "Are you certain?"

Benjamin nodded. "I saw them myself when I returned, near the Rose Meadow."

"We will be careful."

Christian slept fitfully in the loft. Catharine didn't haunt his dreams that night, nor did this Howling Wolf or any of the other Indians. Tonight he dreamed of Susanna. But it wasn't a dream that warmed him, like the ones of Catharine. This one frightened him. He asked for her forgiveness at his deception and she refused to give it, like Elias refused Catharine the peace brought by forgiveness.

So long ago, back in Bethlehem, the men had asked him if he was afraid of his wife. He'd lied. He was terrified of her.

Even so, Samuel was right. He would never be free—he and Susanna would never be free together—unless he told her the truth.

Long before daylight, Christian awoke and he and Samuel hiked out of Gnadenhutten in the darkness. The ridges of the mountains sparkled in the light and ice from a dozen waterfalls clung to rocks, blue crystals glittering like gemmed necklaces adorning the cliffs. There was no snow on the other side of the mountain, so the two men sloshed their way through the valley.

"Will you truly go back to visit Chief Langoma in the fall?" Samuel asked.

"If the Lord wills it."

"Once Chief Langoma tells other clans about what happened with his people," Samuel said, "there will be more who will want to know about the Savior."

"I would like to tell them," Christian replied. "And I would like it if you went with me again."

Samuel was quiet for a moment. "I would like to return as well."

Christian nodded, and they continued their walk in the silence. The pathway grew drier as they hiked south, until they no longer struggled to walk through mud.

Christian was grateful for Samuel's companionship and his wisdom. They worked well together, and until he learned the language—if he ever learned the language—he trusted the man to interpret his message and guide him both along the terrain and within the villages.

He'd never needed another man to protect him before, but he sensed that the Indians might not have been as welcoming to him without Samuel's presence. They didn't trust white men, and Christian couldn't blame them. White men were trying to force them off their lands and kill Indians from the Delaware nation and from nations like the Mohawk and Oneida.

Christian also understood the white men's fear. If an Indian scalped his neighbor or child, he might be afraid too. It was impossible for a European to know the Indians who came in goodwill versus those who killed for spite.

"Who is this Howling Wolf?" he ventured.

Samuel's gaze remained on the path. "Many of our people are not happy with those who tell Indians the story of Christ. Howling Wolf isn't pleased with this new faith that some of his people are embracing, nor is he happy that the Brethren have settled in Nazareth and other places where the Indians were once free to roam."

"But we purchased that land from George Whitefield."

"Howling Wolf doesn't believe Whitefield was the rightful owner of the land."

"Is this Howling Wolf the reason that only one Indian chief would listen to our message?"

"One reason, perhaps, but it is a hard message you deliver, that a god would care about his people and offer his gift of forgiveness for free, when most of the gods my people know require so much of them."

"They prefer a god who is cruel?"

"Some of them prefer a god they understand," Samuel replied. "A god who thrives on division and war and doesn't ask them to give up their rum or their many wives."

"If you think I should speak in a different way to them, Samuel, you need to tell me."

"You didn't preach to Chief Langoma and his people. You told the story of Christ and they understood the power in this story—"

Samuel suddenly threw out his hand in front of Christian, stopping his walk. Christian squinted ahead of them, into dense pine trees, and started to speak, but Samuel put his finger against his lips and motioned for Christian to follow him. They slipped behind a narrow rock along the path, and Samuel pulled his musket over his shoulder, bracing it in his hands.

From behind the rock Christian watched three Indians pass by, and he held his breath. In spite of the cold temperatures, their chests were bare, bows and quivers of arrows strapped over them. Emblazoned across the chest of the first man was some sort of tattoo.

A fissure between the rock and cliff exposed their hiding place, but it was too late to move farther back into the woods. Christian pressed his back against the cliff, but the men were still in sight. If the Indians turned to the side, they would be able to see him as well. But the men didn't seem to realize that they were being watched. They plodded along quietly, their footsteps making no sound. If Samuel, who'd shown no fear in the midst of all the villages they had visited, feared these men, then Christian was wise to fear them as well.

Seconds passed after the Indians disappeared from view, but Samuel kept the gun in his hand.

"Don't move," he whispered, and Christian remained motionless against the jagged cliff.

He didn't know how many minutes went by before Samuel lowered his gun and directed him away from the rock and the pathway.

"Was that Howling Wolf?"

Samuel nodded. "And two of his men."

"But I didn't hear them."

"Neither did I," Samuel said. "I smelled them."

Christian wiped his clammy hands on his new leather breeches. In that moment, he was exceedingly glad for the guidance of his friend.

* * * * *

As she brushed her long hair, Susanna squinted out the window, into the dark morning, as she listened to the trumpets and trombone play. There was no pattering of rain on the window or clumps of snow, but she wished she knew if sunshine would greet them on this Easter morning. Her birthday.

She twisted back her hair before she tied the blue ribbon of her haube under her chin. To celebrate Easter morning, she slipped her blue bodice over her shoulders and tied the ribbons. The other women around her busied themselves, preparing for the early morning of worship.

She lit an oil lantern, and when the bell rang, Catharine stepped in beside her and they joined the other women, also carrying lanterns, who followed Annabel across the plaza. This time though, they didn't stop at the Gemeinhaus. They continued walking up a long slope, past the Disciple's House and through the trees until they joined their brothers at the cemetery they called God's Acre.

Flat stones marked the graves, and they seemed to glow in the lantern light as the people sang. The sun rose over the hills and forest to their east, and as the sunshine warmed her face, Susanna knew it was going to be a glorious spring day. The sisters would take the dyed eggs to the Nursery this afternoon and hide them for the children. And then the community would enjoy them along with a feast for their supper.

She closed her eyes, worshipping their Savior as she felt the warmth of His love wash over her along with the sacrifice of His death and miracle of His resurrection. She was still praying, still worshipping, when Lily elbowed her.

"What?" she whispered.

Lily didn't speak. Instead she pointed to their left, and Susanna followed the trail of her finger to two men who'd joined them in the rear. Her heart leaped within her.

Christian had come home.

Elder Graff began to pray, and Susanna squeezed her eyes shut before he saw her, trying to steady the rapid breaths that rushed out of her mouth. Her heart rejoiced at the safe return of her husband, and she wanted to stand up and run to him, to tell him how much she had missed him, but she sat silently among the others, knowing he was there but pretending she hadn't seen him.

The elder's prayer ended quickly, and then he waved Christian and Samuel toward him. Elder Graff spoke to Christian, and then she watched as Christian's gaze roamed over the crowd of women. She didn't look away this time, didn't cower at his search, and when he found her, she smiled at him for the briefest moment.

"Happy birthday," he mouthed.

As the flame from the lantern flickered in Susanna's hands, a fire sparked inside her and roared through her skin.

"Welcome home," she whispered back.

He smiled at her before she looked away.

She didn't dare look back, not when her eyes would betray all the emotions that blazed inside her. She couldn't let him know, not until the same feelings raged through him as well.

Chapter Seventeen

....

Christian followed the slender figure of his wife as she walked down the hill with the other sisters. Her head was bowed, but before she left the cemetery, she glanced back at him one last time with her gentle smile. And in both her smile and her words, she welcomed him home.

He didn't move from his place among the brothers as he watched Susanna—not Catharine—leave the service. He'd worried that someone would tell her about him and Catharine, but perhaps she had yet to know the truth.

Last night he and Samuel had spent part of the night in a tent, but he'd risen hours ago, wanting to return to Nazareth for Susanna's birthday. In the final hours of hiking, he was propelled forward not by the possibility of seeing Catharine, but by seeing Susanna. He wanted to see her again, to remember what she looked like. He wanted to talk with her and thank her for letting him go to the Indians. Most of all, he wanted to tell her what had happened with Chief Langoma and his clan.

Then when they were finished celebrating, he would tell her about Catharine.

His own joy dimmed at the thought of telling her, at her disappointment, but he had to confront his own sin, expose his darkest secret with her, and ask for her mercy. One day, perhaps, God would give her the strength to forgive him and maybe even love him.

Brother Edward directed the married men back toward the village, and Christian hurried around his fellow brothers so he could speak with the laborer.

"I want to see Susanna," he whispered to the man. "Today."

Edward shook his head. "I can't arrange a time with her laboress on such short notice."

"It's her birthday, Edward." His mind wandered to her face in the sunrise this morning, holding his gaze. He must see her, speak with her. "And I've been gone for six months."

"You should rest on the Sabbath."

"I'm not asking something improper," Christian insisted. "I only want to visit my wife—in the kitchen or in the bedchamber, it matters not to me."

"You must calm yourself, Brother Christian."

"Calm?" The word came out like a shout, but at the moment, he didn't care.

He'd spent the past six months apart from this community, and during that time he'd made most of his own decisions and learned to be flexible for the sake of the Gospel. He'd walked and paddled hundreds of miles in the rain and then the snow. He'd spent three nights instead of one with Chief Langoma and his people so he could answer their questions. He'd met with Indians who had scalped men for being white, and he'd hidden from those who might scalp him even with Samuel at his side.

And now, all he wanted to do was see the woman he'd married.

"I brought her a gift," he said. "It will only take minutes to give it to her."

"I will speak with Annabel as soon as I'm able." Edward clapped his back. "She will be there after Sabbath, Christian."

Christian slowed his pace, letting the laborer walk in front of him. As they descended the hillside, his gaze wandered toward the stone house across the grass. What would Edward do if he strayed from the pack to knock on the ladies' door? He didn't care so much what Edward did, he supposed, but he knew Annabel would dismiss him as Edward had done.

But at least Susanna would know he tried.

Sunlight reflected off the windows of her dormitory, and he stopped on the steps of his house, searching for a face in the windows.

Susanna would know he tried, but his efforts might embarrass her, humiliate her even, among the other sisters. He'd already done enough harm to his wife.

"Go rest." Samuel placed his hand on Christian's shoulder. "Edward is right. She will be there tomorrow."

"I wanted to see her when I returned."

"You did see her this morning, my friend. And you will see her again very soon."

The fatigue from his long journey washed over Christian. Perhaps it would be better if he visited his wife after he had rested. *If* he could rest.

He stepped up into the house. Tomorrow morning Edward would have to let him see Susanna, or he would find a way to visit her on his own.

* * * * *

"Wake up," someone whispered with a nudge to her side.

Susanna turned under her heavy quilt. After being up most of the night, shaken by Christian's presence and then disappointed that he hadn't called for her, she finally fell asleep. It was too early—and too cold—to get up now.

"Wake up, Susanna."

The voice was more insistent this time, and she opened her eyes although she could only see the shadow of Annabel's face in the darkness. "Is something wrong?"

"Your husband wants to see you."

She pushed herself up on her elbows, trying to process her words. "What time is it?"

"A quarter till five."

Susanna pressed her hands against her head, pushing back her tangled hair. "Are you certain he wants to see me?"

"Oh, I'm certain." Annabel sniffed. "He's been awake for over an hour now, pestering Brother Edward for a visit."

Susanna threw back her covers and her toes touched the icy floor. "When—" She chattered. "When does he want to see me?"

"Right away if he could, but I told him to meet us in thirty minutes in the chamber room."

Susanna forgot the chill on her feet and her skin as she stood. "I must hurry."

Women slept on both sides of Susanna as she washed herself with cold water and brushed her hair. She pulled her petticoat on over her shift and then she laced her blue gown. She almost didn't put on her haube—after all, Christian was her husband and not even Annabel could insist that she wear her cap into the bedchamber at this hour. But she felt too vulnerable without it, so she brushed her hair one last time and then lay the brush down on the bureau before tying the ribbons of her haube under her chin.

She glanced down the rows of women, and all were in their beds except Lily. Lately Lily had been leaving the dormitory while the rest of them slept. She didn't know where her friend went on these nights nor how long she was gone, but she imagined her out dancing in the cool air, spinning in the fields, when no one was watching as she worshipped God in her own way.

Three beds down, Catharine inched herself up on her elbows. "Where are you going?" she whispered.

"To see Christian."

"Oh…" Catharine's voice was sad. "Elias hasn't called for me since we returned."

Susanna edged around the beds and sat down beside Catharine. "Someday soon, you and Elias will reconcile."

"I don't know."

Catharine's hands covered her belly, and Susanna wrapped her hands over those of her friend's. Underneath, the baby moved. "When the littlest Schmidt arrives, it will be better."

"Susanna—"

She kept her fingers over Catharine's, alarmed at her friend's solemn tone. "What is it?"

"I never meant to deceive you."

She leaned closer to Catharine. "What are you talking about?"

"Never mind." Catharine shook her head, pushing her hand away. "Go—before Annabel changes her mind."

Chapter Eighteen

· ·

Susanna's heart fluttered as she quietly followed Annabel up the stairs and down the hall to the bedchamber. Not only had her husband returned, but he wanted to see her. Perhaps he had missed her like she had missed him.

There was much to tell him—about Lily and the beautiful songs that were teaching her the language of the Delaware, about her hours in the Nursery, about the renewal of her health. There was much to tell and much to hear about his journey, stories that could probably last for hours. But more than anything, she wanted to be near him, even if it were only for an hour. She was grateful beyond words that he had come back safely to her from the wilds.

The door to the bedchamber was already open. She paused in the doorway, and Annabel nudged her forward. Breathing deeply, she stepped into the room, and then her breath seemed to escape her.

Instead of leaning back on the pillow with his legs stretched out on the bed like the last time they were together, Christian paced the few steps between the bed and the window. When he turned and saw her, his eyes seemed to swallow her in the lantern light. Her heart leaped at his gaze.

They eyed each other silently, waiting for Annabel to close the door, but when she did, neither of them reached for the bolt. Christian motioned to the stool, and after Susanna sat down, he sat on the bed. Instead of leaning back, though, he arched forward, his hands together. She looked at the shadows along the wall, swaying with the firelight. The quiet engulfed them as she waited for him to speak. When he didn't speak, she met his gaze again.

"Thank you—" she whispered. "Thank you for coming home for my birthday."

He nodded. "I wanted to see you, Susanna."

Her heart stirred again. "You did?"

"The past few nights," he started, rubbing his hands together, "I couldn't stop thinking about you."

"Nor I you."

He smiled at her, and she was glad for his smile. He had changed during his months away, though she didn't know exactly how. It didn't matter, she supposed, as long as he wanted to be with her.

"I brought you something." He reached under the pillow and took out a necklace of sorts. It was shiny with color.

She ran her fingers over the smooth beads and shells. "What is it?"

"The Indians call it wampum."

"It's beautiful," she said as she clutched it to her chest. "Please tell me about the Indians."

He inched closer to where she sat. "What do you want to know?"

She strung the necklace over her head, fingering the beads. "Catharine said you and Samuel spent most of your time traveling to visit clans who never heard the story of Christ before."

"The Indians love stories, but most of them wanted to be entertained more than they wanted to hear the truth." His lips turned up in another smile. "There was one clan though, not far from Gnadenhutten. The chief decided to follow Christ, and when he did, his entire tribe followed his lead."

"Oh, that's wonderful," she said with a clap. "I want to go visit them."

He reached for her hand, and when he took it, her skin warmed with delight. "One day I will take you there."

"Perhaps in the summer months."

His smile dimmed. "There is much talk of war outside our community."

"You won't be able to go visit them?"

"I will go, but I don't want to take you until it is safe."

"But Rebecca went to the Indians," she insisted. "And Catharine."

"They both stayed in Gnadenhutten."

She couldn't imagine saying good-bye to her husband again for six months, not knowing when or if he would return. God had planted the desire to go the Indians in her heart as well, just as He had done with Christian. She wanted to go with him like her mother had gone with her father, visiting this chief who had found Christ and sharing God's love with all the women in his settlement and settlements who had yet to embrace the great story.

Christian took a deep breath, releasing her hand. "There is something I must tell you."

She put her hand back in her lap as she studied the drawn lines of his face, the worry in them.

The warmth from his grasp faded away. "What's wrong?"

"A long time ago, back in London, something happened." In his grasp for words, her heart began to plummet. It was too much to hope that all would be well between them now that he returned.

"What happened in London?"

He lowered his gaze. "I met Catharine Weicht and her family."

The way he said Catharine's name sent a shiver down Susanna's spine. Catharine had never mentioned that she knew Christian before Marienborn. Was this what she trying to tell her this morning, that she'd never meant to deceive her? But what was there to deceive her about?

Her head felt faint, and she prayed that she wouldn't slip away again like she had done in Bethlehem. No matter what Christian had to tell her, no matter what he had done, she had to stay strong.

When Christian looked up, he watched her expectantly, like he wanted her to say something—but she didn't know what to say.

"Her father was ready to join the Brethren, but his wife and daughter weren't quite ready, so I spoke with them."

She let out the breath she'd been holding, scolding herself silently for doubting her husband and friend. So Christian had brought them into the fold of the Brethren. That was to be commended. But she still didn't understand the solemnity in his eyes.

She folded her hands in her lap. Part of her longed to flee the room, yet she remained. She wanted to hear what he had to say; she knew so little about this man she had married. Yet she didn't want his story—their story—to involve Catharine.

"Catharine and I—we courted during this season."

Her breath was sharp. "Courted?"

"During this season, her family seemed to become my family and we talked of marriage."

She blinked. She would not allow her husband, this man she barely knew, to see her pain at his revelation.

She stiffened her back. "Did you make plans?"

"Nothing was certain."

"But—," she started, knowing her voice sounded as wounded as her heart felt. "Back in Marienborn, why didn't you ask for Catharine as your wife?"

When he hesitated, her heart seemed to stop. "You asked for her?"

At his nod, as slight as it was, her heart crumbled within her. Her husband had wanted to marry her best friend, and somehow he'd gotten stuck with her instead.

"What did the lot say?"

"It refused me."

She stood up and walked slowly to the window.

"So when the lot didn't give you the woman you wanted," she

said slowly, her eyes on the dark pane, "you agreed to marry me instead."

In his silence, the truth was finally known. She could never compete with a woman like Catharine. Her friend's beauty was like a garden filled with roses while Susanna was more like a wilted flower. Or a weed.

The laboress in Marienborn was wrong—she had nothing to offer Christian Boehler.

And he had nothing left to offer her.

"You should have told me." She stepped toward the door. "The elders, they should have told me when I agreed to marry you."

"You're right," he said. "You should have known before we married."

The strength drained out of her along with her tears, down her cheeks, smeared onto her sleeves. She couldn't offer him anything right now. She reached for the latch on the door.

"Susanna—," he called out, but she didn't turn back.

She'd agreed to love this man, but he...

How could she do that when he loved someone else?

* * * * *

Christian didn't move from the bed. Part of him wanted to chase Susanna down the hallway to tell her how sorry he was for his deception and his ineptness. He should have told her about Catharine long ago...or perhaps he shouldn't have told her at all.

He banged his head against the wall. He hadn't known how she would react to his confession, but it seemed the news frightened more than angered her, sending her away from him. When she walked into the chamber, he'd seen the pleasure in her eyes. She'd wanted to be with him. He'd also seen the concern in her eyes—she had missed him while he was gone. He'd welcomed her with his words, and then he'd sent her running away.

Samuel had been right; he couldn't withhold the truth from her. Not if he wanted to grow a strong marriage with her to last a lifetime. They needed a foundation of truth between them, but what if the truth destroyed what little they had, like it had with Elias and Catharine, instead of building it back up?

He raked his fingers through his hair. For someone who traveled around telling stories, he was horrible at communicating with those closest to him. Not that he expected Susanna to forgive him right away— he hadn't even had the opportunity to ask for her forgiveness. He had wounded her, and he didn't know how to heal the wound he'd inflicted.

He wished he could speak to Samuel, but the Indian had returned already to Bethlehem. While Brother Edward was a good spiritual advisor, he was also a single man who didn't understand the relationship between a husband and wife. And Christian and Joseph never talked about anything more substantial than weather and crops. Joseph followed after God, but he held private the spiritual matters in his life as well as the marital ones.

Christian had begun to wonder if marital health and spiritual health went hand in hand.

Over the months, he'd begun to believe the lot was right in its direction for him. Even with her beauty and charm, Catharine was not a good companion for him or any other missionary. During their time in Gnadenhutten, she'd almost shunned the Indians instead of encouraging them, and he'd heard her complain to Rebecca several times about their living conditions.

He couldn't imagine what Catharine would think, traveling with Samuel to the villages and sleeping on the benches among the Indians or in the forest with the animals. He was frustrated with her actions and he clung to the frustration—much better to be frustrated with her than long for her. She would do better with Elias in Bethlehem or Nazareth than alongside Christian in the Indian villages.

"'They that wait on the Lord shall renew their strength.'" He spoke the words of Isaiah in the darkness. "'They shall run, and not grow weary; and they shall walk, and not faint.'"

He prayed that, in time, Susanna would forgive him for what he had done, but he wouldn't push her. He would wait on the Lord and pray that God would not allow him to grow weary.

Chapter Nineteen

....

Susanna slipped into the spinning room and slammed the door behind her. How could Christian have done this to her? How could Catharine? Catharine could be selfish at times, but she thought there was kindness in her friend's heart as well.

She closed her eyes and tried to erase the image of Christian and Catharine in her mind, but the image persisted. She couldn't blame Christian for wanting Catharine—any man would prefer Catharine over her. But it didn't stop the despair from welling up inside her.

She leaned back against the timbers, breathing fast yet not able to catch her breath. She tried to make sense of the words Christian spoke. He and Catharine had once loved each other, back in London. They'd even talked of marriage. She should have asked him more questions, probed deeper about their history, but the shock of it stole away her resolve.

She sank to the floor and pulled her knees close to her chest. Christian told her the truth now, but before, in the first months of marriage, had he and Catharine been making a mockery out of their spouses? They'd loved one another and yet they had been selected to marry people they didn't love.

No wonder Christian had been so distant to her, why he didn't even want to be alone with her until today. Not only did Christian not love her, but his heart longed for another. She was a product of his disappointment, the rejection of the lot. The only reason they had married was because he didn't get the woman he desired.

Oh, why hadn't the elders told her about his affections for Catharine? Or did Christian guard his secret from them as well? If she'd known the truth, she would have refused the lot.

No wonder Christian had been so ambivalent at their wedding. He must have spent the morning looking at the bride next to Susanna, wishing he stood behind Catharine instead.

He could have asked not to marry her, before they selected the lot, except for his need of a companion. She wished he would have declined. He should have remained unmarried if he didn't want to marry her, even if it meant he couldn't come to Pennsylvania.

Maybe she wasn't even Christian's second choice. She'd heard of men who had selected a dozen women before the lot finally concurred with their choice. By the time Christian had agreed to marry her, his heart might have been torn into pieces. He had nothing left to give her.

As she sat on the floor, her legs curled close to her chest, the room felt unsteady around her. She wished now that the darkness would swallow her again, like it had back in Bethlehem, but the darkness didn't take her this time.

She leaned her head against her knees. Even if there had only been one woman before her, Christian should have told her. He should have let her know that this marriage was for companionship only, with no hope of growing into love. Maybe she would have accepted, knowing those terms, so that she could come to Pennsylvania as well. Except she would have to spend a lifetime knowing that her husband wished to marry another.

Oh, it was a miserable affair. Even though they hadn't yet consummated the marriage, the elders would never allow her to end it. Plenty of the Brethren married without love and their marriages survived. But she didn't know how a woman could remain married for the rest of her life if she knew her spouse loved another.

Susanna slowly stood up and leaned toward the closed door, listening for footsteps. When she didn't hear any, she opened the door and rushed back down to the security of her dormitory. There would be no more secrets for her, for them. No more hiding.

Catharine slept in her bed like the rest of the women, and Susanna stared down at her. If Catharine loved Christian, why hadn't she told Susanna before they both married? And if Catharine loved Christian, why did she marry Elias Schmidt?

Her mother had once told her that love made people do strange things. Susanna's heart had never erupted with love like many of her friends, but if Catharine had loved Christian, no matter if the lot concurred or not, she should have told her the truth.

As she sat down on Catharine's bed, she scanned the row to her right. Lily was back in her bed and the rest of the sisters were still asleep. She shook Catharine's arm to wake her friend.

Catharine opened her eyes slowly, reluctantly, and Susanna realized she hadn't been sleeping at all. Only pretending, like she had been doing all along.

"You and Christian—"

Catharine shook her head. "Nothing happened between us in Marienborn."

"Not in Marienborn, Catharine, back in London." She sat on the bed, facing her friend. "Why didn't you tell me you knew Christian before Marienborn?"

"I wanted to tell you earlier," Catharine said. "But I thought it would wound you."

"Of course it wounds me." Susanna arched her back, not sure exactly what to say to her friend. "You knew my husband."

"Not in the biblical way," Catharine whispered. "Not in any way that matters."

"He wanted to marry you."

"He only thought he did," Catharine replied. "He has a much better bride in you."

But Christian didn't think so. As nice as he had been to her in their few times together, he had treated her as he would any sister. And he should treat her as a sister when he loved another woman.

"I didn't think any good would come out of telling you," Catharine persisted. "It—it seemed so long ago that I knew Christian. I didn't know he'd come to Marienborn to marry—"

"But you'd talked of marriage."

Catharine was silent for a moment. "Not for a long time."

"But you must have guessed."

Catharine folded her hands over her stomach. "I thought the elders might come with the news that the lot had confirmed our marriage, but if they did, I was going to decline the offer."

Susanna flinched. She'd never heard of any woman declining the will of the lot in marriage, nor could she imagine someone refusing to marry a man like Christian.

"There wasn't anything wrong with Christian," Catharine continued. "It's just—Elias and I had begun to sneak away to the fields near the castle months before our wedding. I wanted to marry him."

"What would you have done if the lot had said you couldn't marry Elias?"

Catharine didn't hesitate. "We would have left the Brethren."

Susanna looked out the dark window. The selection of Catharine's husband was more important to her friend than the bond of their faith. No wonder the elders didn't want a brother and sister to court prior to going before the lot. It made things messy on this side of their marriage.

"I promise you," Catharine said, "I never did anything in Marienborn to make Christian think I loved him."

Susanna studied her friend in the dim light. She wanted to believe that Catharine hadn't seduced her husband or led him to believe they would marry, but she didn't know what to believe.

Susanna stood up and reached for her shawl, pulling it tight around her shoulders. Then she walked away from Catharine and out of the Sisters House. She didn't even realize where she was going until morning dawned on the Nursery in front of her.

She climbed the Nursery steps, and when she went inside, to the tables where the children were eating breakfast, one of the girls shouted her name. They surrounded her with hugs, and she understood why Mariana loved her job so much. The children were honest in their love.

Maybe it would be better if Christian went back to the Indians alone. He was doing what he loved, and perhaps she could move to the Nursery like Mariana requested and help with the children. She wouldn't be reaching out to the Indians on a mission like she'd envisioned, but she could tell the Brethren's children about how Christ loved them. And how He would never deceive them.

* * * * *

Christian pored over the Scriptures in Edward's office, trying to find solace in the words he knew in his heart, words that often struggled to reach his mind. With most of the snow gone, the men had gone to work on completing a storage building for the summer's grain. Edward insisted that Christian stay inside to rest, and Christian hadn't argued. During the past six months he'd rarely been alone, and only in the aloneness could he ask God to renew his spirit. And grant him wisdom in how to love his wife.

He lifted his head, looked across the grass to the Sisters House, and wondered what Susanna was doing today, which tasks she preferred and what talents God had blessed her with. He'd been married for almost a year now and he knew very little about his wife.

He hadn't seen her since the day after Easter, five days past. Not even at worship. He'd knocked once since then to ask about her well-being, but Sister Annabel had sent him away without a response. And he supposed he didn't deserve a response, not after what he had done.

Someone pounded on the front door of the Brothers House, and he closed the Scriptures to answer it. In his heart he hoped that perhaps Annabel had come already, requesting another meeting for him and his wife. He hoped she wanted to meet soon—there was so much more he wanted to say.

But when he opened the door, there wasn't a familiar sister waiting outside, nor was there a brother. Instead, before him was a white woman and two children—a boy about three or four and a girl a year or so older. Their faces were smeared with dirt, their hair tangled, and they smelled of smoke. Even with the cool weather, none of them wore coats. The woman carried a small bundle wrapped in a wool blanket. Christian looked over their shoulders to see if the children's father accompanied them, but he saw no one. Nor did he see a wagon or cart or even a horse.

He opened the door wide and motioned them into the common room. Then from the side of their residence, a man rushed toward him. His clothes were torn, his face an ashen-gray color. And in his hands he held a musket. Christian asked him to leave the gun outside, but the man didn't acknowledge him or his request as he hurried up the steps to join the family.

The children huddled close to their mother, who was still clutching the bundled woolen blanket. The man sat in a chair with his rumpled fur cap low on his head and the musket in his hands. None of them spoke.

When the front door opened again, Edward walked inside.

"I thought I saw company." Edward held out his hand and the man shook it. Edward eyed the musket as well, but he didn't say anything.

"Where are you from?" he asked.

The man blinked, like he didn't understand the words, and the woman spoke for him.

"Ten miles, west of here." She choked on her words. "Indians came yesterday…and they burned down our home."

She stared at Edward and then Christian, like they might know what to do. Her eyes were void of tears. Christian didn't know what to say, but he thought back to Howling Wolf and the other Indians they had seen in the forest. Dangerous men, according to Samuel.

Had they taken revenge on this family?

"You're blessed to be alive," Christian said.

"No—" She clutched the woolen bundle to her chest, and for a moment, he wondered if there was a child inside; no baby could survive being wrapped so tightly.

He glanced back toward the window, wishing Susanna were here with him. She would know how to comfort this woman in the loss of her home and probably her land.

"Our baby," she cried, and then he knew. There had been a baby in her arms, yesterday perhaps. And now the baby was gone.

The daughter and son hugged her, trying to comfort her. Edward stood silent beside Christian, seemingly unable to help them with their sorrow. Christian had heard many stories of Indians attacking colonists in their homes, but never so close to Nazareth.

Christian hurried toward the door and then jogged across the plaza, rushing into the Sisters House without knocking and then down into the basement, where he found Susanna among those who were cleaning up after breakfast. He wanted to tell her again how sorry he was, how he would do whatever he could to win her trust again, but right now, they needed to focus on the family across the plaza.

Annabel stepped in front of Susanna, protecting her from him. "You already had your visit."

"I need her."

"Another time, Brother Christian."

He shook his head, trying to clarify his words. "A family just arrived in our community."

He scanned the women working in the room and found the Indian girl who lived among them. He didn't want to condemn her along with the Indians who had killed this family's child—good and evil dwelt among every group of people—but he had to speak the truth.

"Indians burned down their home."

He heard Susanna's soft gasp, and he couldn't bring himself to tell her and the others that the Indians had killed their baby as well. His eyes lingered on Susanna even as he spoke to Annabel. "I need a sister who can comfort them."

Susanna stepped around the laboress, but she didn't look at him when she spoke. "I will go."

Annabel turned toward her. "Are you certain?"

When Susanna nodded her head, Annabel waved her on. "Then go to them."

With Susanna at his side, Christian rushed back across the plaza and into the house. Edward still sat in his chair, watching the family, but Susanna didn't take a seat. Instead she knelt before the woman. Christian marveled as Susanna took the woman's hands into her own and the woman leaned into her shoulder. Susanna wrapped her arms around this new sister as she cried.

The husband shifted his muzzle in his lap, his eyes staring out the window. Christian wished he knew how to comfort him like Susanna had done with his wife, but if he tried to take his hands, the man might shoot him. So he prayed silently instead.

The minutes turned into a half hour, the men quiet as Susanna consoled the wife. When Susanna finally stood, she motioned Christian and Edward into the office. There was no timidity in her voice now.

No reluctance. She was ready to fight for these people, and he knew the moment she started speaking that he would back her in the fight.

"Where will we house them?" she asked.

Edward sat in the chair behind his desk. "We will need to send them to Bethlehem."

She looked at him like he had lost his mind back in the hallway. "They can't walk another ten miles."

"We have no room for another family," he said. "Or food for them."

Susanna frowned at the laborer, the strength in her eyes not willing to cower to his position. If Edward insisted they send them on, there would be a battle.

"They could live among us, in the Brothers and the Sisters Houses," Christian suggested. "They could live and work among us for a week or two. Surely we could lesson our portions a bit so these four can eat."

Edward contemplated his words and then slowly nodded his head. "They can stay for a week, until they are ready to go to Bethlehem or return to their land."

Susanna crossed her arms. "I don't think they will want to return."

"They will need to rebuild eventually."

"In a month or two they can decide," she said. "Right now they must mourn the loss of their baby and their home."

"We must consult Elder Graff about where they can stay."

"We can't split them up," Susanna said. "They need to comfort each other."

Edward shook his head again. "But we have no place for them to live together."

Christian turned and followed Susanna's gaze out the window, at the house built for the Zinzendorfs. She pointed toward the window. "We could house them there."

Edward looked out the glass, but his gaze traveled to the building across the plaza. "But there is no room in the Sisters House for a family,"

"Not in the Sisters House." Susanna paused. "In the Disciple's House."

Edward huffed like Susanna was the mad one, but Christian moved toward the window, focused on the crown residence of their plaza. And he knew his wife was right. They didn't know when the Zinzendorf family would arrive, and he was certain that the Count, who had sacrificed so much for those in need, would be angry if, during his absence, they turned these refugees away instead of harboring them in his home.

Christian tapped his fingers on the glass. "Susanna is right—they can live there safely until summer comes."

Edward sighed. "Of course you think she is right."

Christian glanced back at Susanna and saw a glimmer of something in her eyes. Thankfulness, maybe. It didn't matter, he supposed, but he was still glad of it.

"I don't want to turn them away," Edward said. "But I don't know how we will feed our current residents until harvest. How am I supposed to feed four additional people?"

"Even if they don't live with us, they can work among us," Susanna suggested. "The man could help us hunt for food."

Edward drummed his hands on the desk. "I can't care for another house."

Christian cleared his throat, and they both looked at him. "With your permission, I will oversee the Disciple's House."

"If the Count arrives—" Edward continued, but Christian interrupted him.

"Then the Count can decide what to do with the refugees."

Edward looked back at the window, seeming to weigh his options. "Elder Graff will want to send this request before the lot."

Susanna stepped back toward the door, her voice confident. "The lot won't turn these people away."

Chapter Twenty
....

May 1755

The Keatons were the first refugee family to arrive in Nazareth, but as the hostile Indians ravaged farms across Pennsylvania during the months of April and May, more refugees flooded into Nazareth. With no news of Count Zinzendorf's arrival, forty guests took up residence in his house. The children, with their singing, infused life into the stoic manor, and they played along the plaza as their parents helped harvest the wheat and tend the gardens.

Summer was approaching, and most days, Susanna was able to get outside for fresh air even if it was only the brief walk to the Disciple's House. She and her sisters spent much of their days singing as they weaved blankets for the beds and stitched clothing for people who had fled without their belongings. Ruby Keaton, who'd lost her baby to the Indians, busied herself by overseeing the manor's kitchen, and the other refugee women helped her cook.

So many people of different faiths and different languages had settled in Nazareth, and they were all learning to live together as a community. Susanna knew that God wanted them to care for these wounded people, and to her delight and the amazement of all the Nazareth residents, God multiplied their limited supplies of grain as well as their game, several of the men returning almost daily with deer and even bear for them to eat. And their Quaker friends in Philadelphia had sent them extra supplies as well.

As the weeks passed in a feverish pace of work and worship, she and Catharine slowly and sometimes painfully mended the friendship they'd shared for three years. The wound was still raw to Susanna, but she refused to wallow in her bitterness. Living so close to each other could only breed bitterness or healing, and she chose healing.

She only saw Christian during their daily times of intercession, when he wasn't out hunting or harvesting with the other men. With all the activity in the community, Annabel hadn't mentioned the scheduled quiet times for married couples—she hadn't even given her weekly lessons on marriage.

While part of her wanted to see her husband, Susanna wasn't ready to speak to him yet. She wanted to forgive him for his deception, but even when she decided to offer him this forgiveness, she wasn't certain she could ever trust him again. He hadn't crossed the plaza, demanding to see her again, not since the day the Keaton family arrived. He might be kind to her, but she could never live up to his ideal for a wife, not in comparison to Catharine. Except for the late nights when she couldn't sleep in the dormitory and the worship times when she sat across the aisle from him, she refused herself the pleasure and torment of thinking about him.

Catharine stitched on her bed most days, waiting for her baby arrive. When Susanna was there, Catharine talked incessantly about going back to London, but even as her stomach grew larger, she rarely mentioned Elias's name. It made Susanna sad for what the deception had cost all of them.

This afternoon Susanna wasn't inside the dormitory. It was Sabbath, and after worship she and Lily tramped their well-worn path to the Nursery to visit Timothy and Nathan. Wild roses grew on both sides of the path, perfuming the air as they walked, and sunshine warmed their faces and their song.

Lily enjoyed the outdoors as much as Susanna did, except Lily was more comfortable in this world where she had been born. The wilderness of this New World still intimidated Susanna at times as she thought about the snakes and bears and other unknowns around them, but Lily never seemed to worry about the danger. She embraced the outdoors with the same affection that she embraced her son.

Susanna hadn't seen the Indians watching them since last fall, but several of the Brethren had seen them lingering near Nazareth. With Lily alongside her, she wasn't afraid to travel to the Nursery. They sang together as they walked along the pathway, a song about three children who paraded behind their mother and mimicked her every move. The lyrics were silly—children spilling their mother's cittamum and burning the pots of tea—but in the silliness of the words, Susanna was learning much of the Delaware language and about the people.

The Nursery in sight, Lily's song stopped abruptly as she scanned the trees in the distance. Susanna watched the trees also. She saw a blur of color, but it disappeared so quickly that she thought it was a ray of light shimmering among the trees.

Lily took her hand and pulled her toward the Nursery.

"What is it?" Susanna asked.

"I thought I saw something."

Susanna looked back toward the trees. "What did you see?"

Lily shook her head, and Susanna recognized the forced lightness in her tone. "Some sort of animal."

Susanna started singing again, to frighten the animal as Lily had taught, but Lily hushed her.

"Not this time," she whispered, before motioning for her to hurry.

When Timothy saw them, he shouted their names as he ran to greet them. Susanna spent the afternoon playing outside with Timothy and the other children while Lily played with and rocked her child. When Mariana rang the dinner bell, Timothy hugged Susanna and rushed back inside with the others. Susanna stepped into the house, searching for Lily, and she found her friend in a storage room. Mariana waited nearby in the hallway to take the baby, but Lily wasn't ready to give him back yet.

"The sun will be setting soon," she told Lily—but instead of responding to her, Lily whispered something into her son's ear.

It always grieved Lily to leave her son at the Nursery, but over the months her sadness had seemed to lessen. It was almost as if armor had grown over her heart to protect her from the pain, an armor that would be hard to penetrate when she wanted to love another.

Today though, the grief had returned. Tears fell down Lily's face as she clutched her son to her chest, and Susanna worried for what was happening inside her friend.

"One more minute," Lily begged, and Susanna nodded her head. They knew the path back to the Sisters House well. They could walk in the darkness if need be.

Lily turned her back, and Susanna joined Mariana outside the door. "Perhaps it is too hard for her to continue visiting him," Mariana said.

"Oh no," Susanna said with a shake of her head. "She lives for these visits."

"Most of these children never get to see their parents."

Susanna couldn't sense sadness in the governess's words, only a statement of fact. Mariana's mother had been sold when she was a young girl, so she didn't know what it was like to be raised by a loving father and mother. Susanna knew the security and love of a parent... and Lily seemed to know as well.

Susanna couldn't imagine Lily giving up the privilege of seeing her son.

When Lily finally emerged from the small room, she handed her baby to Mariana. Instead of the playfulness that usually danced in her eyes, a curtain seemed to have dropped, ending the dance. There were no more tears or even kisses for her child as she turned and walked out the door.

"They are good to him, aren't they?" Lily asked as they began their walk home.

Susanna nodded. "Yes, they are."

"I love him more than anything."

"You are a good mother to him."

"I'm not a good mother," Lily murmured as she scanned the trees.

They hiked quickly toward the falling sun, and before they reached the Sisters House, Lily began to sing in her language, a soulful song about God protecting her son. Susanna had heard her sing the song before, usually when they were with Nathan, but today her words sounded more like a prayer.

"If something happens to me," Lily whispered, "promise me that you will care for Nathan."

She slowed her pace before they walked up the steps to their house. "Is something wrong?"

"I need to know—I need you to teach Nathan my language and tell him stories about me. I need to know that you will protect him from those who wish him harm."

Susanna studied her friend's face, and in her eyes she saw the craving for reassurance.

"I will take care of him."

The front door of the Sisters House banged open.

"What are you two doing?" Annabel demanded.

Susanna glanced at Lily. "We've been at the Nursery."

"Hurry." Annabel waved them toward the door. "Catharine is about to give birth."

* * * * *

Elias paced back and forth outside the Sisters House like a panther waiting to pounce. He didn't invite Christian to join him in the pacing, but when Christian sat on the porch, he didn't send him away either. So Christian remained on the porch, not sure of what to do for the man who had once been a good friend. Perhaps if he talked to Elias, he could offer some sort of comfort like Susanna had with their refugee friends. Or at least he could get him to sit down before he collapsed. The rapid back and forth motion was maddening.

But like Susanna, Elias remained angry with him. Any comfort Christian tried to offer, he was certain, would be rebuffed—so he remained on the porch, drumming his hands on the steps.

God had scoured his mind over the past two months along with his heart, cleansing the impurities and the yearnings that once plagued him. He still dreamed about Catharine on occasion, but the dreams that once intrigued him now angered him instead. He couldn't tell Elias this, of course, but he was grateful for the cleansing, no matter how painful.

A scream bellowed from the house behind him, and Elias stopped his pacing and stared up at the windows.

"That's normal," Christian said. He tried to sound reassuring, although he had no idea what was normal in childbirth.

Elias stepped toward him, his gaze locked on the upper windows. "I should be in there with her."

"Annabel wouldn't let you near her room."

Elias hesitated and then sat on the step below Christian. "I should have been with her long before today."

Christian folded his hands together, weighing his words before he spoke. "Why didn't you reconcile with her?"

Elias looked up at him. "I was so upset at her—at both of you. I didn't want to be near her."

"Catharine loves you, Elias. Not me."

"You don't know that—"

"Everyone knows it except you."

Elias shook his head. "She loved you long before she even met me."

"I don't know that she ever loved me," Christian replied slowly. "I wanted to think that she cared about me, but that doesn't mean that she did. She wanted to marry you instead of me."

"But you went to the lot before I did."

"Yes, but if the lot concurred with my choice, Catharine was planning to turn me down."

Elias's head snapped up so fast that Christian wondered if the man had injured his neck. "She wasn't going to marry you?"

"Didn't she tell you that?"

Elias shook his head. "For a long time after the night I saw you, I didn't speak to her at all, and when we finally spoke, I never bothered to ask her exactly what happened."

"You should ask her, Elias. She hasn't done anything wrong."

Another scream thundered down on them, followed by a high-pitched shriek.

Elias's voice was low as he watched the window. "I thought she still loved you."

"She loves you, my friend. No one else."

His head dropped to his hands. "I've been so stupid."

Minutes later, Susanna opened the front door and peeked out at the men.

"You have a beautiful little girl waiting for you upstairs, Elias."

"I do?"

"She has your eyes."

A slow smile crept up his face. "Is Catharine all right?"

"As well as can be expected," she replied and then waved him toward the door. "They both want to see you."

Christian gave a light push on the man's shoulders. "Go."

Elias bounded up the stairs and in the door, but Susanna lingered for another moment. "Is Elias speaking to you again?" she asked.

"God is a worker of miracles."

"Indeed," she said softly. "And a healer of wounded hearts."

She closed the door, leaving him alone to wonder at her words as the bell rang overhead to announce the birth of Elias and Catharine's daughter.

Chapter Twenty-One
....

November 1755

Even though she was a tiny creature, Juliana Catharine Schmidt was more vocal than her mother. Her lungs blared like the trumpets at daybreak, and when she wasn't happy, the octaves she reached were monumental.

Some nights, though, even as Juliana's crying woke almost every sister in the house, Catharine didn't seem to hear her daughter. Nights like tonight, Susanna had to retrieve Juliana from the wooden crib that Elias had carved for her and cradle the baby in her arms.

Susanna swung Juliana gently, trying to calm her. She didn't mind holding the baby during the dark hours, but her attempt at soothing words rarely comforted Juliana's cries. The girl wanted her mother's voice and the milk from her breast.

Susanna looked down at Catharine, huddled in a ball on her narrow bed, and wondered if she was ignoring the cries or if she was truly asleep. Elias had been a doting papa over the past five months—visiting whenever Annabel would allow him—and most days, Catharine cared well for Juliana. But during the nights, when Elias wasn't around, it seemed that Catharine often forgot she was a mother.

The other sisters were aggravated with Catharine's lack of care for Juliana during the night, especially when Catharine was allowed times of rest during the daylight hours. The other sisters had to work throughout the day, no matter how many hours little Juliana kept them awake.

Annabel slept in her office on the first floor of the building, but even she had been awakened at times by Juliana's cries. Annabel had agreed to set up a mattress for Catharine in the spinning room so that she and Juliana could sleep there during the night, but this arrangement worried Susanna even more than the waking of the sisters. What if, like tonight, Catharine didn't wake to feed her daughter? What would happen to Juliana?

"Catharine," Susanna whispered, nudging her friend's back with her toes.

When Catharine didn't respond, Susanna shifted Juliana into her other arm as the baby alternated her wailing with attempts to suckle Susanna. She shoved Catharine with her foot, and her friend slowly rolled over.

"Can't you hold her?" Catharine moaned.

"She needs to eat."

Susanna bounced Juliana, singing one of Lily's songs to her as Catharine buried herself under the covers, but the baby's crying increased. If Catharine wasn't going to feed her baby, Susanna needed to find something to soothe the pains in Juliana's stomach.

Perhaps she could put some maple syrup on Juliana's tongue, just until Catharine was ready to feed her.

With Juliana in her arms, Susanna rushed to Lily's bed for help, but when she reached it, she saw that Lily was no longer under her covers. A shadow of worry crossed over her, but the baby's cries chased away her concern. She couldn't wait until Lily returned from wherever it was she escaped to at night.

"Rebecca," she whispered to the woman who slept next to Lily.

"You don't have to whisper," Rebecca said as she sat up. "Everyone is awake except that baby's mama."

Susanna shifted Juliana again to her other arm. "Will you help me get her down to the kitchen?"

Rebecca wrapped her cloak around her nightdress, and they retreated to the hallway. After lighting a candle, Rebecca escorted her down to the basement.

"The syrup's on the left, top shelf," Susanna instructed from the doorway of the pantry. "Toward the back."

Rebecca stepped on a stool to retrieve the jug of maple syrup and brought it to Susanna. Susanna dipped her finger into the brown sweetness and then slid it into Juliana's mouth. The baby's crying stopped immediately, sucking Susanna's finger until it was clean. Then Juliana's mouth puckered again.

Rebecca pushed the jug toward her. "Give her some more."

Susanna dipped her finger again and again until Juliana's cries faded into sleep. Susanna turned and leaned her back against the table.

Rebecca handed Susanna a spoon as she sat down beside her. "You can't keep rescuing her."

They both dipped spoons into the maple syrup, something neither of them had tasted until they moved to Pennsylvania. Annabel would be furious if she found them hovered over this jug, but if the syrup soothed Juliana, perhaps it would soothe her caregivers as well.

"I'm not rescuing Catharine," she insisted. "I'm rescuing Juliana."

"Catharine needs to care for her baby."

"It's only a season," she replied. "In time she'll be ready to care for Juliana."

"I don't know if she will. I don't think it's the same darkness that some of the other new mothers experience. It seems like she expects someone else to care for her child."

Susanna took another spoonful of maple syrup, a small one,

and the sweetness calmed her. If she weren't careful, she could eat their entire stash.

"Catharine was raised with a nursemaid."

"And now she expects you to be Juliana's nursemaid for her."

Susanna looked down at the auburn curls of the baby, her rounded face so endearing as she slept. It wasn't Juliana's fault that her mother walked in the presence of the enemy known as despondency. Or sloth. Pregnancy had taxed Catharine, childbirth even more. And while the move to Nazareth had invigorated most of them, it seemed to sweep away the life and charm that once embodied Catharine.

But was her mother taking advantage of the friendship that Susanna offered her? Surely, Catharine would do the same for her when…if Susanna ever had a child.

Over the months, Susanna had begun to wonder if Catharine had embraced the Brethren's faith after her parents joined their community, the faith that Susanna and so many others had clung to as children and now as adults…or if their faith had been forced upon Catharine back in London. Catharine seemed to love their Savior, but perhaps she was rethinking her service to Him.

"One day you will have a child of your own to care for," Rebecca said.

"I—," she stuttered. "I don't know."

"You and Christian will be good parents, if you ever find time to be together." Rebecca studied her face. "Are you glad you married him?"

Susanna brushed her hand over Juliana's hair, knowing she could be honest with Rebecca but not sure she wanted to be honest with herself. "Most of the time I don't feel like I am married."

"You and Christian need to schedule a time in the chamber."

"Annabel has stopped scheduling couples."

"Not for those who request it." Rebecca smiled. "He needs to be with you."

"He doesn't need me."

Rebecca's eyebrows arched. "Every man needs his wife to support him, especially after he's failed."

"Christian said an entire clan decided to follow Christ."

"Yes, but hundreds upon hundreds of Indians refused to listen to him."

Susanna twisted the pot of syrup slowly with her free hand. "He didn't speak of them."

"In all his travels and preaching the Gospel, only this small village decided to follow Christ. All that work and effort and prayer and yet so few listened."

Susanna pushed the pot away.

"He needs you to love him, Susanna, in his triumphs and his failings."

Rebecca could say that, but she didn't know everything about Christian's failings. "Back at Marienborn...you didn't want to marry Joseph, did you?"

Rebecca brushed her hands across the table and then put them back in her lap. Her voice sounded sad when she spoke again. "My first marriage was very hard."

"Why was it hard?"

"I tried to love my husband, but he was a—" She hesitated. "He was a difficult man."

Susanna rocked Juliana in her arms. She'd never heard Annabel or the others talk about the more complicated marriages. "And yet you agreed to marry again."

"Because God knows much better than I do of what I need, and Joseph...Joseph is a very good man for me."

The words settled between them. "Have you begun to love him?"

"Very much, but our love didn't begin to grow until we spent those together months at Gnadenhutten." Rebecca glanced down at

Juliana and then reached for the candle. "We'd better get that little girl into her cradle before she wakes again."

Before they slipped back into the dormitory, Rebecca turned to her one last time and whispered, "You and Christian make a good team, Susanna."

The words refreshed Susanna like a soft rain, and as they walked into the room, she wondered if perhaps they could work together as a team.

Susanna glanced toward Lily's bed when they walked into the dormitory, and it was still empty.

"What time does Lily usually return?"

Rebecca shrugged. "It depends."

Susanna tiptoed to Catharine's bed and placed Juliana into the cradle her papa built for her. Catharine didn't stir.

She kissed Juliana's forehead and tucked the blanket around her. "Rest, little one," she whispered.

She lay back down but she couldn't sleep. Instead, she listened for Lily's footsteps until dawn.

* * * * *

After breakfast, George Keaton helped Christian haul two barrels of water from the wagon into the basement kitchen of the Disciple's House. George was the strongest among them in body, but his spirit had been crippled with the Indian attack on his family. Still, he helped willingly whenever Christian asked, and Christian had begun to rely on the man's assistance in almost every aspect of managing the refugee house.

As the laborer of the refugee house, Christian's tasks over the past months included everything from obtaining the necessary supplies for the refugees to helping them resolve the conflicts that arose frequently when so many different kinds of people tried to live in community together. Their refugee friends didn't have the same respect for the Brethren's authority or for their peculiarities, such as the lot.

Not that the refugees were trying to wreak havoc on their community. In actuality, they were quite grateful for the safe haven the Brethren offered, but they didn't understand the Brethren's way of living, nor did they follow the necessary rules of Nazareth. Christian's new role drained him of energy at times, while other days he was exhilarated by the tasks. Through everything, God provided both the physical and spiritual needs of the Brethren and their guests.

George Keaton hadn't spoken to Christian about the night the Indians burned his family's house. In spite of his willingness to help, George hadn't spoken much at all since his family arrived in Nazareth. This morning, though, as he sat beside Christian on the wagon's bench, he began to speak.

"Ruby and me—we want to rebuild our house."

Christian flicked the reins, and the horse moved forward. "Perhaps it will be safe for you to return to your homestead in the spring."

"It's awfully hard on a man to lose his home."

"I can't imagine," Christian said, and he meant it—he didn't know what it was like to have his own home or lose it.

"I couldn't even protect my own son."

Christian nodded, wishing Susanna were here. He didn't know what to say to this man who had lived in silence for five months.

The story, trapped inside George for so long, seemed to pour out. "We were out in the forest, gathering chestnuts to store, and when we looked back at the cabin—when we looked back, it was on fire. Ellie ran before the men saw her, but little Jacob—"

"There was nothing you or Ellie could have done."

George didn't seem to hear him. "I wanted to chase those Indians and kill them for what they'd done to our child, our house, but it was almost as if God stopped me and told me I needed to care for my family who remained."

The heat of his vengeance probably would have resulted in the end of his life as well as the lives of his wife and other children, but even so, Christian couldn't imagine what it must have been like to watch the fire that consumed his son. "We can't always protect the ones we love, can we?"

"No, but we must do the best we can to care for our family."

"For our family and our community," Christian said, but even with his correction, it didn't sound right. Was it more important to care for his family than for the community around him?

George glanced at him. "I appreciate all your community has done for our family, more than I can ever say, but I don't understand how you can live apart from the people you love."

Christian paused for a moment. He rarely thought about the logistics of the way the Brethren lived, but he knew it seemed odd to the people outside their faith for the married sisters to live with other sisters and for the brothers to live among other brothers instead of with their wives and children.

"It gives us an opportunity to serve the Lord without conflict," he tried to explain.

"But don't we grow in our faith through conflict?" George asked, and in his question, he sounded genuinely confused. "The Bible says we are supposed to sharpen each other."

Christian's mind wandered with the man's words. During his hours in the manor, he had observed firsthand what George referred to as "sharpening," though it sounded more to him like the sin of anger as husbands and wives barked at each other and their little ones. At the time, he'd been grateful for the Brethren's structure of separation so its families didn't fight with one another.

But was it possible that God could use conflict in marriage and families to sharpen each other? Could God use his relationship with Susanna to strengthen him? As he mulled over the thought, he slowly realized that God had already begun to strengthen him as a result of their marriage.

Now that some time had passed between them, perhaps she would meet with him again. Perhaps she would even forgive him. Either way, like Elias had done with Catharine, he needed to let Susanna know that he cared about her.

He didn't want them to be like the couples who were officially married but lived very separate lives with their choir houses. Somehow, even if they lived in different houses, the small hope remained inside him that he and Susanna could meld their hearts together as one.

George hopped off the bench to join the dozens of men and women working in the orchards and field. Christian began to ride away, to return both the horse and wagon to the barn, when he saw a woman wave her hands and hurry toward him from the apple orchard. He pulled back on the reins, stopping the horse. His heart pumped even harder when he realized it was Susanna coming toward him.

He smiled at her until he saw the redness in her eyes. Climbing down from the bench, he hesitated for only a moment before he reached for her hand. "What is it?"

"Lily— she's gone."

"Lily?" he asked, trying to remember which of the many sisters went by that name.

"Lily," she pressed. "The young Indian woman with a son."

He dropped her hand. "Where did she go?"

"I don't know. She often slips away at night, but she always returns…" Fresh tears ran down her cheeks. "This morning she didn't return."

"This sister, is she a friend of yours?"

She nodded. "A very good friend."

"Do you think she went back to her clan?"

"I—I don't know, but one time, weeks ago, she asked me if I would care for her son if something happened to her."

If only he had earned the right to touch his wife, to soothe her in his arms.

"Where is her husband?"

"She told me he is a great warrior and that one day he would come for her."

His voice was low. "Perhaps he finally came."

"Perhaps, but she would never leave her child." She lifted her eyes, locking him in her gaze. "Do you think you could help to find her?"

He swallowed hard. Even though he wanted to help her, he wasn't certain that he could find a missing Indian girl if she wanted to disappear. "I will do everything I can to locate her."

"Thank you, Christian." She stepped back toward the orchard. "Lily's name is Wingan in the Delaware language. It means 'sweet.'"

Her eyes lingered on his face for a moment longer, like she wanted to say something else, but one of the refugee children wrapped herself around Susanna's leg and escorted her back to the orchard.

Chapter Twenty-Two

....

Elias met Catharine on the top floor of the Sisters House like he'd promised her, and they stole away into the chamber together. The light in the room was dulled from the gray clouds, and she dreaded the grayness of the winter months. It was in the spring that she thrived, in the many colors of the flowers and the birds and the blossoms on branches.

Elias situated the chair for Catharine to sit, but his gaze wasn't on her. It was on their baby girl. Since Juliana's birth, Elias had doted on both his baby and his wife, but things still weren't the same between them, not like it had been before Gnadenhutten. When he visited them down in the hall, he seemed mesmerized by their daughter. While Catharine loved him for his affection for Juliana, she was also a bit jealous of it.

She knew it was silly. His love for Juliana was different from his love for her, but Catharine couldn't help feeling that his love for her had changed. He seemed to love her more as Juliana's mother than as his bride. Even now, when they finally had time alone together after so long, it was to see Juliana, not her.

But God was slowly healing the relationship between Elias and Catharine, restoring the trust between them. Their love for each other was still fragile, and she would do nothing to hurt what she'd worked so hard to strengthen.

He sat on the bed, his arms outstretched. "Can I hold her?"

She gave him their daughter, and Juliana laughed. Elias loved Juliana more than Catharine did, and in return, Juliana seemed to love her father more than her mother.

He tickled her cheeks and grinned at her, babbling with her as the minutes passed. When he looked back up at Catharine, his smile faded. "Edward says you are neglecting her care during the night."

She bristled at the condemnation in his tone. "I feed her plenty."

"But Edward says—"

"Brother Edward doesn't know how to care for a baby. It's none of his business how I care for mine."

"Our baby, Catharine," Elias said. "She is my daughter as well as yours."

Catharine's callused fingers balled into fists beside her skirt. He had helped create the baby, but he left her alone to care for what they'd created. She was so tired of the feedings and the crying and the demands the other sisters placed on her in her role as nursemaid. And now Annabel had her slaving in the field with the others every morning too, expecting her to care for the baby the rest of the day.

She crossed her arms over her chest. "You have no idea how hard it is—she cries all day and all night."

He looked down into the eyes of a daughter who exuded nothing but sweetness in the arms of her father. And Catharine knew what Elias was thinking—that she was a liar.

"Most of the day," she reneged. "She cries whenever you're not around."

"I wish I could be there to help you, Catharine." He was looking at her now, his eyes wide with the sincerity and kindness that she loved in him.

"We could move into one of the rooms in the Disciple's House like the rest of the refugees," she insisted. "We could live as a family."

He brushed his hands over Juliana's cheek, and she smiled at him. "We aren't refugees, Catharine. We belong with our choirs."

She stood and moved toward the gray light at the window. All she wanted was her privacy. Not to be by herself, but to be with her family. Didn't God understand? Even as she fought with admitting her need for anyone, the truth was that she did need her husband, needed him desperately.

Her gaze was still out the window when she spoke again. "I don't think I can stay here any longer," she said simply.

"What do you mean?"

"Everything is so plain here, everything as gray as the sky."

"It's winter," he replied. "It's supposed to be gray."

"But not like this, Elias," she tried to explain. "Not in my heart."

Elias set Juliana on the bed beside him and opened his arms. Catharine folded into them, like a lump of flour into the smoothness of gravy. She wanted to dissolve into him, to become one with him again, but his touch felt awkward instead.

"If you don't like it here—where is it that you want to go?"

She hesitated, fearing he would think she was too rash with her words. She wanted him to think she was contemplating his question right now instead of the hours she'd spent planning the answer. "I think we should go to Philadelphia."

"Philadelphia?" he said slowly. "But there are no Brethren living in Philadelphia."

"Perhaps not, but there are plenty of Lutherans. Even Count Zinzendorf speaks at the Lutheran Church when he is there."

Elias thought for a moment. "We would have to leave the Brethren."

"But you could manage or even open a business in the city. I could hire a nursemaid for Juliana and oversee the running of our home. It could be a simple but beautiful and warm place for the Brethren to stay when they traveled through Philadelphia...and we could live as a family."

He looked back at their baby, and she knew he wanted to be with them.

"I must take it before the lot."

"No lot," she insisted. "We should pray and ask God to guide us."

Elias thought for a moment, and then he bowed his head and began to pray right there for their Savior to guide them. He asked God to keep Catharine's heart content if they were to stay in Nazareth or to open up a door if they were to go away.

Juliana stirred on the bed and Elias rested his hand on her belly, but he kept praying.

And Catharine loved him for it.

* * * * *

Susanna hiked up to God's Acre and sat on the flat rock that overlooked the cemetery and the valley. As she rested, she hummed one of Lily's songs about God providing both the sun and the rain. The sun was out today, shedding light on the fields and forests below, but the storms seemed to pound inside her. Even as she sat, even as she sang, she prayed for her friend, that God would protect her and guide Christian and the elders to find her.

Her gaze swept across the wooden markers of the Brethren, and she wondered again where Lily had gone. Her friend would never get lost in the wilderness, but something else could have happened. Perhaps Lily had already gone home like these brothers and sisters.

Christian had said he would try to find Lily, but two days had passed and neither Christian nor Annabel had given her any more information about her friend. Annabel had lectured their entire choir about the free choice the Savior gave to them. They could choose to leave the community whenever they liked. They could even choose to sin. The Savior never forced a brother or sister to remain, though He continually tried to woo a wanderer back to Him.

Something rustled behind her, and she leaped to her feet. Annabel also lectured the women about roaming outside of the settlement. After listening to the horror of the refugee stories, even Annabel had become concerned about the hostile Indians.

Susanna scanned the brush to see if it was an Indian or if an animal was watching her...and an Indian girl stepped out. She didn't recognize Lily at first. Instead of her bodice and petticoat, she wore a leather dress and moccasins. There was no smile on her face.

"Lily," she whispered, rushing to her friend.

She kissed Lily's cheeks, but Lily didn't return the affection. Instead she pushed her away, not harshly, but with an intensity that surprised Susanna.

"Where did you go?"

"Nathan's father," she began, her voice as cool as the November air. "He has come for me."

Susanna slowly tried to understand her words. "Your husband is here?"

"Not my—" she started. "Nathan's father wants me, and he wants his baby."

Susanna cringed at her words. "Nathan is your baby as well."

Lily nodded slowly. "I must protect him from this man."

Protect him from his father?

The coldness of Lily's words turned into a plea. "If he becomes angry, he might hurt Nathan just to spite me. If he doesn't kill him, he will teach our son how to hate the white man. How to kill them. He will turn my sweet boy into a savage."

"Oh, Lily—"

"Howling Wolf—he talks of raiding the Nursery so he can take Nathan."

Susanna clutched her hands to her chest. The refugees often talked about the possibility of a raid on Nazareth, but none of the Brethren thought the Indians would attack their Nursery. "We need to move the children."

"And you need to—" she whispered. "Could you please take

Nathan away from here?"

"But where would I take him?"

"My father, he will take care of him in their village."

"I don't know where your father lives."

"My father is Langoma. Samuel knows." Lily camouflaged herself in the forest's overgrowth though her voice was still clear. "You must hurry."

Susanna stepped toward the trees. "You don't want to go with this man, Lily."

"You would not understand."

"But I want to."

"I can't explain in your words," Lily said. She hesitated and then began to sing about a love so great, a love so powerful, that nothing else mattered, including one's life.

Her implication pierced Susanna—Lily thought she didn't understand the power of love. While her friend was willing to risk her life to be with this man.

Susanna held up her hand to stop Lily's singing. "You love him more than your life, and you love him even more than the life of your son."

The brush rustled in front of her. "I love Nathan with all my heart. That is why you must take him from here."

Leaves and branches rustled again, and Susanna knew Lily was gone.

Susanna glanced back one more time at the wooden markers, and she cringed at the thought of burying Timothy or Nathan or any of their precious children alongside them. Lifting her petticoat, she rushed back down the hill. Elder Graff and the others must move the children today.

Chapter Twenty-Three
....

A burlap bag dangled from Catharine's shoulder as her little bag of treasure banged against her hip. She scooped up a handful of the seed and dropped it into the tilled dirt. Her back ached, and even though the coolness of fall was upon them, sweat poured from her face. Elias hadn't promised her that he would take her away, but if they didn't go—

Even as she brushed her fingers over the bag hidden under her clothes, she refused to consider the possibilities.

Her father had been proud when Elias had been selected to oversee the building of Count Zinzendorf's manor, and he'd been proud when she had been selected to accompany Elias as his wife. Her parents had guessed that Elias would one day become a leader in the church on the new continent, and she'd planned to support him in this leadership.

But what would her parents think of her now, covered in sweat and planting wheat alongside the rest of the women? She'd done every task assigned to her since she'd been in Nazareth, and even though she'd grumbled some, she had done most of them in silence.

Last week Annabel insisted that Catharine get off her bed and start working again among them. The woman couldn't understand how tired she'd become. Her nights never refreshed her. Instead of welcoming her, the mornings mocked her. And her baby, the pretty girl that had formed in her womb, drained any ounce of energy that she could muster.

Rebecca Wittke trailed her, covering the fallen seeds with dirt, but the woman didn't speak to her. They had never been good friends, not even during their months in Gnadenhutten when Rebecca spent much of their little free time visiting with the Indian women and their children, as if she preferred the company of the natives more than Catharine's. Now that they were back in Nazareth and Catharine was a mother, Rebecca had stopped speaking to her altogether.

Rebecca had stopped speaking with her, and Christian had stopped watching her from across the Saal. Part of her wanted to be rid of his admiration, but another part of her, a part she'd never reveal to a soul, wondered if she had lost her allure. It had been so long since she'd seen a looking glass. Had her beauty faded in the wilderness… or perhaps after Juliana was born?

She needed to get out of here before Elias stopped looking at her as well.

She sprinkled another handful of seed on the dirt, a bit more than their supervisor had instructed; but the more she tossed onto the ground, the faster she would finish this chore. Maybe she could go back to rest for an hour or two before she went to get her baby.

Nursemaids were caring for Juliana in the Nursery, women who had been trained in how to care for children. Catharine had been trained to care for servants, but her ability to run a household didn't matter here in Pennsylvania. Nor did her ability to stitch beautiful clothes or dance a waltz or banter with London's elite. The laboress wanted her to work like a mule, not speak or dress like a lady. A strong back was prized over finery or clothes or conversation.

She was far from her home, both in location and in attitude. And all she wanted to do was go home.

Even though she wouldn't be here to eat the harvest of her work, she threw another handful of seed and Rebecca silently covered it with dirt.

"Catharine!" she heard Elias shout. She turned to see her husband walking toward her. She shoved the burlap bag at Rebecca and turned back toward him.

"Where are you going?" Rebecca called, breaking their silence, but Catharine didn't acknowledge the question.

She rushed to him. "What is it?"

He handed her a mug of apple cider, and she gulped the sweet liquid. He directed her away from the field, toward a large tree, and she leaned against it.

"Is something wrong?" she asked.

"Elder Graff wants to see us right away."

"Is he sending us away?"

"I'm not sure."

She lifted her skirt and followed him through the remaining field, to the Gemeinhaus. Elder Graff and Edward were waiting for them along with Benjamin, their Indian brother from Gnadenhutten. Her husband greeted Benjamin and then they sat on the bench, waiting to hear why the elder had beckoned them.

"The wheel on the gristmill has stopped turning," the elder said. "Benjamin has requested that you come and help fix it, Elias, so they will have enough flour to last the winter."

Catharine leaned forward. "And what will I do?"

"You will stay in Nazareth and care for Juliana."

"Oh no," she insisted. "I'm going with him."

She trusted Elias now, but she no longer trusted herself. If he left her here, there was a good chance she wouldn't be here when he returned.

Elias reached for her hand, something he had never done in public before. "Catharine?"

"You are my husband, Elias. I need to be with you."

And he must have known it, because he jumped to her defense. "If I go," he said, "my family goes with me."

She smiled at him, softening her voice. "We can't take Juliana to Gnadenhutten."

A trace of sadness crossed his face. "The Indian women can help you care for her there."

"It will be too cold. And too dangerous."

"I will protect her," Elias insisted, but she shook her head.

"She will be safer here, Elias. The Nursery workers will care well for our daughter."

Much better than she ever could.

"If we go to Gnadenhutten," Elias said to the elder, "I have a request to make upon our return."

He glanced at her for approval, and she nodded her head. She didn't know exactly what he was going to ask, but she hoped it was for them to go to Philadelphia.

"What is it?" Elder Graff asked.

"I would like to take my family to Bethlehem...to stay."

She lowered her gaze. There would be no home for her and Elias to live together in Bethlehem, but it would be so much better than here. In time, perhaps, they could continue south to live in the city.

Elder Graff considered his words. "You were sent to Nazareth to help us build."

"And the Disciple's House was almost finished when we arrived."

"But we will have other buildings—"

He squeezed her hand. "My wife, she longs to live in a bigger village."

"They may not have room for all of you when you get to Bethlehem."

Maybe they would have to go to Philadelphia.

"When we get there, we will decide about accommodations."

"Or we can pay for them," Catharine muttered. Elias shot her a look, and she stopped talking.

Elias stood, and the elders agreed to put his request to relocate before the lot. The lot would decide whether or not she would join Elias in Gnadenhutten and whether they could move on to Bethlehem when they were done.

* * * * *

Christian waited until the Schmidts left the Gemeinhaus and then he joined the other men inside. He'd already spoken with both Edward and Elder Graff about Lily's disappearance, but neither man knew where to look for her. But now that Benjamin was here, perhaps he could help them search.

Elder Graff instructed him to speak.

"Do you know the Indian girl named Wingan who lived among us?" Christian asked Benjamin.

The man nodded slowly.

Elder Graff took off his spectacles and placed them on the table. "Her name here is Lily, and she has left us."

"Not left," Christian corrected him. "She disappeared in the night."

"Lily is a free spirit," the elder said. "She came to us in need and left when she no longer needed us."

Christian leaned forward, trying to make them understand. He had told Susanna he would help her, and he meant to keep his word. "Maybe she has gone back to her clan."

Elder Graff shook his head. "Samuel brought her to us, and it would be almost impossible for her to find her way back home without a guide."

The door on the back of the Saal opened and Susanna rushed to his side, and when she sat down, she gasped for air. He smiled at first, glad that she had joined him, but his smile turned quickly to alarm. "What is it?"

"I just saw Lily, up by God's Acre." She took several breaths. "She was dressed in her Indian clothes."

"What did she say?"

"That her husband is a dangerous man—and he's looking for his son."

Benjamin scooted forward on the bench; his voice was low when he spoke. "What is her husband's name?"

"Howling Wolf."

At Benjamin's low whistle, Christian fell back against his seat. Perhaps that is why they had seen the man so close to Nazareth.

Elder Graff interrupted the men. "This Howling Wolf," he began. He rubbed the bridge of his nose. "This man is not her husband."

* * * * *

"But—" Susanna began to protest the elder's words and then she stopped. The quiet in the room was agonizing after his announcement, and she refused to look at Christian. She was frustrated at her naïveté, frustrated that she continued to swallow lies from those whom she was supposed to trust. "Lily said her husband brought her to Nazareth."

The elder shook his head. "Howling Wolf is not her husband. When Samuel brought her to us, he said that Howling Wolf never planned to marry Lily."

And so the sisters had taken her in and sheltered her from this man.

Susanna supposed she understood why Lily hadn't told her the truth—no one in Nazareth had ever given birth to a child before they were married. Susanna would have been among those who judged and condemned Lily for her sin. But after they had become friends, after they learned to love each other, Lily should have told her.

And now Lily had chosen to run away with this man, the father of her child who was still not her husband. She had seemingly chosen to return to this sin instead of staying with her child and the sisters who welcomed her.

"Why did she come to you now?" the elder asked.

"The children are in danger," Susanna said. "Her hus— This Howling Wolf is planning to raid the Nursery to find his son."

Elder Graff shook his head. "We can't trust Lily's word."

"There are fifty children there," Christian said.

"Where are we going to put fifty more children and the workers and all their belongings?"

When Christian looked out the window, toward the Disciple's House, Edward shook his head. "It's already full."

"It would just be temporary," Christian said.

"We could move them on to Bethlehem before winter," Brother Graff said. "When Catharine and Elias return from Gnadenhutten."

"But we must trust her," Susanna said. "She doesn't want her son to be hurt."

"Or she is being used by the people who want to hurt us," he replied slowly. "To gather us together for an attack."

"No," she insisted. "Lily wouldn't want any of us to be injured."

"My wife is right," Christian interjected. "We must move the children."

"It won't stop him," Benjamin said. "Howling Wolf doesn't care who he wounds or kills."

"Lily—she asked that we take Nathan back to her people."

"We don't know where she came from," the elder said.

"She said her father was a chief by the name of Langoma."

"Langoma?" Christian turned toward her and then looked at Benjamin.

"Langoma has three daughters," Benjamin said. "I don't know their names."

"When I was there, he said he lost a child."

Susanna forgot everyone else in the room. "You've visited her people?"

"They were the clan that decided to follow Christ."

"They will care well for him?" the elder asked.

Christian nodded.

Susanna's eyes filled with tears. She would keep her promise to Lily, but she'd grown to love both Nathan and his mother over the past year. She didn't want to say good-bye to either of them.

"The other children will not be safe as long as Nathan is kept among us. When he is gone, there will be no reason for his father to threaten us." Elder Graff leaned forward. "Benjamin, can you escort him back to his village?"

"I must stay in Gnadenhutten and help Elias with the gristmill," Benjamin said. "I could wait to take him, but if Howling Wolf finds out we kept him from his son, he will bring harm to our people as well."

Christian spoke rapidly. "I will go with you tomorrow to Gnadenhutten. I can take Nathan back to his people."

Tomorrow.

Her mind spun. Now Lily was gone and her son would follow in the morning. It was too much change too quickly.

Elder Graff tapped the desk, looking at all of them. "You don't know the language, Christian."

"I know enough, and Chief Langoma speaks English."

Still the elder didn't seem to be convinced. "I'm not sure it is safe for you to travel by yourself."

"It is not safe for us to stay in Nazareth either," he said. "And yet God's angels continue to protect us."

Susanna cleared her throat. "He doesn't need to travel by himself."

The men turned and looked at her.

"I would like to visit this village with him."

"You can't go," Christian murmured.

Her hands embedded themselves into her hips. "Why not?"

"It's not safe, like Elder Graff said, and it might snow. I don't want you to get sick again."

"I haven't been sick in months." The elder was listening, but she didn't acknowledge him. "If Catharine can make it to Gnadenhutten, then I can make it to this village."

"It's a six-hour canoe ride upstream from Gnadenhutten to Tanochtahe."

She shrugged. "Then I will canoe for six hours."

When he protested again, she inched closer to him. "Do you know how to care for a child, Christian?"

He leaned back against the bench. "I will figure it out."

"How are you going to paddle a canoe and care for him?"

"He will ride in front of me."

She laughed softly. "He will tip over your boat."

"I will figure out a way."

"I want to go with you, Christian. To meet these people and help you care for Nathan on the journey."

Elder Graff tapped his hand on the table. "This is a decision that neither of you will make," he said. "We will take it before the lot."

Susanna sighed, her hands balled in her lap. She wanted to continue arguing, fighting for her position, but she would wait first to see what the lot would say.

The elder slipped the papers into the tube, but before they could draw a lot, Joseph rushed into the room with his face white with worry.

"What is it?" the elder demanded.

"Several Indians have been spotted near the Nursery." He glanced at Susanna, seemingly weighing whether he should continue, but he spoke. "They were carrying muskets."

"Did they speak to you?"

He shook his head. "They were just watching."

When Christian looked up again, worry replaced the sadness in his face. "We must get the children to safety."

This time the elder concurred without using the lot.

Chapter Twenty-Four

....

Christian waited on the bench as Susanna slipped out of the Saal. The lot had granted her permission to go with him to the Indians.

He wanted to go back to Tanochtahe and he wanted her companionship, but he was worried for her safety—her safety and her health. She didn't realize how treacherous a journey like this could be, especially with winter approaching and so many Indians attacking their neighbors. More than he wanted her company, more than he wanted to spend time with her to mend their relationship, he wanted her to be safe.

But the elders—and the lot—wanted her to go with him, and he had no choice but to honor their direction. It was too late to move the children tonight, but they would move them at first light. And then he and Susanna and the Schmidts would follow Benjamin out of Nazareth. As they snuck out of town, the Indians, they hoped, would be focused on the commotion of moving both the little ones and their belongings.

When the elders finished the meeting, Edward asked Christian to wait. The laborer left the room with the others, but when he returned, he held a musket in his hand.

When he handed the gun to Christian, the brass and iron felt cool. He hadn't held a musket since his short stint in the British Army before he had joined the Brethren.

He pushed the musket back toward Edward. "I don't need a gun."

Edward held up his hands, refusing to take it back. "Joseph said the Indians were carrying guns."

"Perhaps they were hunting."

Edward shook his head. "They were making themselves and their weapons known."

Christian dropped the gun to his side. "I'm here to tell the Indians about Christ. I can't kill them."

"I don't want you to kill anyone," Edward said. "You can shoot over their heads or on the ground or wherever you like, but if they become hostile, we have to protect the children."

Sighing, Christian crossed the strap of the musket over his back and walked out the door. He wanted to protect the children, of course, but he'd come to Pennsylvania to share the good news with the Indians, not hurt them. How was he supposed to bear arms against the very men he wanted to save?

Night had begun to fall when he joined nine of his married brothers for the first shift of guarding the Nursery. As he stood in the darkness, scanning the still forest, he thought about Chief Langoma and his people. Indians had been known to become hostile to other tribes who decided to follow Christ, claiming they had given in to the ways of the white man. Saying they should be fighting the white man instead.

Did Indians like these warriors stalk their brothers as well, since they embraced the so-called faith of the white men? He prayed that Chief Langoma and his tribe had stayed strong in their faith, even in the face of persecution from their people. And he prayed that he would be able to spend a day or two encouraging them after he and Susanna carried Nathan to them.

* * * * *

Long before midnight, Susanna lifted Nathan from his crib and held him in her arms. He was almost two now, walking and even talking, but she still felt the urge to protect and care for him like he was a baby. Her baby, even. As the other children in the Nursery slept, she sang one of Lily's songs to him—a song about a flower budding in the spring, of its strength to face the wind and the rain, of the beauty that emerges once it stands strong. A tiny bud that transforms into a flower.

A child who would soon become a man.

Would that man threaten others like his father, or sing like his mother? Would he follow the God of his grandfather, or the many gods of his father?

If only she could steal Nathan away and protect him from the trials he would face.

She sat in the rocker and whispered to the sleeping boy. She told him how much his mother loved him and how much she herself loved him as well. How she wished she could keep him and raise him as her own.

As she looked at his face in the dim light, the black locks of hair curled at his temples, she couldn't imagine him becoming a warrior. If only there were a way she could stop him from hating the white men, especially those who loved him.

She placed Nathan carefully back in his bed, pulling the blanket up over him, and then slipped outside to the small portico that overlooked the woods. There were plenty of women to watch over the sleeping children tonight—she was only a guest among them.

Many of the sisters were afraid to be outside in the darkness, but she wasn't afraid, at least not tonight. Not only was her husband watching over them, but she imagined a fiery ring of God's army beyond, guarding the children while they slept.

Susanna wasn't afraid for herself, but she did fear for the men guarding the Nursery. Squinting into the darkness, she searched the men who guarded them, for Christian. God was replacing her fear with power and love and even a sound mind, like the Scriptures said. Perhaps it was time to tell her husband that she had forgiven him.

The months had turned them into colleagues of sorts, brother and sister if not husband and wife. In their few times together, they hadn't spoken of Catharine or of Christian's longing for her, but his desires still seemed to haunt Susanna. Perhaps this journey would be a time of healing for her.

Perhaps she needed to start now, before they began walking with the others.

She stepped off the porch, into the darkness. Even though she didn't see the brothers, she knew they were there.

"Christian?" she whispered and then she took another step.

"You need to go back inside," he replied quietly, and her heart leaped at the sound of his voice. He had been even closer, guarding her, than she'd imagined.

"I need to speak with you."

When he walked toward her, she could barely see his face in the darkness. He didn't touch her, and while part of her was glad—she didn't know how to respond to his touch—another part of her was disappointed. She wanted to be close to him tonight.

She pulled her shawl tighter over her shoulders. "Have you seen anyone?"

"Not tonight," he replied. "Joseph said there were eight of them earlier. They stood in the field all afternoon, watching us, but they never approached nor did they shoot their weapons."

"Maybe they want something else, something other than Nathan."

"Right now, it seems they want to scare us."

"Maybe they want to scare us," she repeated, as she thought of all the food they'd worked so hard all summer to stockpile for the winter months. Much of it was stored in barns near the Nursery. "Or maybe they want to raid our supplies."

"Or perhaps Lily was right and they really are looking for the boy."

She thought of little Nathan, wrapped in a blanket on the third floor, his dark crown of hair growing longer each day. She stepped closer, whispering now. Just in case someone was near. "His father wouldn't really harm him, would he?"

"I don't know what he would do to the child, but I know for certain that he wouldn't want him to be raised by white men."

"What if we adopted him, Christian? We could take him away from here and care for him."

"If his father wanted to, he could find us, no matter where we went."

"Not if we went back to Europe."

"Nathan isn't our baby." His words were kind, but they were still painful to her. "He belongs to Chief Langoma and his people."

"Does the chief even know he has a grandson?"

"It doesn't matter. Nathan is part of their family."

She pulled her hands to her chest, and in that moment, her arms longed for a child to hold. She'd never before realized how much she wanted to be a mother, not until she thought of having to give Nathan away. There were many other children to hold in Nazareth, but she'd loved Nathan more than the others. Perhaps because he was Lily's son, or perhaps, like Timothy, because he called her name and ran to her whenever she visited the Nursery. Perhaps because God placed the desire in her heart to love him like a mother would.

"We should take it before the lot," she said. "Let the lot decide whether or not we can adopt him."

"Susanna." His voice quieted. "We already know what is right. The lot is only used when we are unsure of the right choice."

She wrapped her arms around her waist. This choice—her choice—to keep Nathan and care for him, wasn't of God. Then why did she want it so badly?

Her heart ached as she turned away.

"Susanna?" he called softly to her.

"I must sleep," she said before she ran back into the house.

She curled up on the floor beside Nathan's bed, but with her tears, sleep evaded her for most of the night.

Chapter Twenty-Five
....

At first light, the Brethren began to escort the children and their knapsacks to the Disciple's House along with a wagonload of mattresses and food. None of the chaperones wanted to scare the children, and they realized that no matter how quiet they tried to keep them, it would be impossible to sneak the children past the Indians. So instead of hushed whispering, one of the brothers brought a trumpet and led their parade as they laughed and sang along their half-mile journey to the Disciple's House. If nothing else, they would confound those who watched them.

Susanna and Mariana led the first ten children behind the trumpeter, and five Brethren with muskets trailed them. The children giggled and skipped along their pathway, excited to be out of the Nursery on the cool autumn morning. She hoped they would enjoy the fervor in the Disciple's House and all the new children to play with.

In a little over a year, their settlement had transformed from a rather subdued village into a hub of noise and excitement. And it didn't seem like it would quiet again for a long while.

With a quick glance behind her, she saw Christian with two young boys flanked to his sides. Timothy was four now and had grown so much in the past year that she didn't think David would recognize him during his next visit. Nathan held Christian's other hand, his arms covered by the long sleeves of his jacket just like the other children. Most of his face was hidden by an oversized coonskin cap—one would have to examine him closely to see the reddish tint of his skin. The brothers would do anything they could to keep the warriors from examining the child.

Once all the children and workers left the Nursery, the Indians might raid the food supplies left behind, but God could supply them with food if necessary, like He had done last year. But if they lost Nathan to Howling Wolf, she feared they would never see him again.

Susanna stole another glance back at her husband laughing with the boys and the surrounding children as if there were no threat in the autumn-colored trees beyond. It had seemed like Christian was everywhere this morning as they prepared to move, helping the children store their belongings and collecting bags for the wagon and even stopping to help Nathan when he tripped on a step. As she watched him, she couldn't help but think what a fine father he would make one day. The stern look that often hardened his face seemed to melt away when he was helping the children.

As their little troop walked up the long plaza to the Disciple's House, the community rallied around the children, just as they had done with the hundreds of refugees who had joined them. In that moment, as the community surrounded them, she had never been more proud of her husband or of their Brethren. While the refugees who lived among them had no place else to go, the people in Nazareth and Brethren around the world relied upon each other in times of need. They were never alone among their brothers and sisters unless they chose to be.

As they walked into the house and up to the rooms reserved for the children on the second floor, she watched Christian lay out a mat for Timothy. A smile stole across her face, and she wondered at what was happening inside her.

Before she'd found out about the ruse of their marriage, she'd thought Christian handsome, but this feeling inside was something new. It was desire mixed with admiration. A longing she'd never felt before, and in its wake she quickly turned away from him.

Backing into the hallway, part of her wanted to stay watching him while another part of her wanted to run to a place where she could think.

She'd always wondered what it would be like to love a man. Perhaps this was what it felt like to be in love, warring emotions of confusion and admiration, frustration and delight.

If only she could be with her mother one last time. She would have helped Susanna sort through the conflict inside her.

"Sister Susanna!" Timothy exclaimed, rushing to her with his arms opened wide. She gave him a second hug since he'd awakened this morning, and then Christian was beside her, along with Nathan. She looked down at Timothy, afraid of what Christian would see if he looked too long in her eyes.

"Will you play with me?" Timothy asked.

"Nathan and I have to go on a journey." Nathan reached up, and she took his hand. "But when I return, I will play with you."

Nathan smiled at her, not knowing where this journey would take him.

"But when you return—," Timothy insisted.

She nudged his chin. "Of course."

Then she took a deep breath and glanced at Christian. "I must go pack."

"We're meeting by the Gemeinhaus in an hour."

He reached for her other hand, squeezing it gently, and she flinched. She had to get out of the house. She tugged her hand out of his grasp before hurrying Nathan down the hallway, away from him.

* * * * *

Christian glanced down at his hands and then back up at Susanna's retreating figure. He'd only wanted to console her, not hurt her, but it was almost as if he'd burned her with his touch. If only she knew how grateful he'd become that the lot had chosen her to be his wife.

But Susanna didn't give him an opportunity to speak. It was as if her anger had turned into fear, though he didn't know why she would be afraid of him. He had done everything he could to reassure and encourage her.

Turning, he offered to help David's son untie the small pack that he had on his back, but Timothy galloped away from him, around the room and then over the bed.

Christian pointed to the pack. "Can I help you unload that?"

Timothy shook his head. "Sister Mariana said I must keep my sack with me."

"Only until we reached this room," he tried to explain. "This will be your home for a few weeks."

Timothy gazed around the room, at the straw mattresses strewn across the floor. "Is my papa coming back?"

"Not today," he said. "But maybe sometime soon."

Christian glanced out the window and watched Susanna rush toward the Sisters House. "I need to leave in a few minutes."

At his words, Timothy slipped out of the cords that bound his pack over his shoulders and held it out to Christian. "I need help."

Christian lifted the pack and untied the knots that held it together. He understood what it was like to crave attention. For him, it had been trying to get the attention of his father when he was a boy. For a child like Timothy, it was trying to get the attention of any adult, since his parents were so far away.

He needed to pack for his journey, but he took the boy's clothing out of the bag, trying not to rush as he folded it in the bureau, to show the child he cared.

Timothy stood tall beside him. "Can you be my papa?"

Christian turned slowly, examining the boy's earnest face. If only they could choose their parents. Or parents, their children.

"I—I wish I could." He didn't want to hurt the boy any more than he'd already been hurt, but he had to be truthful with him. "You have a papa who loves you."

"But I never see him."

"Perhaps he will come again soon."

Timothy reached for his hand. "Can we pretend you're my papa?"

Christian knelt down beside him, unsure of what to say to this child, unsure of what David would want him to say. "I have an idea."

The boy's eyes grew wide as he waited for Christian to speak.

"Do you know what an uncle is?" Christian asked.

The boy shook his head.

"It's almost like a papa—more like a grown-up friend," he tried to explain. "Why don't we pretend that I'm your uncle?"

Timothy nodded.

Christian stood and stepped toward the open door. "And as soon as I return from my journey, I will come back and visit you."

The boy stepped with him. "Like Sister Susanna?"

He paused. "Has Sister Susanna been coming to visit?"

Timothy nodded again, the smile on his face growing bigger. "She loves to play with me. Like a—like an uncle."

Christian smiled and glanced back toward the window. Susanna continued to surprise him. "Maybe Sister Susanna and I can come together to play with you when we return."

* * * * *

Catharine stood at the edge of the manor hall, Juliana squirming in her arms. It had been seven months since her daughter was born; it wouldn't be long before she would need to take up permanent residence in the Nursery.

As she looked into the blue eyes of her child this morning, both tender and strong, she knew she would miss her. Juliana had been her companion for almost the entire seven months of her life. Even though she wanted a nursemaid to help her care for the child, she also wanted to spend time with her, especially as she grew older. She wanted to teach Juliana how to dance and how to sew and, most of all, how to love her husband.

She understood why Elias needed to go to Gnadenhutten—he didn't want to leave Nazareth as a failure—but after he accomplished this task, they would leave with the blessing of their elders. They could go live in Bethlehem for a season and then perhaps they could move on to Philadelphia.

When they went to Bethlehem, they would have to leave Juliana in Nazareth until she was five. At that thought, she pulled her baby close to her again. They must separate, but she would miss her. She had never allowed her heart to get too close to her child, like some of the sisters did with their babies. From the day Juliana was born, Catharine had been preparing herself for the day they must part.

And that day had finally come.

They would surely be allowed to visit her again before they left for Bethlehem, but she didn't know if she wanted to. The saying good-bye over and over would be almost too painful to bear.

Rebecca Wittke walked out of the manor to take Juliana. She was one of the women who'd been newly assigned to watch the children.

Catharine clung to Juliana a moment longer, not wanting to

say good-bye to her, not wanting to give her to a woman who had slighted Catharine for so long. A woman who'd looked down on her because she'd been too tired to be a mother.

She hesitated. "You will take good care of her, won't you?"

"I will care for her as well as you have done."

"No." Catharine glanced down at Juliana resting her head on her shoulder. "Please care for her better than I have done."

Slowly she released her daughter to Rebecca. And Juliana began to cry.

Catharine's eyes filled with tears like her daughter. Rebecca reached out, hugging her, and what remained of Catharine's strength dissolved at the woman's touch.

She felt Elias's strong hand secure her elbow, and she turned to her husband. His eyes were on Juliana, his tears reflecting those that dampened her cheeks. This was why she shouldn't allow herself to think of the possibilities. Even to think of this girl any more as her daughter.

The saying good-bye was even harder than she'd imagined.

"We'll be back soon," Elias said before he kissed Juliana on the cheek. Then he whispered that he loved her, as if Juliana could understand his words.

As Catharine kissed her daughter, the void expanded across her heart. As long as they lived among the Brethren, she was a mother without a child. And her child would have no mother.

But it was only temporary, she reminded herself. One day Juliana would know how much her mother loved her.

Chapter Twenty-Six
....

Another group of children would be leaving the Nursery at any moment, the trumpeter leading their parade, and Susanna prayed quietly that the Indians would be focused on the commotion instead of on the small group preparing to vanish into the woods.

She turned from the window of the Gemeinhaus, back to the five adults and little Nathan, who continued to cling to her hand but seemed oblivious to all that was happening. His life was about to change in ways that none of them could imagine, and she prayed they were doing the right thing, taking him into a world he had never known, a place where they hoped he would be safe.

"It's time," Elder Graff said, directing them toward the door.

There would be no send off today for them. No crowd to wave them good-bye. They would leave quietly in pairs, away from the Nursery and the crowds, strolling into the woods in the daylight without looking back.

Elder Graff prayed for them one last time, and then Benjamin walked through the door. Minutes passed as he scoured the woods to the west of the Gemeinhaus, and then he motioned that it was safe.

Elias and Catharine left next. They walked hand in hand, talking casually together as if they were going on an afternoon stroll as they disappeared into the woods.

Then it was time for Susanna and Christian and Nathan to join them.

Nathan looked up at her, his brown eyes round. "Mama?"

She leaned down to kiss the top of his head. "She's not here right now, but can I take you for a walk?"

His lower lip trembled, and for a moment she worried that he would cry out for Lily. They couldn't take him into the forest if he were whimpering for her. But then he nodded, and she smiled at him. Her head high, she squeezed his hand and they moved through the door.

She wanted to carry him, but the others concurred with Benjamin that it would be better for the boy to walk the first part of the journey so it didn't look like they were stealing him away. They were all simply taking a slow walk, gathering nuts in the forest.

Christian walked a few feet behind her and Nathan, and she knew he was scanning the forest as they walked, staying alert for a threat. She was glad for his quiet presence, taking care of them.

She feared that Nathan might cry out again for his mother, but he continued to follow her without another sound, as if he knew something grave had happened and the possibility of danger quieted his lips. Or at least he stayed quiet until they walked into the trees. Then he began to sing quietly like his mother.

One of the brothers had hidden their packs in the woods, under piles of leaves, and they quickly strapped on their loads—food for their travels, canvas for the tents, and a warm change of clothes. Christian carried the ax for firewood, and Elias held a musket.

Susanna's shoulders curled away from her neck as she walked, heavy from the pack and the anxiety that threaded through her as she listened for footsteps around them. She knew she would never hear the Indians coming, not until it was too late, but she continued to listen as they moved farther into the forest, away from the settlement.

Nathan stopped his quiet singing, and when he did, Christian leaned forward. "Are you all right?"

The boy shook his head. "Go home."

She took a deep breath. How was she supposed to explain this to him—that his mother was gone and they were taking him away, that he would never return to what he had known all his life?

When Christian stopped walking, she stopped as well. He knelt beside the child. "Did you know you have a grandfather?"

Nathan shook his head.

"He is a great man. An Indian chief and a follower of our God."

His eyes grew wide again. "An Indian?"

As she watched the boy, she realized that Nathan didn't know about his mother or his father being Indians. The life of the Brethren was all he had ever known. Susanna leaned back against a tree, resting her shoulders from their load. The others waited for them ahead.

"We're going to a safe place," she said, trying to reassure him. And trying to reassure herself, that they were doing the right thing.

Christian stood and nodded to her. It would be a much safer place than keeping him in Nazareth.

They continued on. The farther they walked from Nazareth, the lighter her load felt. Nathan walked in front of her for a bit, searching for sticks and rocks and bringing her his favorite finds. She breathed deeply of the wilderness and it strengthened her.

This was where she was supposed to be, out here in God's creation with her husband. After all this time, she was finally going to the Indians. It wasn't how she had planned to visit them and yet maybe, maybe it was exactly what God had planned.

Her heart began to race. The past hours had been so busy, preparing and keeping watch over the children, that she hadn't stopped to think about the implications of this journey. She was finally going on a mission, and after they stopped in Gnadenhutten, Christian and she would be alone, escorting Nathan back to his tribe.

She rubbed her hands over her arms. She and Christian would be alone, and she must learn how to be around him without reacting to his gaze or his touch.

Elias and Catharine talked quietly in front of her as they hiked, and she wondered if she and Christian would feel comfortable in each other's presence one day, like the Schmidts did. Elias had forgiven both Christian and Catharine for their deception.

Christian no longer needed to carry the burden of his guilt. God had forgiven him for what he had done, and soon, when they were finally alone, she would tell him that she had forgiven him as well.

A rock wall fortified the mountain ahead of them. At first she assumed that they would walk around the mountain, but Christian handed Benjamin his pack and Benjamin strapped it on himself. Christian picked Nathan up and put him over his head, securing the boy's legs as he carried him on his back.

"Hold on," Christian instructed him.

Susanna was afraid that Nathan would topple over and land on the rocks, but he clung to Christian's neck. She reached for a tree limb among the rocks and started the climb behind them.

When they reached the peak, Catharine sat down on a rock while the men included Nathan in their discussion. Susanna didn't want to sit nor did she want to talk. Instead she walked to the edge of the mountain and savored the view below. She'd never been up this high in her entire life—like a bird soaring over the trees. Or a star hanging above the earth.

A river snaked below them, in and out of a grand forest that stretched to the horizon, and the mountains looked as if they had tumbled from the sky, falling over one another in a pile of stair steps meant for God Himself to climb, up into the clouds and whatever lay beyond. They'd climbed one of God's grand steps and the others didn't seem to care.

Christian joined her side. "You need to rest."

She clapped her hands together, invigorated by the view and the air. "How could I rest with so much beauty around us?"

He may not understand it, but the beauty of God's nature, the coolness of the autumn air, made her feel alive.

Instead of pressing Susanna to sit, Christian stood beside her, looking out over the valley and the haze of mountains beyond. "His majesty is all around us."

Nathan held out his arms to her, and she picked him up. "Around us and deep within us."

Nathan pointed down at the trees. "Mama?"

"She's not here right now," Susanna tried to explain again, not knowing what else to say. She held him close to her, pointing out the hawk circling below them, the sun creeping toward the edge of the world.

Catharine pulled off her shoes and rubbed her feet. "He won't miss his mama for long."

Susanna moved toward the smooth top of the rock, holding the boy a little tighter. "I don't know...."

"Someone will take her place." Catharine's voice sounded hollow. "Someone else will care for him."

Susanna didn't answer. It was hard enough for Catharine to leave Juliana behind. She didn't need to tell her about the nights she'd spent as a young woman longing for her own mother to talk with, to hold her during the hard times. How she'd once confided in her mother about all the details of her life, and how much she missed her confidante when her mother left for Africa.

Nathan might not remember his mother's face, but if Lily never returned, surely God would allow him the memory of her beautiful voice.

"Every child needs a mother."

"Not in Nazareth," Catharine said.

She thought of Timothy, of Nathan and Juliana. The sisters cared well for them, but there was still something special about experiencing a mother's love. "A child needs his mother, especially in a place like Nazareth. Even if they only visit."

Benjamin stepped toward them, as if he knew what she'd been thinking. "Chief Langoma will make sure this boy is cared for."

Susanna nodded her head. But Chief Langoma wasn't a mother.

Christian removed a bag of chestnuts from his pack and offered them to her. She ate a handful of the sweet, peeled nuts before they continued hiking, using torches to guide them as far away from Nazareth as possible that night. Nathan slept in Christian's arms as they walked, and even as the hours passed, her husband didn't complain about the extra weight.

She reached her arms out to him. "Let me take him, Christian."

He shook his head. "It will wake him."

"You've been carrying him for too long."

"He doesn't weigh much."

Susanna knew well the weight of a sleeping child, but Christian continued to carry him until they stopped for the night.

Dinner was hastily prepared as Elias helped Christian string the canvas over the poles and stake it into the ground to erect two tents, side by side. After they ate, the men slept in one tent while Nathan joined Catharine and her in the second tent. But in two nights, she knew, there would be no second tent.

Where would she and Christian sleep when they got to Chief Langoma's village?

*   *   *   *   *

Catharine hurled to the side, trembling in her sleep. She screamed at the eyes that haunted her, eyes that flashed between a fierce orange and a red, and then she awoke, her body shivering under the blanket, though she knew not if it was from the cold or from fear. She'd never had a nightmare like this before.

She pulled her blanket to her chin, but the eyes continued

to haunt her. She turned over, trying to think about Elias instead. And Juliana.

Susanna had said it was important for a child to have a mother to love her, to comfort her. Catharine had a mother, but the woman had never been around long enough to offer any kind of comfort. During her childhood, Catharine had always felt more like a doll to her mother, a toy she could dress and play with and then put back into her crib until the nursemaid came for her.

In that moment, she wished she'd had a mother who loved her for more than a toy, a mother like Susanna had. When Catharine had nightmares as a child, there was no one around to comfort her, to help her fight the demons of the night.

She rolled over again and closed her eyes, trying to fall back asleep, but all she saw was a wild animal stalking them, stalking her. The animal glared into the darkness of her mind—the fierce orange eyes of an animal she didn't recognize.

And then it attacked.

She jolted upward on her bed, looking wildly around the tent. She was awake and yet the eyes were still there, circling around her, and she was terrified for herself and for Elias. For their daughter.

She glanced over at Susanna, who was sleeping peacefully beside Nathan, and she kicked her leg.

Susanna moaned. "What is it?"

"I've had a nightmare," Catharine said. "Something was trying to hurt us."

Susanna rolled toward her, but Catharine couldn't see her friend's eyes in the darkness to see if they were opened or closed; she saw only the eyes of her dream. "The men will protect us," Susanna murmured. "God will protect us."

Catharine squeezed her fingers together. "But what if they don't— what if God doesn't protect us?"

"Then, I suppose…" Susanna's voice trailed off, and Catharine thought she had fallen asleep again. But Susanna continued. "I suppose it means He's calling us home to Him."

Catharine leaned back on the clothing she'd balled into a pillow. What would it be like to finally be home with their Savior? A place without sorrow or tears? She would no longer mourn the loss of her life, no longer be sad at the thought of losing Elias or her daughter. She'd drifted far from their Savior over the past months, but she didn't want to be far. She wanted to be near Him. Only God could chase the fierceness of the eyes away, along with the despair that had settled around her heart.

"Susanna," she whispered again.

"Yes?"

"When Juliana gets older…I want her to know that I loved her."

"You will tell her."

Panic rushed through Catharine again.

"But what if I'm not there?"

Susanna paused. "Then I will tell her."

Catharine tucked the blanket under her body and shifted again to avoid the rock that poked into her back. When she closed her eyes this time, the orange eyes vanished in the light of their Savior. An image of the cross broke through, and she took a deep breath, sleep embracing her once more. She rested secure the remaining hours of the night, knowing the Savior was with her no matter what she faced. And knowing He would be with Juliana as well.

Chapter Twenty-Seven
....

Seated in the front of a bark canoe, Susanna paddled up the Lehigh River with Christian and Nathan behind her, toward Chief Langoma and his clan. Before they left Gnadenhutten that morning, Elias had already begun work on the wheel of the gristmill. He predicted that the wheel would begin turning again by the morrow, and then they would return together to Nazareth.

Their journey to Chief Langoma would be much shorter than she and Christian desired, but the visiting was secondary to this new mission. When they left Tanochtahe, they would leave Nathan in a safe place.

Her husband sat behind her, paddling the canoe and shouting out commands for her to pull her oar through the water on the right or the left. She'd never been in a canoe in her life. She didn't tell Christian, pretending she knew how to paddle, though he must have guessed at her ineptness. She obeyed his instructions, hoping every moment that he didn't regret bringing her on this journey.

The hours passed rapidly. Nathan entertained them from the floor of the canoe with an assortment of songs; the wall of leaves around them were ablaze with color. They stopped to eat a quick supper, and by the time they finished, the temperature had begun to fall. She tucked a blanket around Nathan and he fell asleep on the bottom of the boat between them. Dusk would soon be upon them, and she hoped they would be able to find the village before dark.

As Nathan slept, she glanced behind her. "Do you have any siblings?" she asked Christian, breaking the silence between them.

He dipped his paddle into the water. "Three brothers."

"And they are married?"

"Last I heard, two of them married, but it has been ten years since I left home."

"That's a long time."

"When I left my home, I never intended to return."

"My family never planned to return to Moravia either."

The river lapped against the rocks, and they paddled around a fallen tree branch. When she glanced behind her again, Nathan was still asleep.

"Thank you," she said softly. "For taking such good care of him."

He stopped paddling as she continued. "Thank you for caring for Nathan and Timothy and all the children back in Nazareth."

His voice filled with concern as he dipped his paddle into the water again. "Before we left Nazareth, Timothy asked me to be his papa."

"What did you tell him?"

"That he already had a papa."

Her heart felt sad for the child. He had a papa, a papa he never saw. "Was he upset?"

"A little, until I told him I could be his uncle instead."

"Oh, that's perfect."

"He said you've been visiting him at the Nursery." He spoke slowly as he paddled, as if every word was weighted.

"Brother David said he would like it if I kept watch over him."

"You have a good heart, Susanna," he said, and her skin warmed at his words. "You will be a good mother."

The warmth stole up her cheeks, and she was grateful he was sitting behind her. "And you will make a good father."

Hours passed and then she saw red markings on the trees in front of them, pictures of birds and bear and deer. Christian directed their canoe to the landing underneath. Together they worked to lift the sleeping child from his bed, and when they did, he awoke with another cry for his mama. Susanna pulled Nathan to her chest, humming one of Lily's songs to him, but this time the song wouldn't console him.

Christian lifted the large pack from the canoe and looped it through his arms, around his back.

"How far is it?" she asked over Nathan's cries.

He pointed at a narrow path leading away from the river. "Just up this hill."

As darkness rained down on them, she began singing again, but not a song of the Delaware language like she did when they were alone. Instead, she sang a hymn about the Savior's light in a dark world. Nathan settled into her shoulder and fell back asleep.

* * * * *

Through all the months of travel earlier in the year, Christian had never enjoyed himself more than he had today. With the beauty of Susanna's voice trailing him, the picture of her carrying the boy in her arms, something was happening inside him. He'd known for a long time that he and Catharine would never have made good partners on the mission field, but perhaps he and Susanna could be good partners. Perhaps they could even be good parents together.

Perhaps he'd been missing the truth all along.

As they hiked up the hill, a harsh voice called out to them from the trees. Guttural words of the Delaware, but he didn't understand them. He flung out his arm to stop Susanna's walk.

"Who is there?" he called as Nathan cried out behind him. Susanna hushed the boy to no avail.

When there was no response from the woods, he reached for

the ax strung alongside his pack. He hoped the man who called was from Langoma's clan, but he had no way of knowing if he was a friend or a foe.

"Auweeni," he said to the darkness, hoping the man would understand the Delaware greeting Samuel had taught him.

The voice responded this time, but Christian struggled to understand his words.

Then he felt the gentle pressure of Susanna's fingers on his arms. But instead of speaking to him, she called out to the voice over Nathan's cries, speaking the Delaware language like it was her own.

He looked over at her, stunned. When did his wife learn the language of the Indians?

The man spoke again, and Christian heard the rustling of leaves. Even as he clutched the ax in his hands, he prayed. He didn't want any of them to get hurt.

"Put the ax away," Susanna told him.

"Are you certain?"

"He said he comes as a friend, as one of Chief Langoma's men."

He slowly slid the ax back into its hold as he waited for the man to appear, and when he saw the man's face, he remembered him as one he had baptized in the river. A young Indian named Moenach.

He embraced the man.

Moenach turned to speak with Susanna, and Nathan stopped crying when he saw the Indian. Christian watched in awe as Susanna responded to the man's words, conversing easily with him while he himself struggled to understand the basic words. Not only had Susanna befriended an Indian woman and cared for her baby, but she had also learned to talk with the Indians. She didn't need him to go on a mission—she could deliver the message of salvation alone.

Moenach reached forward, seeming to offer Susanna relief from her load. She shook her head, telling him something that made him smile, and then he escorted them up to the village. When they walked between the huts and up to the lodge, Christian felt like he had come home.

The two Indians inside greeted Christian when they walked through the door, and then they scooted back as he and Susanna walked toward the fireplace.

A woman dipped a wooden ladle into a kettle hanging over the fire and offered it to Susanna with a slight bow of her head. Gripping the ladle in her fingers, Susanna sniffed the drink. The Indians made powerful teas of herbs and roots to heal, but there were also poisonous herbs and roots that held the power to steal away a life instead.

Susanna glanced over at him, questioning him with her gaze. He nodded at her, and she thanked the woman before she took a sip of the tea. Then she yawned.

The Indian woman, seemingly pleased by the effects of her tea, led Susanna and Nathan to the animal furs in front of the fire. Nathan cuddled close, dozing back to sleep in her arms. More men entered the lodge, and Christian shook their hands until Chief Langoma entered the room.

The chief extended both arms, shaking Christian's hand as he spoke in English. "It is good to see you again, my friend."

"Are you well?"

The chief nodded. "Our faith is still strong."

"Faith will keep you well."

Chief Langoma's gaze wandered to Susanna and Nathan on the bear rug. "You brought guests with you."

Susanna looked up at the man with her warm smile and spoke to him in the Delaware language. The chief's eyes widened in surprise as he spoke with her.

Then the chief turned to him. "This is your wife?"

"Indeed."

"She speaks our language much better than you do."

"I am a blessed man."

The chief looked at the boy in the dim light, his eyes squinting. "We didn't know you had a son."

"He is not mine." He paused, not knowing exactly how to introduce Nathan to him. "But I believe—I think he might be your grandson."

No one spoke as the chief took another step closer. Nathan was asleep now, resting on Susanna's skirt, and the chief studied his face. "Who is his mother?"

Susanna wiped her hand across her eyes before she spoke in words that Christian understood. "I knew her as Lily, but you would know her as Wingan."

"Wingan." The chief whispered the name, his gaze locked on the child. Then he looked back at Susanna. "Where is my daughter?"

"Samuel brought her to the settlement at Nazareth before Nathan was born, and she lived among us for almost two years."

"She is still in this Nazareth?"

Susanna shook her head. "She left with a man known as Howling Wolf."

The chief clutched his hand to his chest, like the pain was too much for him to bear. "There is no good in this Howling Wolf."

There was no good found in any of them, not without the Savior, but Christian didn't say the words. It would only discount the man's pain, and he would never discount a father's sorrow at the loss of his daughter.

The chief began to speak rapidly in the Delaware language, and Susanna began to translate his words.

"Wingan's mother and I—we were already old when we had her. My other daughters were all grown and had children of their own, and when my wife died, I didn't know what to do with our youngest one. She was supposed to marry the son of a friendly tribe, but she met Howling Wolf instead—

"When I discovered she was with child, I was very angry and she ran away. Howling Wolf came here after she left, but when he couldn't find her, he killed one of my granddaughters for revenge. I thought he would kill Wingan as well when he found her."

Susanna spoke in English for him and then in Delaware for the Indians. "Wingan asked us to protect Nathan, but we are afraid that he won't be safe in Nazareth, not with Howling Wolf searching for him."

"Howling Wolf is not a man easily deterred."

"Maybe he will marry her?"

The chief shook his head. "He already has three wives."

A gasp escaped from Susanna's lips, and Christian put his arm around her shoulders. Perhaps Lily's eyes would open; perhaps the truth she'd learned in Nazareth would penetrate her actions. Perhaps she would still come for her son before she became the fourth wife or not a wife at all.

"Will you keep Nathan here," he asked, "until Wingan returns for him?"

"She will not return," he said sadly. "Howling Wolf doesn't love my daughter, but she still runs back to him whenever he asks."

One of the women offered them a platter filled with roasted meat and boiled corn, and both Christian and Susanna ate so quickly that he didn't stop to wonder what type of meat they'd eaten. Then the woman handed the chief a ladle filled with the tea. He sniffed it before he took a long sip. "Wingan is like a child herself. She doesn't think about how her actions impact those around her. She brought destruction on our village, and now she brings it to you as well."

"She hasn't brought destruction on us."

The sadness in his eyes deepened. "It will come."

Christian shook off the ominous words. The Lord would keep watch over them—they didn't need to be afraid.

The chief took another long sip of the drink. "I will continue to pray that the Christ Child will protect her and her baby."

"God can't protect someone who doesn't obey Him, and sometimes, for reasons we don't always understand, He doesn't protect those who do love and obey Him." Susanna held the baby out to Langoma. "But He did protect Nathan."

Langoma eyed the baby for a moment, this son of Howling Wolf and his daughter. "Howling Wolf won't stop searching until he finds him."

Christian nodded. He didn't know this warrior, but he remembered well the fear on Samuel's face at the sight of him, the fear that laced his friend's words. Howling Wolf's search would inevitably lead him to Chief Langoma and his people.

"Perhaps we can still take him back with us." Susanna looked at Christian, hope cresting in her gaze. "We could go to a faraway place, like Mariana's St. Thomas."

"He will only be safe among his people."

But even as Christian said it, he realized that the chief hadn't offered to allow Nathan to stay with the clan. Perhaps he feared that Howling Wolf would kill another member of his family if the child remained among them.

The boy stirred, and as he sat up on Susanna's lap, his gaze roamed around the room, searching the strange faces, perhaps looking for his mother. Then his eyes rested on the chief.

At first Christian thought the boy might cry again, afraid of the weathered face. But he seemed to study the wrinkles on the man's face instead. And then he smiled.

They stared at each other for a moment, grandfather and child, the fire flickering behind them.

And then the chief reached out his hand.

Chapter Twenty-Eight

....

Nathan rested against Susanna's side by the fire while the chamomile tea warmed her insides. And then her eyelids began to droop. Christian picked up Nathan and held him in his arms while the chief offered his hand to her. His skin was rough, yet the hands were strong as they helped her stand. Several of the Indian men reached for the visitors' packs, and then the chief guided her and Christian and Nathan outside the lodge to a small hut next door.

The chief must have known that love for Nathan entangled her heart, that it would be hard for her to part from him so soon. But just as the chief seemed to understand the bond that had formed between her and this child, she understood that she must leave him here for his protection as well as the protection of their community in Nazareth. But it didn't mean the leaving would be easy.

With Nathan in her arms, she stepped into the mud-and-bark hut, and the chief hung a lantern on the wall. There was no bureau or even a bed, only straw mats on the floor covered with deerskins and a bench along the wall. Rows of dried herbs hung on strings across the ceiling, like a canopy of leaves from the forest.

Christian set his pack along the wall and then pulled a curtain made of animal skin over the doorway and secured it. He helped her lay Nathan on one of the mats, but she stood frozen by the worn curtain, her eyes taking in the surroundings. They were far from the bedchamber in Nazareth and the pressure that came with it, but she didn't know exactly how to prepare for bed with her husband in the room.

Her fingers brushed over the ribbons laced across her bodice. She couldn't sleep in her dress and yet she couldn't disrobe in front of this man, even if he was her husband. She stared at him, not knowing what to do. He must have seen the distress in her gaze, because he turned to dig in his backpack. Then he tossed a blanket onto the mattress beside her.

"I meant to ask the chief one more question," he said as he moved toward the curtain. "Do you mind if I step out for a few minutes?"

She shook her head. "Please don't feel like you must rush."

He flashed her an awkward grin. "I won't." Then he left her.

She tucked a blanket around Nathan and undressed as quickly as she could, hanging her dress and cape on a hook. She wrapped another blanket over her shoulders, covering her shift, and lay down on the mattress away from the light of the candle and the curtain. She closed her eyes.

Nathan scooted to her side, and she sighed. The room smelled sweet, the aroma of savory and thyme, and she thought back to the women who'd served her tea and roasted veal so graciously, and of the chief who was wounded by the choices of his daughter. She thought of the closeness of their community in the lodge, the informality of their welcome and their evening prayer together before they retired to their huts. And she loved it all.

Nathan's little hand reached out for her, circling her arm, and she squeezed it.

Chief Langoma and the others would do all they could to keep Nathan safe from Howling Wolf, but even so, as she lay on the mat, she prayed that God would blind Howling Wolf's eyes from the truth. She prayed that no matter where Howling Wolf searched, he wouldn't be able to find the child.

* * * * *

Christian stood outside the hut until he no longer heard Susanna moving. When he slipped back through the curtain, his gaze rested on Susanna's back. Nathan snuggled close to her. Sitting on the bench, he removed his boots as he watched her, wondering if she really slept or if she were pretending.

When had his wife learned the language of the Delaware? How did she care so much for these people she hardly knew? There were so many questions he longed to ask her.

Contentment flooded his soul as he leaned against the bench. Even as he'd begun to appreciate Susanna during the past year, he hadn't loved her as he should have. He was cold, abrasive even, and so focused on his tasks that he often wounded those around him.

There was no doubt that if Susanna could forgive him his past, she would love him well as his wife. But could he figure out how to love her?

He rubbed his hands together, admiring the curve of her back in the lantern light. He longed to take Susanna in his arms—a woman he barely knew but someone he admired beyond words. He longed to hold her as only a husband holds his wife. The lot had given her to him as a gift, and he'd failed her.

He blew out the candle and lay down on the bench. Perhaps his deception had cost him Susanna's love, but still, he wanted to try to learn how to love her well.

* * * * *

Catharine heard the savage Indians long before she saw them. They shrieked outside the door of the Gemeinhaus, the sound snaking through her skin and shaking her core. She squeezed her eyes closed and blocked her ears like it would make the sound disappear. Sisters abandoned their beds around her, fleeing down the steps as they shouted instructions to bar the doors and windows.

Catharine picked up the bag of gold and belted it around her shift. Then she pulled her hooded cloak over her nightdress. Elias met her at the top of the stairs as the screams outside turned into chanting. She didn't know how many Indians surrounded them, but in the darkness, it sounded like a legion.

He kissed her and then prodded her down the steps. "We have to be ready to run, Catharine."

There would be no running from these savages and they both knew it, but she nodded her head, trying to be strong.

Something pounded against the door below, and the sisters rushed up toward them. Several men stayed downstairs, and she could see a solitary musket pointed at the cabinet that blocked the front door. A pile of chairs and the table had been stacked around the cabinet as a fortress against their enemy, and she prayed it would hold.

"Hurry," Elias said, leading her back up into the dormitory for the brothers. He opened the shutters, and below them, she could see the Indians circling the house, their war paint glowing in the light of their torches. Like the eyes from her nightmare.

There would be no escape through the window either.

She fell to her knees, begging God for help, and Elias prayed beside her. At first they prayed that God's angels would rally around them, protecting their house from the evil one, but then she smelled smoke below. It was too late. Instead of rescuing them, God seemed to be calling them home. They would suffer, and they would probably die. And perhaps, like the Count had told them, they would even be forgotten.

She prayed that God wouldn't forget them.

A woman screamed, and then she pushed Catharine aside as she flung herself out the window, jumping into the arms of their enemy. Catharine refused to look below.

"I'm so sorry," Elias said, tears smeared across his face. "I should have made you stay in Nazareth."

"Hush," she whispered. "I wanted to be with you."

"If I hadn't insisted..."

Then he would have come alone. And she would be a widow. There would be no life for her without Elias.

"I'm ready to go home with you," she said.

Smoke filled the room, the heat burning her skin, and she leaned into Elias. Fear clutched her in the heat, the smoke.

"The enemy can kill the body," Elias whispered, "but the Savior owns the soul."

Catharine no longer heard the screams around her. Elias was kneeling beside her, his arms wrapped around her, whispering his love to her.

She wouldn't be going to back to London or even to Bethlehem. God was taking her to a place much more grand.

Chapter Twenty-Nine
....

Susanna woke before Christian or Nathan. Threads of moonlight crept around both sides of the curtain, and in the faint light, she dressed quickly in the dark. Her husband's arm dangled over the bench, and she smiled as she draped her heavy shawl over her dress and slipped out of the room and down to the river to wash her hands and face in the cold water.

Light eased across the horizon, water rushing over the rocks and under branches that hung over its path. As she stood on the riverbank welcoming the dawn, she imagined herself on a warm summer day, dipping her toes in the water and splashing the Indian children.

She wished she never had to leave this place.

After she helped the Indian women prepare a breakfast of corn bread and dried berries, Christian brought Nathan to her. Fifteen more people in the clan wanted to be baptized, so in spite of the frigid temperatures, Christian took them outside and down to the river.

From the shore, she and Nathan watched him wade into the cold water, and one by one he baptized men, women, and a few children. Their Indian friends didn't seem to notice the cold when he dunked them under the river. Their faith was fresh as they emerged praising their Savior, reminding her of the children that must have gathered at Christ's feet. She couldn't see God, but she imagined Him with his arms outstretched, welcoming these followers to Him.

Nathan clapped his hands every time someone went under the water, and as Susanna clapped with him, she prayed that God would bring them back here again soon. She didn't mind the cold weather or even living in a hut. She wished she could serve the Savior here, alongside Christian.

If only they had more time, she would ask the Indian women a hundred questions about their customs and heritage. Life was more unscheduled here. Free. The women seemed to work just as hard as those in Nazareth, but the time wasn't as structured here.

Even as she wondered what it would be like to live in Tanochtahe, she knew it would be hard to leave Nazareth, hard to leave her friendships with Catharine and Rebecca and Mariana and her time playing with Timothy and the other children in the Nursery. Yet the Savior had put the desire in her heart to be with the Indian people and she must follow, no matter where He took her.

She spent the day working with the women in the kitchen house. They showed her how to boil venison with handfuls of rice and how to grind roasted corn into a powder. As they worked, the women assured her that their chief would keep Nathan safe. That evening, while she tended to Nathan in the hut, Christian stayed up late talking with the chief and his council of elders. Nathan rested on the mat beside her, but it was a long time before he closed his eyes.

"There are so many things I want to tell you," she whispered.

He looked over at her, probably for the last time. "Mama?"

He was too young to understand all that was in her heart, but she still needed to speak. And she prayed God would give him the ability to remember, remember and understand, as he grew older.

"Your mother loved you very much," she said. "She didn't want to leave you."

How could she explain to him, when she herself didn't understand exactly why Lily had to go? But then she remembered one of the songs that Lily had taught her—the song about a mother bear who loved her cub so much that she left him to chase the hunter away.

And so she began to sing.

It was a sad song, because as the bear rescued her cub, she was slain at the hands of the hunter. For the first time since Lily had taught her the words, Susanna understood what Lily was trying to tell her. By leaving Nathan, by going to the hunter, perhaps she too was trying to protect her child.

Nathan fell asleep as she sang, and she closed her eyes. He was home now, and in some strange way, for the first time since she was a child, she seemed to have found her home as well.

* * * * *

Susanna clutched Nathan in her arms as she walked beside Christian to the edge of the village. Christian watched her blink back tears as she tried to be strong, but he knew the turmoil in her heart. When Susanna loved, she seemed to love with all of her being.

The chief took his hand and shook it. "Visit us again soon," he said.

"I would like that."

The chief nodded at Susanna. "And bring back your wife."

Susanna clutched Nathan in her arms a little longer, and then slowly, reluctantly, she kissed him on the forehead and handed him to the young woman who would care for him. When she turned, Christian saw tears in her eyes, her strength beginning to falter.

He was certain that Susanna wouldn't let him come back to Tanochtahe without her.

After a final wave good-bye to the men and women gathered at the perimeter of the village, he took Susanna's arm and quickly escorted her away from the small crowd, to the canoe below them.

He helped her into the front seat and then he picked up his oar and climbed into the back. The sun shone this morning, but the leaves above their heads masked most of the light as they paddled away from the village. Susanna was quiet, and he wondered if she was angry at him for not letting her keep Nathan in Nazareth with them. Or if she was mourning the loss.

"Perhaps we could return soon and visit him."

She shook her head. "If we return, Howling Wolf might follow us. He might find Nathan."

He hadn't thought about the man following them, but she was right. He might trail them all the way to Tanochtahe to find his child.

"You took good care of him, Susanna."

She dipped her oar into the water twice before she replied. "Thank you."

"How did you learn to speak the Delaware language?"

A ray of light streaked through the leaves, and she lifted her hand as if she could catch the beam in it. "Lily taught me."

"Can you teach me how to speak it?"

"I can't teach you how to speak it." She turned around to him, and the hint of a smile lit her face along with the light. "But I can teach you how to sing it."

"Sing it?"

"That's how Lily taught me."

"God didn't bless me with a voice for singing."

"But He still wants us to lift our voices, no matter how poorly we sing."

"You might disagree after you hear me."

She sang a line, and he mimicked her words. Then she laughed. "You are terrible at singing."

He laughed along with her. "If only you were honest with me—"

"You'd rather I lie to you?"

"I never want you to lie to me, Susanna."

She brushed her hand over her sleeve, a slight smile on her

face when she turned back to him. "Singing is still the best way to learn."

And so they sang as they paddled through the woods, him with his gruff voice, her with a melodic voice that could probably calm both sailors and angry seas. And in the hours of their singing, Christian began to feel the healing between them.

They paddled around a curve, and two animals were drinking from the river, horses without manes. Susanna lifted her oars and watched them.

"Samuel called them elk," he said.

"They are magnificent."

There was a plain of flat rocks around the elk, and he paddled toward it. They stopped along the riverbank, in the sunlight. He unwrapped the bread and dried strips of bear meat their Indian friends had packed for them and spread the food over one of the rocks.

"I'm glad you were able to come with me."

She nodded, but in her eyes he saw a bit of sadness. Tonight they would be back in Gnadenhutten with the other brothers and sisters, with Catharine. He didn't know when he would be alone with Susanna again.

He put down the chunk of bread in his hands and turned to her.

"Please forgive me," he begged. "I should have found a way to tell you about Cath—about my past before we married."

She lifted her head slowly. "I've already forgiven you, Christian."

He searched her blue eyes, the smoothness of her skin.

"Do you still love her?"

He shook his head. "God has given her to Elias, and I am happy for both of them."

"And what about you?" she asked.

"God has given me a most wondrous blessing," he said quietly. "A blessing I don't deserve."

His hands twitched and he reached out, taking her small hands within his own. He feared she would pull away, but he held her hands, and her skin felt so soft to him. He worried that he might hurt her if he squeezed too hard.

"I still don't know how to be a husband to you, Susanna."

Her lips quivered. "All I want is your love."

"I don't want to hurt you again," he whispered, but even as he caressed the top of her hands, he knew that he would. In his bullishness, in his pride, he would do something to hurt her again. If she could continue to forgive him, if she could dare to love him, he would do everything he could to be a good husband to her.

Susanna looked down at their hands. "You must forgive me as well."

"There is nothing for me to forgive."

She shook her head. "I was so angry at you, angry at both you and Catharine. I thought you were trying to hurt me."

"I never wanted to hurt you."

"It took me awhile, but I slowly realized that what happened between you and Catharine was so long ago. You couldn't help continuing to care for her after we married."

Maybe he couldn't stop his emotions back then, but he should have worked harder to extinguish the desire that had controlled him for so long. He couldn't tell his wife this, not as he was basking in the grace of her forgiveness, but with the Savior's help, his love would be for his wife.

"It is you I love, Susanna. It is you I want to be with."

Her chin fell, and he nudged it up with his fingers. The intensity between them was strong, stronger than he'd ever felt before. If he tried to kiss her now, he might hurt her, but his lips longed to feel hers.

"Catharine said—" Her words faded into silence, and he knew Susanna was silently reprimanding herself for mentioning her name again.

"It's all right. You can talk about her."

She started again, her voice quiet even in its boldness. "The helpers are assigning times in the chamber for couples who request it."

Her words registered slowly, his wife asking him to join her in the chamber. His skin tingled at her invitation, and he marveled to himself that after all he had done, a woman as beautiful and pure as Susanna would want him.

"We could meet—," she continued, but he reached out and stopped her nervous words with the touch of his fingers to her lips. And he felt her tremble.

He leaned close to her, and he thought about the wonder of being alone with her, both of them willing to consummate what God had brought together. But then he thought about someone pounding on the door, interrupting their time as husband and wife. He thought about the pressure from all those who knew they were scheduled to be together.

He wanted to love her for hours, not an hour. He wanted to woo her to him and savor their moments together, not rush before someone knocked on the door.

"The first time we are together," he said, his voice resolute, "will not be in that chamber."

* * * * *

At his words Susanna's fingers shook inside the strength of her husband's hand, and she closed her eyes, remembering their wedding day so long ago at Marienborn—the day he'd wanted to marry Catharine.

But Christian no longer loved Catharine. He loved her.

The fortress she'd built around her heart crumbled at his touch, and in that moment, she knew he was telling the truth. His indifference to her, his deception, it was all in the past. She was grateful that

God had brought them together, grateful that Christian Boehler was her husband.

"Not the chamber, then," she said softly.

He looked at her again, and she could see the longing in his eyes.

"They are expecting us in Gnadenhutten," she said. It was more a question than a statement.

"They are."

"We should leave soon."

"Very soon."

His gaze traveled over her shoulder, and her body trembled when she realized he was scanning for a clearing among the rocks and trees. He untied the blanket roll attached to his pack and took her hand, leading her away from the riverbank to the tall dry grasses, beside a patch of huckleberries. The blanket waved like a sail in his hands as he shook it over the rocks.

"Christian," she began. Her emotions soared even as her nerves seemed to tumble down upon themselves. "I'm scared."

He dropped the blanket. "We will wait, then."

She looked up at the golden specks in his eyes, the stubble that had grown on his cheeks and chin, and she wanted him to wrap her in his arms. She wanted to feel his skin against hers.

"I don't want to wait."

"Your haube." He looped his fingers around the blue ribbons. "May I take it off?"

Something sparked within her at the suggestion in his words. The intensity of them.

"You may," she whispered.

He slowly brushed his hands over her head, and she melted into his chest. She wanted nothing more than to be close to him, to feel his body against hers. To love Christian Boehler as a wife loves her husband.

She tried to remember all that Annabel had said, what she was supposed to do. But her mind seemed to go blank as he held her in his arms.

"Susanna," he began, and then she put her finger over his lips.

At first she only wanted to stop his penance, but when he went quiet, she heard another sound behind him. A rattling sound from the earth.

A curse slipped through Christian's lips as he picked her up and rushed her away from the snake coiled at their feet. And away from the second snake that slithered into the thicket nearby.

He set her down by the rocks and then hurried back for their blanket. When he returned, his voice was husky. "Are you all right?"

A tremor rushed through her, and for a moment, it felt like she couldn't breathe...but they couldn't stay here on the rock. They had to return to Gnadenhutten before dark.

When he touched her arm again, she pulled away. "We—we must go."

He pushed the canoe into the water and held it close to the rocks for her. "Did I do something wrong?"

"No," she replied, before climbing back into the canoe. He most certainly hadn't done anything wrong.

As they paddled away, nervous laughter slipped from her lips, and then he began to laugh alongside her. They slid through the rocks, the river rushing by them, and they laughed together.

The laughter felt so good to her. She and Christian could sing together and they could laugh together. Maybe one day they could learn to love each other as well.

Chapter Thirty

....

Christian smelled smoke. The aroma welcomed him back to Gnaden-hutten, and after he pulled the canoe out of the river, he took Susanna's hand and they hurried toward the village and what he hoped was a kettle full of hot soup.

A new longing replaced the desires that had once infected his soul, and this new longing was like a healing balm. He didn't want to be apart from Susanna again—not in the Brothers House or when he journeyed again to the Indians. He wanted to be with her wherever he went, whether or not they shared the bedchamber. He wanted to sing with her and laugh with her. He wanted everyone, including Catharine, to know that he loved his wife.

The village of Gnadenhutten was beyond the trees, but before they reached it, he stopped Susanna one last time. "We have to find a way to be together in Nazareth."

"The chamber?" she whispered.

"For more than an hour," he said with a shake of his head. "For hours."

"We'll find a way," she promised.

Her fingers entwined in his. The river forked before them, and they walked to the left. As they grew closer to the village, the smell of the smoke turned foul. He couldn't identify it, but the stench was black, like the terrors of the night. Like death. And there was no pounding of hammers or whirl from the mill or laughter or song.

"Something's wrong," Susanna whispered.

Christian untied his heavy pack and dropped it to the ground. Susanna ran with him, forward through the trees, until Christian threw out his arm, stopping her.

On a tree stump before them was a blanket and a black hat, pierced through with a knife. He yanked the knife out of the wood, and his stomach rolled when he saw the blood on its blade. Dried blood. Susanna stepped back, and he dropped the knife, reaching for her. She rested her head on his shoulder and trembled against him.

Whatever had happened in Gnadenhutten, he couldn't let her see it. As he held his wife, he looked at the forest ahead, wondering what the trees hid, wondering what they had seen. He couldn't leave Susanna here either.

She pulled away from him, her voice barely a whisper. "They might need help."

Whoever had been here was probably gone, but he couldn't risk losing Susanna if someone had remained to hurt them. Hours had passed since someone had used the knife, with the blood dried, but he didn't know how long ago the knife had been thrust into the stump.

He didn't want to take Susanna, but he couldn't leave her here either. They would be cautious, but she was right, they must see if someone needed help. So they walked quietly toward Gnadenhutten, hand in hand, listening for life or sounds of hostile Indians on the attack.

When they reached the forest's edge, Christian stumbled backward into a tree.

"God help us," Susanna whispered.

Instead of the circled village built by the Indians and missionaries, a smoldering pile of logs lay blackened beside the river. The Gemeinhaus was gone, along with Elias's gristmill. The kitchen was gone. So were the bakery and the blacksmith's shop and the smaller dwellings that housed their Indian friends.

And the people were gone too.

"Stay here," Christian told her, and she remained hidden in the trees as he crept forward, searching the ruins for his fellow missionaries and their Indian friends, his mind alert for the enemy. Ashes fluttered like mist in the air, covering his coat and his shoes, and the silence was deafening.

Then he heard the bark of a dog behind one of the burnt buildings that stood above the rubble. He rushed over to the sound. The dog was guarding the burnt remains of a man.

At the sight of the blackened body, Christian balled over. His stomach emptied beside the remains, and then he rushed away from the horror of it.

The dog followed him back toward the ruins, whimpering beside him. Anger surged inside Christian. His brothers and sisters here, they had done nothing wrong. They chose to live peacefully instead of warring like many of their neighbors. How could their desire for peace be more of a threat than muskets and knives?

He stood in the midst of the ruins, shouting Elias's name. Then he cried out for Benjamin and Catharine and the others. The silence broke when a man, wrapped in a blanket, shuffled out of the trees. Christian braced himself for what may come from this stranger.

As the man neared, Christian realized he wasn't a stranger at all. It was Benjamin, with his long face covered in soot.

Christian embraced the man and then stepped back. "What happened?"

Benjamin whistled, and dozens of their Indian brothers and sisters crept out of the forest. Christian looked into their desperate faces, searching for Elias and Catharine, but the Schmidts weren't among them.

Christian clutched his fingers into fists. "Where are Elias and Catharine?"

When the man's gaze fell to the ground, Christian heard Susanna gasp beside him, and he was glad she had joined him. He needed her.

"Where are the Schmidts?" she demanded.

"The Indians, they burst into the Gemeinhaus, and we couldn't stop them. A few of our people escaped through the windows, but most of them…"

Christian surveyed the damage again, the terrible scars the savages had left from the attack. Then he pointed toward the burnt building. "I found a body over there."

"They killed many of our people."

Christian didn't want to ask, but he knew he must. "Did they kill Elias and Catharine?"

"Elias was killed in the fire, but Catharine—"

Susanna stepped forward. "What happened to her?"

"She was injured in the fire, and the Indians…the Indians took her away."

Took her away?

His blood raced. "Where did they go?"

"We don't know."

A sob escaped Susanna's lips, and he reached for her, pulling her to him as her strength seemed to dissolve. As she trembled against him, his neck dampened with her grief.

When she stepped back from him, her gaze bounced between him and Samuel. "We have to find her."

Benjamin shook his head. "They won't let us find her."

"Please!"

"All of these people," Benjamin said as he swept his hand before them, "all of my people. We need to get them to a safe place before the savages return."

Ashes fell down on them as the day turned into night. Would the hostile Indians really return, after all the damage they had done? Perhaps if they knew how many Indians remained on the hill above the village, they would come back to destroy all of them.

Christian took off his hat and pulled his hands through his hair, praying out loud for wisdom for all of them. He couldn't go raging through the woods alone, in search of the Indians who took Catharine. They had to get their brothers and sisters to a safe place, but they also couldn't leave Catharine in the hands of the Indians.

Susanna looked up at him. "Samuel could find her."

Benjamin nodded at him, and Christian realized they were right. If anyone could find Catharine, it would be Samuel.

He glanced at each person gathered around him and then said, "We will leave for Nazareth at first light, all of us together."

* * * * *

The night air clung to Catharine, the cold piercing her skin as she hobbled barefoot through the forest. When she asked for a blanket, the savage slapped her and then tightened the cords that held her wrists together, like she was a prisoner being led to the chopping block.

Perhaps that was exactly what she was.

Blood trickled down her cheek and seeped into the edge of her lips. The Indian in the front of their pack had held a knife to her head, so close that it pierced her skin. She thought for certain that he would scalp her like he had done with the other woman who jumped through the window.

But for some reason, he had let her live.

She never should have jumped. She should have lain down beside Elias and let the fire consume her as well. But she panicked after Elias passed out, her lungs screaming for air. And the window was the only way to get it.

Why hadn't God taken her with Elias, back in the fire?

A groan escaped her lips and the guard rewarded her with

another slap, this time across the cut on her face. Pain pulsed through her body, heat overpowering the cold. But she didn't cry out again.

They'd been goading her since daylight, and part of her wanted to fall down and refuse to move another muscle. They would kill her if she did, she knew they would. It was as if her pain was a kind of sport for them, like they were waiting for her to lie down so they could savor one more death on their rampage. She didn't want to give them any more reason to kill her yet, not that they needed a reason. They would kill her when they wanted to.

The only reasons she could think of for their keeping her alive terrified her even more. She forced herself to think of something else. Of Elias. But thinking of her husband in the fire, his life stolen away by her captors, was even more painful. So she forced herself to think about nothing at all.

Her kidnappers must be getting tired, having slept so little before they began their journey into the wilderness. Last night they had spent hours terrorizing the Christian Indians with their fire and their blades. They had taken pleasure in killing those who escaped the fire, like they fed on their fear.

Then, when there was nothing left to burn except the barns, they raided the village's food supplies and gorged on the bounty.

The screams of the people and the animals rattled in her head. No matter how many years she lived, she would never be able to rid herself of the terror or of the smell that had filled her very being with the stench of death.

She was terrified, but as she trailed the men, she didn't want them to see her fear.

Her mind wandered again to her dream of going to Philadelphia or London. These men had stolen her future from her. They'd taken away her husband and any hope she had for their future.

The man in front, the man they called Iachgan, stopped them

and listened. Then he barked out a command to the others. She didn't know what he said, but they began moving again, even more rapidly this time.

She was so glad Juliana was in a safe place tonight. Her daughter might never remember her parents, but Susanna and the other sisters would take good care of her.

Another moan bubbled in her throat but she swallowed it before they heard.

Why hadn't God protected her husband and her people from the arrows and knives of these Indians?

She heard the beating of drums ahead, and fear rushed through her once more. She stopped walking, her feet unable to move forward. Her warden shoved her, and when her face hit the ground, dirt mixed with blood and filled her mouth. She spit it out.

Iachgan grabbed her hair, pulling her back to her feet and yelling something to her that she assumed meant to walk. She spit again, to her side, and she realized that one of her teeth was gone. She didn't feel the pain of it, didn't feel much of anything anymore except for the sorrow that flooded her soul.

She didn't see God in the faces of her abductors, didn't hear Him in the pounding of the drums. She didn't even feel Him inside her body that had been beaten and torn. But He must be here somewhere.

She longed to feel Him somewhere in this darkness. Longed to know He was here.

Her arm bumped her thigh, and she felt the bag of coins still hidden under the shreds of her skirt. Her small treasure no longer offered a way of escape. She had nothing except her Savior.

Moving forward, she begged Him to forgive her for all the times she had grumbled like the Israelites in Egypt. She should have been thankful for her bed in Nazareth, for the food and the safety. She should have thanked Him every day for her baby and her husband

and His many provisions. And she prayed, in the midst of her sorrow, that God would show Himself to her.

In the clearing ahead were several huts circled around a large bonfire. The beating of the drums stopped when the Indians saw them. And they greeted her captors like victors coming home from a war. Iachgan and the others dumped bags of food on the ground, and then, their hands securing her arms, they pushed her toward a man seated in a large cane chair like she was one of many spoils taken after a battle instead of a woman stolen away from men who never fought back.

The ugly man in front of her was old, his cheeks wrinkled on both sides of his bulbed nose, his dark eyes slightly crooked. As his eyes traveled over her body, he licked his lips and opened his mouth in a toothless smile.

She wrestled against the hands that bound her, but this time the men didn't slap her. The ugly man laughed in the face of her struggle, and the others laughed with him.

She stopped fighting, glaring at the man instead.

He motioned toward a hut and Iachgan pushed her toward it. Inside, he barked orders to the five women before he shut the door, leaving her with them.

The women stared at her, and she could only imagine what they saw. A white woman's face smeared with blood and dirt. A torn dress exposing her stomach and her legs.

She backed against the door and then collapsed to the floor. Putting her head into her tied hands, she sobbed.

One of the young women stepped forward with a knife in her hands. Catharine looked up at her in expectation, wanting nothing more than to be with her Savior. She hoped the woman would kill her quickly.

Instead of wounding her, though, the woman lifted the knife and sliced through the cords that bound her.

Stunned, Catharine blew on the raw skin where the cords had rubbed it.

"Come." The woman spoke in English.

Catharine's legs wobbled as she stood, and she followed the woman into the hut, into a separate room. The woman pointed toward a mat, and Catharine lay down. Then the woman covered her with an animal skin.

The warmth engulfed her, embracing her, but in the warmth, her numbness began to dissolve. And the pain from her many wounds blazed. Her feet hurt. Her head hurt. Her mouth hurt from the loss of her tooth.

The woman whispered to her. "My mother used to call me Mary, from the Scriptures."

"You know the Scriptures?"

"Only a little." She paused. "Are you one of the messengers?"

"My husband is—" She choked on the word. "He was one."

"They killed him?"

She nodded.

"He is with the Savior now," the Indian woman said softly. "The Savior will heal all his wounds."

The woman took a rag from a bucket and began to gently wipe Catharine's face and her hands. "One of your messengers came here last year and told our people about the Christ Child. He told us this child was our Savior, but my people refused to listen."

"Was his name Christian?"

She nodded.

"He told you the truth."

"None of my people wanted to follow Christ, but after he left, I decided to serve this Savior. It is a secret, though. The others would kill me if they knew."

Catharine coughed, and the pain rippled through her skin. "He is a God of love...and forgiveness."

Mary studied her. "My mother, she was an English woman. A captive like you."

"What happened to her?"

The woman reached for a small wooden tub with some kind of ointment in it and rubbed it on Catharine's wrists and then her ear. It soothed some of the pain. "It is not good to speak of her."

When the woman turned, Catharine reached for her arm. "What are they going to do to me?"

"I shouldn't—"

"I can face it, if only I know."

Mary pulled her knees to her chest, sitting beside her. "They will take you from here in the morning, but I don't know where you will go."

"And what will they do to me there?"

"They will make you run through a gauntlet."

"A what?"

Mary didn't explain. "If you survive, they will probably give you to an Indian man, like they did my mother."

Catharine cringed at the woman's words, at the terrible thought of these Indians forcing her to be with another man. It would ruin everything she and Elias had shared.

And what would Juliana think of her when she returned home, knowing that her mother had been raped by a savage? She didn't know how she would escape, but she couldn't let them do this to her. She wouldn't let them.

There was a shuffling noise outside the door, and over Mary's shoulder she saw the smile of the ugly man who had assaulted her with his eyes.

Mary turned around and said something to him in their language. His smile turned into a sneer, and they seemed to argue between them. Catharine felt compassion for the woman also trapped within her circumstances. Maybe she wanted out as much as Catharine did.

After he left, Catharine whispered. "Who is he?"

"Our chief."

"What does he want?"

Her eyes were sad. "You."

She began to tremble again. "What did you tell him?"

"That you were sick and needed to rest for a few hours before he took you to his hut."

She clutched her hands to her chest, looking again at the door. The last time she'd tried to escape, she'd been taken captive...but she couldn't sit here, waiting for the man to come back for her.

She reached out to Mary again, pleading. "I can't be with him."

"I know."

The two of them sat silently, each of them lost in their wondering until Mary stood up.

"I will make you some tea so you can rest for a while."

It hurt when she nodded. "Thank you."

Catharine had already drifted to sleep when Mary returned, but the woman woke her.

The ladle close to her lips, Catharine hesitated at the pungent smell of the tea, but Mary lifted her head higher, prompting her to drink. "It will make you well again."

Catharine slowly took a sip and then another. As she drank, the agony seemed to drain from her body.

"Forgive me," Mary said as she lowered the ladle. "There was nothing else I could do."

Her words seemed muffled, but Catharine still understood. She reached out, taking the young woman's hands in hers. There was nothing for her to forgive.

"Bless you," she whispered.

And then the darkness welcomed her again.

Chapter Thirty-One

....

Two red-coated soldiers stood guard outside the Gemeinhaus in Nazareth. On their left shoulders were braided gold epaulettes, and each of them held a pistol. Christian approached them first to explain why they were bringing the Indians into the settlement, and Susanna cringed at the disdain in the men's eyes as they glared at the brothers and sisters.

Didn't they understand that there were kind Indians in the midst of the hostile ones, just as there were malicious British men and women among the upright? But all Susanna could see in their eyes this evening was the same fire that had burned down Gnadenhutten, the same fire that threatened to burn inside her if God's Spirit didn't douse it.

The grief mixed with her anger as the devastation at Gnadenhutten played through her mind. And the loss of her best friend. She wouldn't say it, but she almost wished Catharine were dead like Elias instead of taken captive by the Indians. Benjamin gave no hope of her return, but there was always hope. Christian would find Samuel and then Samuel would find Catharine.

The wounds were so fresh that they seemed to ooze from inside her, but she couldn't let the bitterness consume her. God had sent her and Christian to share the good news with the Indians, and they could not let the animosity of a dozen savages stop them from loving so many who needed Christ.

The soldiers finally stepped aside, and Susanna helped an elderly woman named Abigail up the steps of the Gemeinhaus and into the meeting room to deliver their terrible news. As they passed by the soldiers, one spat at them, and Susanna stopped and glared at the man for demeaning her friend. But then she realized that the soldier wasn't looking at Abigail. He was looking at her. The soldier was infuriated at her for befriending the Indians instead of fighting them, for sharing the good news with them.

You must be content to suffer, to die....

The Count's words came back to her. She had expected to suffer on the journey, to be persecuted, even, at the hands of the Indians, but she'd never believed that other Europeans would persecute them for their work.

Tears rushed to her eyes as the soldier's glare hardened against her. The tears were not as much for the soldier's disdain, but for Catharine and Elias and the Keaton family and all the Indians who suffered because men chose to war with each other instead of seek peace, because they loved land or money more than the lives of their fellow man.

This was why the Savior came to die, so they could conquer the lust of their flesh, the lust of their eyes. He came for the soldiers as well as the Indians, for the adults and the children. Why couldn't they all stop fighting and learn to love one another as Christ loved them?

Christian was beside her then, his arm around her waist, as he escorted both her and Abigail through the door and to a bench among the other Indians.

Six British soldiers flanked the table where the elders sat, and the men looked up at them, surveying the guests who accompanied them back to Nazareth. Elder Graff held a parchment in his hands, and he placed it on the table before he spoke.

His voice was hesitant as he eyed the Indians over his spectacles. "We weren't expecting so many to return."

Christian stepped up to the table. "Hostile Indians attacked our Brethren at Gnadenhutten."

The elder removed his spectacles and placed them on the parchment.

"They burned down the houses and killed many of our people," Christian said.

The elder didn't speak as the sorrow of the news seemed to overcome him.

One of the soldiers drummed the parchment with his knuckle. "We told you."

The elder lifted his head. "You didn't tell me they were going to attack our Brethren."

"They are attacking anyone aligned with the British."

"We are not aligned with anyone except Christ."

The soldier ripped the parchment from the tabletop and the elder's spectacles clattered to the ground. One of the soldiers bent to pick them up, but the captain stopped him.

The captain lorded over the elder. "You must choose sides."

Elder Graff shook his head. "We cannot."

"It may be days, it may be weeks," the captain said. "But they will attack you here like they did along the Lehigh. And we will not be around to protect you."

"I cannot send our men to fight with you," the elder said. "Our Savior did not come to fight with the sword."

"We don't fight with swords." The captain raised his pistol. "We fight with guns."

The elder's voice grew stronger. "We will not fight."

The man rolled up the parchment and slid it into a sheath. "The Delaware are your enemies."

The elder glanced at the forty or so Indians among them. "Our Savior commands us to love our enemies."

Love your enemies, do good to those who hate you.

"They will kill you," the captain insisted.

"They are our sisters and our brothers," the elder replied. "If anything, we have not done enough to love them."

With a loud huff, the captain motioned for the other soldiers to follow and they stomped across the Saal.

After they marched out the door, Susanna fell back against her seat. It seemed no one wanted to serve the Savior.

Elder Graff stood up and moved slowly around the table, bending down to retrieve his spectacles. He put them on the table and then he motioned Christian forward.

"Did they kill the Schmidts?"

"Elias perished in the fire, but the attackers took Catharine— Sister Schmidt—captive."

Elder Graff nodded slowly, seeming to digest the news.

Christian rubbed his hands together. "We must send someone to find her."

"Where did they take her?"

"We don't know, but we think Samuel could locate her." He paused. "Please let me get Samuel."

"It's too much, Christian. You need to rest."

"No." He glanced at Susanna, and she returned the questioning in his eyes with a slight nod of her head. She wanted him to find her friend.

He turned back toward the elder. "I need to help find Sister Schmidt."

The elder sat down in his chair. "You must take Joseph with you."

"I will."

"And when you return, we will remember the brothers and sisters lost in this massacre."

* * * * *

Christian met Susanna's gaze and mouthed the words that she needed to hear. Even though his love couldn't remove the pain, it began to strengthen her again.

"Sister Boehler," the elder called. It took her a moment to realize that the man was speaking to her. Standing, she walked toward him and Christian, and the elder asked her to escort their Indian brethren to the Disciple's House for food and rest.

Rebecca greeted them at the door of the manor house with Juliana in her arms, and tears filled Susanna's eyes at the sight of the child who would never know her father. A child who might never know what happened to her mother.

No girl should ever grow up without her mother.

As Susanna told the story, Rebecca shed her own tears. Then she handed Catharine's baby to Susanna as she guided the weary travelers up the steps.

Juliana squirmed in her arms, but still it felt good to hold Elias and Catharine's child. It made her feel close to the woman who had been her friend and to the man Catharine had loved.

Juliana began to cry, and Susanna paced along the hall at the bottom of the stairs. Maybe instead of Nathan, God would have her and Christian care for the Schmidts' baby, at least until they found Catharine. If the Savior willed it, she would care for the child as her own.

She bounced the child as she paced, but Juliana didn't stop crying until Rebecca came to relieve her. And then she rested in Rebecca's arms.

* * * * *

Christian left the next morning at daybreak and returned from Bethlehem the same night with David Kunz. Upon hearing the news of Catharine's capture, Christian said, Samuel left Bethlehem within the hour. He'd been brutally honest about the assessment of Catharine's well-being. If she were still alive—and he doubted she was—he had little hope of freeing her, but he said he might be able to find out where she had been taken. If so, perhaps they could convince the British soldiers to bring her home.

Before Samuel left, he encouraged Christian in the midst of his confusion and grief. He assured Christian that he could love his wife even as he fought for Catharine. And if he prayed for her, it didn't mean he was betraying his wife. He no longer loved Catharine as anything except as his sister. Even if she returned to them as a widowed sister, even if something happened to Susanna, Christian would never again ask the lot to marry her.

Still, Christian wanted Samuel to find her. He wanted Catharine to be safe.

The moment they arrived in Nazareth, Christian took David to find Timothy…and the moment David saw him, he engulfed his son with his arms. Christian could see the initial surprise in Timothy's eyes at the affection and then the satisfaction of knowing that he was loved, that he could call this man *Papa* instead of *Uncle*.

With Timothy at his side, David followed Christian outside. They found Elder Graff in the office at the Brothers House. Because of the massacre at Gnadenhutten, along with the concerns of the British soldiers, David wanted the elder to release Timothy and the other children to return to Bethlehem until the threat of an Indian attack had passed.

Neither Elder Graff nor Edward found fault in the man's request to remove his son to a safer place. They asked several questions about where the children would stay, and David told them they'd moved the widowed sisters into the house for the married sisters to make room for the children.

"There are fifty children," the elder said. "It would be another massacre if the Indians found them."

"There could be a massacre anytime," Christian said quietly. "Because right now they know where to find them."

Joseph nodded. "We would have to go as quietly as we can so they won't hear us."

"We need to take it before the lot—" Elder Graff began. But at the distraught look in David's eyes, Christian stopped him.

"We don't need to take it before the lot," Christian said. "We need to keep the children safe."

The elder seemed to be relieved by Christian's words. Even while their community believed that God worked through the lot, Christian wondered how many times they should have made a decision based on the wisdom God gave them, based on His direction. It seemed clear to all of them that the children needed to be in Bethlehem where there were hundreds more people and stone buildings clustered together like a fortress above the river. Howling Wolf and his men could come, but it would be much harder to penetrate that village.

"David and I and some of the other men can escort them to Bethlehem tomorrow," Christian said.

The elder concurred. "Take all the Nursery workers with you and any of the women who would like to go to a safer choir house."

Only a dozen Indians had attacked Gnadenhutten, and the damage was colossal. What would happen if the nations banded together and attacked, hundreds or even thousands of Indians? Even in Bethlehem the Brethren wouldn't be completely safe, but it would be much safer than here.

Christian's gaze wandered to the Disciple's House. Susanna would want to join them—not because of the threat of attack, but because she would want to help him keep the children safe. And he didn't want her to stay in Nazareth another night without him near.

Chapter Thirty-Two

Snow fell the night before they left for Bethlehem, blanketing trees and the path in white. Christmas Eve was less than a week away now, but nobody in Nazareth talked about the celebration any longer. The love of their Savior seemed far away this year.

David drove the wagon, with Timothy sitting on the bench beside him, and Susanna rode in the back with Mariana and two toddlers close to her. Christian walked in front of all of them with a musket, but the gun wouldn't do much to stop an attack. As they rode, she prayed that Christian wouldn't have to use his musket, that God would blind the eyes and deafen the ears of any Indians around them.

Many of the refugee families followed them by foot to Bethlehem. There were only about fifty or so people left in Nazareth now, and she prayed it would be enough to deter the Indians from stealing their livestock and food supplies.

As she watched Christian forge ahead, Susanna's heart swelled with pride for the man God had given her. In the midst of the trials, of the loss and destruction, he remained strong both in his commitment to God and in his commitment to help the Indians. And he'd gone to Samuel to help them find Catharine.

With everything inside her, she loved Christian Boehler. Though she wouldn't admit it to him, she'd begun to love him the moment they met for the first time in the chamber and he didn't demand more of her than she wanted to give. Even when she realized he didn't love her, even when he told her his heart had longed for another woman. Even when her love faltered, it still remained.

Christian stopped in front of her and held up his arm. Susanna didn't understand why he was stopping until she saw an Indian step into their path. A man whose open jacket revealed a wolf tattooed on his chest.

She tried not to gasp, but the noise slipped from her lips.

"Susanna," Christian murmured, his eyes focused on the Indian. "Please come here."

She scooted the toddler on her lap over to Mariana and quickly climbed off the wagon. Standing beside Christian, Howling Wolf stood a good foot above her, and he glowered down at her with his dark eyes. His glare was different than the one she'd seen in the eyes of the British solder, molded of hatred instead of disdain. And she realized he would kill her, probably kill all of them, if he could. He didn't spit like the British soldier. His anger was calm, calculating.

"What do you want?" Christian asked.

Howling Wolf barked an order in the Delaware language and several Indians joined him, including Lily. At the sight of her friend, Susanna wanted to rush forward. She wanted to hug Lily, to beg her to come back to them, but when she reached out her arms, Lily gave a slight shake of her head. Susanna dropped her hands back to her sides.

Howling Wolf turned his eyes to Lily, his gaze still fiery, and Susanna pretended not to understand what he said to her. Howling Wolf knew that Lily had lived among them, but perhaps the familiarity would anger him even more.

Lily translated his words. "Where are you going?"

"To our Brethren in Bethlehem," Christian said, and then he waited for Lily to translate his words.

Howling Wolf scanned the dozens of children and refugees behind them before he spoke again. "I want my son."

Christian looked surprised at Lily's translation. "Your son?"

Howling Wolf picked up his gun and stepped closer to him, meeting his eyes. "Where is the one you call Nathan?"

Christian waited again for Lily's words and then he glanced over at Susanna, his eyes desperate. She knew he wanted to protect Nathan from harm but didn't know how to do it without lying to the man. And he probably knew, like she did, that Howling Wolf would unravel any lie.

Christian began to pray beside her, petitioning the Lord in a loud voice for deliverance as she prayed silently. Howling Wolf looked over at them again, and this time his gaze rested on the wagon. Moving as quietly and as swift as a deer, he rushed toward the first wagon, to Rebecca and the child in her arms. He ripped off the blanket that covered Juliana's head. When he saw the blond curls, he grunted and she began to cry.

Turning, he examined another child and then another, and she knew he would search all of them, looking for a boy with skin the color of faded autumn leaves. In his anger, what would he do when he didn't find Nathan among them? Or what would he do if he thought one of the children was his?

"Wait!" Susanna called, and Howling Wolf turned slowly on his heel. He critiqued her with his gaze, critically, like he wasn't sure if he would lower himself to talk with a white woman.

"Be careful," Lily whispered.

"When Lily left," she said. "We didn't know what to do with Nathan."

Lily quickly translated her words, and he stepped toward Susanna. She inched up her chin, staring up at the warrior.

"So we took him to some Indian friends." She bowed her head, waiting for Lily to finish.

She took a deep breath. "In a place called Gnadenhutten."

Worry flashed across his sneer, and he reached for Susanna, shaking her.

"Stop!" Christian demanded.

Howling Wolf shoved Susanna backward, and Christian caught her. She massaged her arms as Howling Wolf frantically questioned his men and then turned to Lily.

"There was a fire in Gnadenhutten," Lily repeated in English.

Susanna nodded.

"Howling Wolf wants to know what happened to this baby."

"He—" she hesitated as she met Lily's eyes and saw the tears in them. "He survived."

Susanna saw the relief flicker across Lily's face when she nodded, but her gaze twisted into anger when she turned to the man she'd given her life to.

"*Gunt pluphillela,*" she spat. "*You killed him.*"

Her words echoed like thunder around them, and then Howling Wolf let out a scream, loud and eerie and vacant.

"I didn't kill him!" he screamed in the language of the Delaware. "Iachgan killed him. Iachgan and his men."

"You told him to go."

The Indian screamed again, his minions scurrying farther away, but Lily stayed right beside him. Susanna wanted to hug her, to thank her for her bravery, while at the same time she wanted to scold her for her stupidity.

Howling Wolf slid a dagger out of the sheath on his leg, his eyes wild as he searched again the faces of the children.

She caught her breath at the realization of what he was doing. He was examining the children to see which one would avenge the death of his son.

Instead of lifting his musket, Christian bowed his head and began to pray again. In the midst of the Indian's cries, in the midst of the fear, he begged God for protection and for redemption. For a miracle.

Lily screamed at Howling Wolf, telling him to stop, but the man raced past Christian, toward the wagons, toward Timothy and his father. David pulled Timothy close to him, and the boy buried his head in the father's chest.

Susanna wanted to yell at her husband, to tell him to shoot the man, but she knew if he fired a shot, a bloodbath would follow, killing both Indians and Brethren alike. Yet if he didn't shoot, then she was certain Howling Wolf would take the life of one or more of their children.

Christian fired his gun into the air, and Howling Wolf stopped. When he turned back to Christian, the sneer had returned. Then Howling Wolf looked at the men who cowered in the trees and commanded them to fire.

Susanna bowed her head, her hands splayed at her side as she prepared for the bullets to pierce her skin. But the bullets never came. Instead, the earth began to tremble under her feet. It rocked her back and forth and then it sent her crashing into Howling Wolf. The Indian man dropped his knife, flailing as he tried to keep from falling as well.

Christian reached for her, and they both tumbled to the ground.

Howling Wolf grabbed Lily's arm and then yelled for his people to run, but the men were already gone. Lily lifted her eyes one last time to Susanna, as if to thank her.

Susanna reached for Christian's hand, and he helped her to her feet. His eyes were on the retreating backs of the Indians. "What just happened?"

She'd heard of the earth quaking, but she'd never felt its power before.

"Providence, my friend," David said from the bench of the wagon.

Timothy pulled on his father's shirt. "Can you do that again, Papa?"

David gathered his son in his arms. "Only God can make the earth shake."

Susanna was shaking herself as she climbed back into the wagon, and she was still shaking when they entered the town of Bethlehem.

From the Gemeinhaus, they heard the music of an organ, and then the beautiful voices of their Brethren singing a hymn. Susanna looked over at Mariana and the two women began to sing their song. Then the others joined in as they marched toward the house and into the Saal, grateful to the Lord for bringing the children safely to Bethlehem.

From across the Saal, Marie Kunz let out a gasp when she saw her son in David's arms. She started to cry as she rushed toward them.

"Mama?" the little boy asked shyly at first, and then a smile slid across his lips before he melted into her arms.

Susanna didn't know whether to smile or cry. And so she did both.

Chapter Thirty-Three

....

Hundreds of cream-colored tallow candles rested in baskets in the room below Bethlehem's Saal. Susanna and a host of other sisters looped a red ribbon around each candle and tied the ribbon into a bow for the Christmas Eve service. She set the candle into a basket and reached for another one.

While her fingers worked rapidly, Susanna's lips prayed that Samuel would hurry back to them soon and that he would bring back word of Catharine. She prayed for her friend's safety even as the truth of the circumstances weighed on her.

If the men who had kidnapped her were anything like Howling Wolf and the earth didn't shake like it had for their Brethren, then she hoped Catharine had gone home to be with their Savior. The children were safe now in Bethlehem, and she hoped the word spread among the hostile Indians about the quaking of the earth when Howling Wolf attempted to hurt their children.

Nathan was safe with Chief Langoma. Hopefully there would be no more reason for Howling Wolf to search for him.

She tied another ribbon around a candle as the women chattered around her. Juliana, who had been quietly sleeping in the corner of the room, stirred and began to cry. Susanna put down her ribbon and walked over to comfort her. She picked up the baby, bouncing her in her arms as she had done with her in Nazareth, but Juliana refused to be comforted.

Rebecca hurried toward them, her arms outstretched. "Let me try."
Susanna reluctantly handed the baby to her friend, and immediately Juliana snuggled into her shoulder.

She sighed, realizing in that moment that she and Christian wouldn't adopt either Nathan or Juliana. If Catharine didn't return, Joseph and Rebecca would care for this baby.

She reached for her cloak and told the laboress that she needed some fresh air. The windows of the buildings and choir houses were lit by solitary candles that glowed against the darkness, and the doors were decorated with wire ornaments and wreaths colored with dried berries and beads.

She leaned back against the stone wall of the Gemeinhaus and watched the lights dance in the windows. She felt so helpless here in Bethlehem, tying ribbons while her friend was being held captive someplace far from here, probably waiting for them to find her. There was nothing she could do to rescue her friend except pray and wait. She was glad to pray, but the waiting was excruciating.

Squeezing her eyes closed, she felt the winter breeze on her face, and when she reopened her eyes, the glowing windows reminded her of the houses in her homeland as the people prepared for their Christmas festivities. Childhood memories flooded her, the smell of pinecones and gingerbread on Christmas morning, helping her mother prepare their dinner.

Christian was her only family now, and she hadn't seen much of him since they had returned to Bethlehem. She missed walking with him through the wilderness, and she missed her hours around the fire with her Indian friends. She missed canoeing through the trees, and she missed hearing God in the quiet. And she missed Nathan, who cuddled to her chest instead of pushing her away.

She should be afraid of the Indians and what they could do, but still she wished she could return to Tanochtahe instead of remain here. Unless the war among the French and the British and the Indians ended soon, though, she didn't know if or when the elders would allow them to return. It was one thing to be willing to be persecuted and die for the sake of the Gospel and a completely different thing to be sent into the face of persecution. She didn't know if she could face what Catharine must be enduring.

In the lights, she turned and saw a man walking briskly toward her. She almost ran back into the Gemeinhaus, but then she recognized him.

Samuel had returned.

When he drew near, she could see that he suffered with the news he bore, and dread replaced any hope harbored in her heart.

They needed to know the truth, for the sake of their healing, for Juliana's well-being, but she didn't know if she was ready to hear it.

"I must speak with Christian," he said.

She nodded. It was only right that Samuel speak to her husband first and allow him to be the messenger.

Time seemed to plod by as she waited outside the door for Christian to come for her. Part of her wanted to run all the way back to Marienborn, where the colonies were still a marvelous mystery, where she and Catharine dreamed of the day they would marry and begin life together with their husbands in the New World, she among the Indians and Catharine in the village. It was the anticipation of this new life that had driven her for so long, but now she had nothing but yards of ribbon to tie along with the memory of what might have been.

After many minutes had passed, Christian opened the door and guided her into the basement of the women's house, to the kitchen. Ashes smoldered in the fireplace, and the room was warm. Too warm.

As she sat near the hearth, she wanted to cover her ears and pretend that Catharine was upstairs sewing in her bed and Elias was preparing to build a new mill. That they would all celebrate Christmas together this year.

Christian took her hands. "Samuel found out what happened to Catharine."

She nodded, unable to speak.

"She was badly injured in Gnadenhutten and the Indians took her to a small settlement about thirty miles west."

"Did he see her?"

He gently squeezed her hands, pulling them closer to her. "They had already buried her."

She yanked her hands away, gulping the warm air. It was what she had expected, and yet it was still agonizing to hear. The Indians had hurt her friend and then they had killed her.

Standing, she began to pace the dirt floor, past the benches and tables and shelves packed with pans and dishes. Never again would she and Catharine eat dinner together or whisper to each other late at night. Never again would her friend join her in worship or make her laugh. Catharine had been slipping away from her for months, ever since she returned from their first journey to Gnadenhutten, but she'd hoped it was only a season, that Catharine would eventually thrive in their new home.

"They don't know—" She stopped in front of him. "How do they know it was her?"

Christian lifted something off the bench, and she saw the brown bag that Catharine tied around her waist every morning. She'd never asked what was inside, and Catharine had never offered to tell her. "One of the Indian women gave Samuel this."

Christian dumped the bag onto the table, and Susanna watched as a pile of gold coins cascaded down and flashed in the remaining light. Her friend had more wealth secured around her waist than Susanna could ever imagine. She could have left the Brethren at any time and yet she chose to remain among them.

He sat at one of the tables, his hands in his lap, as he watched her pace. "Samuel said it is much better that she went to be with the Savior than suffer at the hands of the hostile Indians."

"How does he know she would have suffered?"

"She would have, Susanna, and if the Lord hadn't called her home, it might have been years of torture at the hands of her enemy."

When Susanna reached the wall, she turned and paced back toward Christian. She wanted to be glad, too, that Catharine was with their Savior. She didn't want Catharine to suffer, but even as the others had mourned for her, she'd been harboring the hope that Samuel and the soldiers might be able to rescue her and bring her home. That in time she would heal and devote herself to her love for Juliana, like she'd devoted herself to Elias.

But her desires hadn't aligned with the will of God.

As the shock of this news wore off, tears came quickly. Christian opened his arms, and she fell into them, her tears spilling out onto his coarse shirt.

"I'm so sorry," Christian whispered in her ear.

"She was supposed to come home, for Juliana's sake."

"She is home."

"But why did He have to take her away from us?"

"I don't know." He rested his chin on her haube; her face was buried in his chest. "God's will is often not our own."

She knew the answer might never come, not until they joined Catharine in the presence of their Savior, but she didn't know if she could wait that long. Her faith wavered like a flag in the wind, and she didn't know how she could continue following a God who allowed those who served Him to suffer and die.

"Remember the earthquake, Susanna."

She lifted her head and looked up into the compassion of her dear husband's eyes. She'd never forget the earth trembling in the face of hatred, the terror across the faces of men who had terrorized so many others.

"He protected the children that day,"

She wiped her tears on her shawl. "But why does He allow some to suffer while others are saved?"

"It is not for us to question what God does or does not do." His voice was tender in its truthfulness.

She sat down at the table beside her husband, his words tumbling in her mind. Was it wrong to question God, to ask why an all-powerful God allowed evil to trump His good? Never would she equate herself with God in her questioning, but relationships allowed for questions, for understanding.

"I think we can question, Christian, even if we do not understand."

He considered her words. "Can you question without losing your faith?"

She knew God wanted the Indian nations to experience His mercy and forgiveness. It was the evil one who was bent on killing those who desired to share and experience this love. The enemy wanted revenge, not forgiveness. Death, not life. But the enemy didn't know that removing life from a body only freed the soul to live with Christ forever. That it was a beginning, not the end.

Above all, she knew God was love.

"I can," she said simply.

Then he smiled at her, and in his smile, she saw a glimpse of delight, as if he wanted her to question in faith.

The organ began playing nearby in the Gemeinhaus, calling them to evening worship, and he helped her to her feet. In her grief she would question why God had taken her friend, but her faith wouldn't falter, even if He never gave her the answers.

Chapter Thirty-Four

....

A wooden pyramid stood at the front of the Saal, adorned with evergreen branches, candles, and tinsel sparkling in the candlelight. The women sat on the left side of the room for the love feast while the men sat opposite them.

The dieners served the basket of sweet buns, and Susanna savored the butter and cinnamon along with the mug of black coffee. Then the brothers and sisters sang a hymn about the Christ Child as another diener emerged with a glowing tray of red-ribboned candles.

When the diener handed Susanna a candle, she brushed her fingers over the strands of ribbon tied around its base. In spite of their grief, the candle and ribbons reminded them of Christ's birth and the wounds He bore for them. In the midst of the darkness, He was the light of the world.

The elder read the story of Christ's birth before the trombone choir, with four voices of the instrument blending together, played another song. In the dim light, Susanna looked up. When she found Christian's face among the married men, he was looking her way.

As he mouthed the words again that he loved her, wax dripped onto her finger and she flinched. Even as the light in her hand flickered, the blaze inside her seemed to roar.

Those around her began blowing out their candles, but she held her light firmly in her hands.

"I love you," she whispered back this time, and his face seemed to light up like his candle.

* * * * *

"Christ came to this earth as a child in order to die for our sins," the elder read. "As a baby, He was predestined to suffer and die, and He did it for each of us."

As Christian listened to the words, he wondered if somehow Catharine had been destined, as well, to suffer and die. Perhaps Susanna was right; perhaps it was all right to question why God did certain things. In the questioning, their faith could grow.

He had so much to learn from the Brethren around him, from the Indians, and, most of all, from his wife. His gaze wandered back across the room and he found his Susanna's beautiful face again, her eyes closed as they worshipped their Savior in song. He loved that Susanna questioned him and questioned God. In the questioning, he prayed that God would bring them even closer together.

Seated on the bench next to Susanna, Rebecca held the Schmidts' child, and the girl was content in her arms. When they found out about Catharine's death, he worried that God would require him to raise this child as his own, as a reminder of his sin and perhaps how God used his weakness for good. But the lot had entrusted her care to Joseph and Rebecca.

Their Gnadenhutten friends were still among them, but he sensed their restlessness to return to the wilderness, to a place where they could worship their Savior in the midst of His creation. He understood their restlessness because he felt it as well. Here in Bethlehem it was safe—as secure a place as they could find without relocating to Philadelphia. Their days were perfectly ordered, and he had been assigned to help teach at the boys' school until the fighting subsided.

Like their Indian friends, he longed for the wilderness as well, to be with Chief Langoma and his people, to help them stay strong against those who insisted they fight. The day he and Susanna had spent with them was just a taste of what he wanted to do. He wanted to teach and baptize, and as he grew in his own faith, he wanted to lead them as well. Together, he and Susanna could learn and teach and serve the Indians who wanted to follow their Savior.

And he loved the idea of them doing this together.

David began to play and Christian joined the singing, rejoicing with the angels in Christ's birth in Bethlehem; when the service ended, he filed toward the door with the other men. David stopped him.

"Merry Christmas to you, my friend."

"And a merry Christmas to you."

David put his hand on Christian's shoulder, whispering, "When was the last time you and your lovely wife were alone?"

The question stunned Christian for a moment, and then he thought back to the tangled weeds in the forest. "We paddled a canoe together to Tanochtahe."

David's eyes twinkled. "That's not what I meant."

Christian knew what the man meant, but he wasn't going to tell him about their time along the river. And he was too embarrassed to say that their last time in the bedchamber had been back in April when he returned from his mission.

He cleared his throat. "It's been a long time."

David grinned again. "That's what I thought."

David slipped something into Christian's hand, and he looked down at a clunky iron key. He clasped his fingers around it.

Several brothers remained in the Saal, so Christian whispered, "The bedchamber?"

David shook his head and pointed to the ceiling. "The attic."

Christian glanced down at the key again.

David put his hand on Christian's shoulder, leaning toward him. "There happens to be a bed up there."

"How would you know?"

David threw both hands into the air. "Just a rumor I've heard."

Christian clenched the key in his palm. It had been so long since he and Susanna were together in a bedchamber, and even then they had never really been together. Was it possible that they could really steal away, in a place without rattlesnakes or threatening Indians or even babies to care for? If he went, would Susanna join him?

Leaning back against the wall, he thought of their time together along the river, her timidity along with her willingness to love him. Perhaps she would meet him.

"I can't get Susanna from her dormitory."

"You don't have to," David said. "She's waiting for you."

Christian took a step toward the door, and then he turned and clapped his friend on the shoulder. "Thank you."

"It was Marie's idea."

He turned again toward the door, but this time David stopped him. And then he pointed to the front of the building. "The stairs are over there."

* * * * *

Susanna waited by a locked door in the attic, clutching a candleholder with one of the ribboned tallow candles from the love feast. The flame trembled in sync with her hands as she waited for her husband.

She leaned back against the door. Marie didn't tell her why Christian had requested her presence in this forgotten hallway, and it worried her. Did he want to speak with her again, or did he—was it possible that he wanted something else from her?

The flames danced with her breath, the memory of their time

on the Lehigh as sweet as the taste of tonight's rolls. Their time at the river was before their mostly tidy world seemed to crash down around them, before sorrow soured their bellies like bitter herbs.

Tonight was a taste of the sweet and the sorrow alike, of the joy of their Savior's birth even with the knowledge of the suffering that lay ahead for Him. She hadn't thought she would be able to celebrate the birth of their Savior tonight, but the beauty of the singing, the taste of the sweet buns and coffee, reminded her that God defeated the enemy and that love would ultimately win. Somehow it was possible for the grief and love to coexist, even for love to thrive in the midst of the pain.

More than a year and a half had passed since she had wed Christian at Marienborn. A year and a half of desire and heartache. Bitterness and forgiveness. A year and a half of pursuing hope and healing wounds.

In the past months, she and Christian had become one in spirit and mind, protecting the refugee families and Nathan. They had also shared their desire to demonstrate Christ's love and forgiveness, the forgiveness that had changed their lives, to the Indians.

Perhaps—her skin tingled at the thought—perhaps it was time to become one in body as well.

Footsteps echoed up the stairway, and she heard Christian call her name. He was beside her then, the candle dancing between them. He opened his hand. "David gave me the key."

Her heart raced at his words, but he didn't reach to unlock the door. He waited for her.

"Open it," she whispered, and he slid the key into the lock and jostled it until it opened.

The candlelight revealed an array of steamer trunks lined up under the slope of a low ceiling and dried bouquets of herbs hanging suspended from the ceiling. Moonlight stole through a small window on the far side of the room, wandering over the trunks and herbs to the bed on the left side of the room. A bed big enough for two.

A sharp breath of air rushed into Susanna's lungs, and in her fear, she felt Christian pull away from her and step back toward the open doorway. "We can leave," he said.

He thought he had failed her, but she had failed him. Even after he'd told her the truth about Catharine, she hadn't been a wife to him.

"Christian," she began—and then, not knowing how to explain her feelings or the desire swelling inside her, she reached for the door and closed it behind them. Then she bolted it.

Christian took the candle from her hands and walked it over to the washstand beside the bed. Then he returned for her, lifting her up onto the bed. She sank into the feathers.

Sitting up, she searched Christian's face in the shadows, and then she glanced toward the door, worried that someone would interrupt their stolen time together. "How long do we have?"

Christian slowly reached up and untied the ribbons that hid her hair from him. He tossed her haube onto the floor. "All night."

He removed the pins that held her hair, and it cascaded over her shoulders and down her back. He gently weaved his fingers through it.

No one would knock on their door. No one would tell them they must return to their separate living places. She and Christian could be together for the entire night.

"You are beautiful," he said.

"Only because it's dark."

"No, Susanna." He put his fingers to her lips, hushing her nervous protest. "You are beautiful."

Fire raced inside her at his words, and more than anything she'd ever wanted in her life, she wanted him to take her in his arms and make her his wife.

But he didn't take her in his arms. Instead he stood and moved to the washstand, taking the cloth beside the washbasin. He dipped the cloth into the basin and water pattered softly into the basin as he wrung out the cloth.

When he returned, he knelt in front of her and slowly unrolled her stockings, over her knees and down her calves and over her toes. With the cloth, warmed in his hands, he washed her legs and her feet.

The touch of the cloth on her skin, the way her husband watched her in her pleasure, made her feel the desire of his own love. And she reveled in it.

"Thou hast ravished my heart," he said, the words from the Song of Solomon.

"My heart is yours," she whispered. "I'm not scared anymore."

His eyes were intent on her when he slowly moved forward. The heat from his lips shot through her body, warming her breasts, her toes. Then he blew out the candle, and she welcomed him to her.

* * * * *

Neither the organ music rattling the trunks at first light nor any hunger for breakfast provoked Brother and Sister Boehler to leave their haven. The only longing they had was for each other, and very early on that Christmas morning, they savored the love the Savior had given them, sweeter than Susanna had ever imagined, from a beginning she thought impossible to overcome.

But Christian Boehler was her husband, and in the sprinkling of morning light, regret no longer filled his eyes.

She smiled as she rested her head on the fleece of his chest.

"For the rest of my life," he whispered as he ran his fingers through her hair, "I want to wake up on Christmas morning with you in my arms."

The love of their Savior had replaced his regret and replaced her fears. It forgave them both of their weaknesses and it brought them together as husband and wife.

Epilogue
....

July 1757

Christian and Nathan slept soundly on each side of Susanna as the summer sun stole around the curtain covering the hut's doorway. She shooed a gnat off Nathan's face and then stood before she pulled her short-sleeved buckskin dress over her shift. When she opened the curtain, morning air greeted her like the light flutter of a kiss, and her bare feet padded softly through the grass, toward the river that ran below the village.

Sitting on a rock, Susanna dipped her hands in the water and rinsed her face and the bare skin on her legs and arms. Her Indian brothers and sisters would awaken soon and eat their morning fare of cittamum and berries as they prepared for today's harvesting of corn. But before she joined the wonderful busyness of their harvest, she relished her daily ritual of cleansing and quiet minutes alone with the Savior.

It was hard to believe that almost two years had passed since she and Christian had paddled back up the Lehigh River to Tanochtahe. French and British and many of the Indians continued to war around them, massacring white men and burning houses, but the Christian Indians remained safe in Tanochtahe. Even though months had passed since they'd received news from the Brethren in Bethlehem and Nazareth, the last she had heard they were safe as well, and she quietly thanked the Savior for it.

Because of the earth's shaking almost two years ago and

because of the awe-filled account of God's salvation that had rippled through the tribes—many came to know Christ, and their new Brethren flooded this village in the midst of the turmoil. The elders in Bethlehem had sent Christian and Susanna to Tanochtahe indefinitely as messengers, along with the Gnadenhutten Indians who had relocated from Bethlehem to this village after the massacre. She hadn't seen Howling Wolf or Lily again, but she had heard stories. Howling Wolf's band of warriors may not have been willing to follow God, but they certainly feared Him.

She stood on her toes and pulled down a tree limb. Reaching high, she pulled off a reddish fruit that was about as large as a plum. *Estachioni*, the Indians called it. As far as she knew, there was no English name for the fruit. The tree limb whipped up into the air at her release, and when she took a bite of the fruit, her mouth filled with the tart sweetness of juice. She leaned back against the tree to savor it.

She and Christian felt at home here in Tanochtahe. He loved his work as messenger of the Gospel and servant to the Indian people. She loved living among the women and children and being constantly delighted by the joys in the wilderness around them. And with Chief Langoma's blessing, they both were enjoying their role as parent to Nathan.

The leaves and grass rustled across the river, and she smiled as she took her last bite, waiting for the morning entrance of deer that drank along its shores. But when the heads of the beautiful animals didn't appear through the trees, her smile fell and her instincts sharpened. She scanned the tall grasses and logs along the bank until the leaves rustled again.

"Who's there?" she said in the Delaware language.

A crown of dark hair slowly appeared through the leaves as an Indian stepped into the sunlight. Startled, Susanna hopped backward and scanned the trees again to see who the Indian was with, but no one else appeared.

The Indian was a woman not much older than her, and her heart leapt, thinking perhaps it might be Lily coming home. But as the woman drew closer, Susanna realized that this woman was taller than Lily. There was more cream mixed with the tans of her skin, and the slight smile on her lips was one of nervousness, not familiarity.

The woman slipped off her moccasins and easily stepped across the wide rocks that bridged the river. When she stepped into the water a few feet from Susanna, the gentle rapids lapping over her ankles, Susanna spoke softly to her in the Delaware language.

"My name is Lasuwin," she said. Christian wanted her to be known among the Delaware as "Music." For the songs, he said, that poured out of her mouth.

The woman's smile widened. "Lasuwin," she repeated. She hesitated, glancing up and down the river before she turned back to Susanna. Then in perfect English, she whispered, "I am glad to make your acquaintance."

Susanna's eyes widened. "You speak English?"

She nodded. "I am searching for the messengers from Bethlehem."

Susanna studied the woman for a moment and then directed her up the hill, toward the village. Usually the Indians seeking more information about the Christ Child came to Tanochtahe in groups, but as she trailed the woman up the hill, Susanna knew the Savior had brought her to them. She only wondered why she was alone.

Small fires were burning around the village huts, both for cooking and to chase the gnats away, and several of her Indian friends looked up with curiosity at the newcomer and nodded at her in greeting. Susanna stopped the woman before her and Christian's hut, and she whispered for her to wait.

"Mama!" Nathan exclaimed as she slipped inside. Susanna

reached out her arms for the boy who would too quickly pass into manhood.

As Nathan hugged her, Christian rolled over and edged up onto his elbows, his gaze examining her like he hadn't seen her hours ago. "You are beautiful," he whispered.

She blushed, and for a moment, she forgot about the woman waiting outside and the waking village around them. Back in Nazareth, she had never thought Christian would look upon her as a loving husband did his wife, and now whenever he did, it made her heart flutter. And her cheeks warm with the pleasure of it.

"Come." She motioned toward the curtain. "We have company."

She fanned her face as she returned to the Indian woman with Christian at her side.

"This is my husband, Gachtatam."

"Leader?" the woman asked.

"No—" Christian shook his head. He still got embarrassed when someone questioned the meaning of his name, but Chief Langoma had insisted on *Gachtatam*. And Christian had finally relented.

Christian stepped closer to the woman, and Susanna watched him squint in the growing light. "I know you," he said simply.

The woman's gaze dropped, and her bare toes slowly made an arch in the dirt.

"You wanted to follow the Savior," Christian continued. "You wanted to, but you couldn't."

The woman looked up at Susanna and then at Christian. "I was too afraid."

"Mary?" Christian questioned. "Your name is Mary, isn't it?"

She nodded.

"Your people—they were going to harm you if you chose to follow our Savior."

Susanna reached out and took Christian's hand, worried that he would frighten Mary. She squeezed his hand gently to quiet him.

"I was afraid before," she whispered. "And still I am afraid, but your Savior—He is a God of love and peace and forgiveness. I want to be baptized."

Susanna's heart thrilled at the honesty of the woman's words, at her choice to follow Christ in spite of the threat of persecution.

Sadness crept back onto the woman's face. "Am I too late?"

Christian shook his head. "You will never regret this decision. We can baptize you today."

The smile returned. "I will go to the river, but first—"

Mary hesitated again, looking into the trees like she had at the river.

"Before I am baptized, there is a story I must tell you."

Susanna opened the curtain and Nathan raced outside to play among his many friends. Susanna and Christian sat on one side of the small hut while Mary sat on the bench across from them. And she told them the story of the English captive who had shown her the forgiveness of their Savior.

About the Author

....

 Melanie Dobson is the award-winning author of nine historical and contemporary novels, including *Love Finds You in Amana, Iowa*, *Love Finds You in Homestead, Iowa*, and *The Silent Order*. *Love Finds You in Liberty, Indiana* was chosen as the Best Book of Indiana (fiction) in 2010, and her suspense novel *The Black Cloister* received the Foreword Book of the Year award in 2009 for religious fiction.

Melanie is the former corporate publicity manager at Focus on the Family, and she worked in public relations for fifteen years before she began writing fiction full-time. She spent her high school years living in Iowa where she became intrigued by the Amana Colonies and Amana people, and she now resides with her family near Portland, Oregon.

MELANIEDOBSON.COM

Author's Note
....

The writing of this story was a personal journey for me. My ancestors joined the Unity of the Brethren (later known as the Moravians) in the 1750s, so my travels to Bethlehem and Nazareth were an opportunity for me to research my family's heritage along with researching this novel. As I read about the custom of marrying by lot, I stumbled upon an entry with the names of my fifth great-grandparents, Johann Beroth and Catharina Neumann. The entry said they married by lot in Bethlehem on July 29, 1758. They were married for fifty-eight years.

I don't know if my great-grandparents knew each other before they married, and as I read pieces of their story, I wondered if they were excited to marry or if either of them dreaded their wedding day. I—along with my father and my grandfather and my siblings— are certainly grateful the lot brought them together.

In my great-grandmother's short memoir, she writes of counting the cost before joining the Unity. She knew there would be hardships and yet she felt the draw of the Savior to join the Moravian people in Bethlehem and said she was "serene and satisfied" in her decision even as her family sent a cart and men to carry her away. She refused to leave the Brethren and remained as part of the congregation until her death in 1819.

While *Love Finds You in Nazareth, Pennsylvania* is fiction, I have tried to record and reflect a small but significant slice of the Moravian's vast heritage. The General Economy as well as the separate choirs for families lasted for almost twenty years, another decade after the conclusion of this book. After 1764, husband and wives began sharing households and children often lived with their parents, but even today, when a Moravian goes home to the Savior, they can request to be buried with their choir in God's Acre.

The Moravians continued to marry by lot until 1818 when a devout Moravian man insisted on marrying a woman the lot refused him. He left the church to marry but later he and his wife rejoined, and after that, marriages began to be arranged by families instead of by the lot.

The settlement known as Gnadenhutten (Shelters of Grace) grew to five hundred Moravian Indians and sixteen missionaries until hostile Indians attacked this settlement on November 24, 1755, in an attempt to drive the Indian converts back to their native society. Ten Moravian missionaries and a baby lost their lives in this massacre. A Moravian missionary named Susanna Nitschmann was captured by the attackers, and she died several months later in captivity. Susanne Partsch jumped out of a window that night and hid in a hollow tree by the river until soldiers found her. Miraculously, her husband also survived the attack.

The earth in Pennsylvania shook on November 18, 1755. Beds shook and doors flew open, a foreshadowing, perhaps, of God's grief at the tragic loss of the Indians and missionaries at Gnadenhutten. After the Gnadenhutten tragedy, the Nursery children were relocated from Nazareth to Bethlehem on the first of December.

In spite of devastation across the Lehigh Valley during the French and Indian War, the communities of Bethlehem and Nazareth were never attacked. Nazareth became a safe haven for refugees during this war, as the Moravians sheltered hundreds of people every day as these refugees fled hostile Indians. The Disciple's House, known now as the Manor House, still stands in Nazareth, though both Count

Zinzendorf and his wife went home to the Savior before they were able to live in the house.

Many Moravian women wrote of their reluctance to marry when they received the call to wed through the lot, and yet many of the same women later described terrible grief over losing their husbands. It seems their love for their spouses blossomed within marriage instead of before.

Maria Reitzenbach wrote, "I must admit that I found it indescribably hard to take this step…. Only the thought that it was my duty to do everything for the love of my dear Saviour who had forgiven me my sins and had taken me into a state of grace made me give myself up to this."

Later, Maria wrote, "I was made a widow by the calling home of my dear husband, after we had lived in marriage for twenty-two years happy and content and had shared joy and pain and had been a comfort and a cheer to each other. For this reason I felt his loss very painfully and no one could comfort me but *the* Friend to whom I had often told all my troubles and with whom I alone took refuge" (*Moravian Women's Memoirs*, translated by Katherine Faull).

Moravians continued their mission work to the Indians after the French and Indian War and the Revolutionary War, but another massacre at a Moravian Indian settlement during the Revolutionary War made the resentment and suspicion of white men and their faith difficult for Native Americans in the late eighteenth-century to overcome.

Hundreds of Moravian missionaries have died on the mission field since they began sharing the good news in 1732, but the Moravian church continues to grow and thrive around the world today. As a result of their continued mission work, Moravians are spread out across five continents to often-forgotten places like Suriname, on the north shore of South America, and Tanzania in East Africa, where there are more than 400,000 Moravians.

I have tried to make this novel as factually accurate as possible through interviews and the reading of multiple history books, along with personal journals and town diaries. Some of the facts were changed for the sake of the story, including the date of completion for the Disciple's House (dedicated in November 1756) and the addition of both a Sisters House and a Gemeinhaus to early Nazareth. In the mid-1750s, the Brethren would have worshipped in the Saal at the Nursery, and until the Sisters House was built, the married women lived on the third floor of the Nursery. Also, the Moravians capitalized names like Laborer, Diener, and Sister on all occasions.

I'm so grateful for each person who helped me research this novel and encouraged me through the writing of it. A special thank you to:

My Summerside publishing family—Carlton Garborg, Rachel Meisel, Ellen Tarver, Jason Rovenstine, Suzi McDonough, and Connie Troyer. Thank you for your excellent work in editing and distributing the Love Finds You books. I love working with each of you!

Lyn Beroth—your passion for our family's legacy inspired this story. Thank you for your dedication to uncover the stories of those who have traveled this road of life before us.

Lanie Graf, Barbara Dietterich, Wendy Weida, and Sarah Hriniak—thank you for sharing your heritage with me and for your grace in answering my many questions about the Moravian history. Any errors are my fault.

Virginia at the lovely Morningstar Inn in Bethlehem and Paul and Laura at the historic Lafayette Inn in Easton—thank you for your hospitality.

Sandra Bishop, Michele Heath, Kimberly Felton, Leslie Gould, and Kelly Chang—your honesty and encouragement both strengthen and sharpen me. Thank you for partnering with me in the writing of this manuscript.

Pinn Crawford—it seems there is no book you can't find, no matter how old or how long out of print. You're amazing.

To friends and family who cheered me on as I wrote this book and who prayed for me and my family during the harder moments. Jim Beroth, Christina Nunn, Carolyn Dobson, Jodi Stilp, Allison Owen, and Tosha Williams—I'm so blessed to have each of you in my life.

Karly and Kiki—not only do your smiles fill my heart with joy, but you inspire me every day with your persistence and your enthusiasm. I love being your mom.

Jon—I'm grateful beyond words that God brought us together fourteen years ago. It's a joy to be on this journey with you!

And to the Lord Jesus Christ, our Savior, who is the same yesterday, today, and forever. Religious traditions may change over the years, but the love and grace of our Lord remains the same.

Melanie Beroth Dobson
melaniedobson.com

POST CARD
CARTE POSTALE
Love Finds You

Want a peek into local American life—past and present?
The *Love Finds You*™ series published by Summerside Press
features real towns and combines travel, romance,
and faith in one irresistible package!

The novels in the series—uniquely titled after American towns with romantic or intriguing names—inspire romance and fun. Each fictional story draws on the compelling history or the unique character of a real place. Stories center on romances kindled in small towns, old loves lost and found again on the high plains, and new loves discovered at exciting vacation getaways. Summerside Press plans to publish at least one novel set in each of the fifty states. Be sure to catch them all!

Now Available

Love Finds You in Miracle, Kentucky
by Andrea Boeshaar
ISBN: 978-1-934770-37-5

*Love Finds You in Snowball,
Arkansas*
by Sandra D. Bricker
ISBN: 978-1-934770-45-0

Love Finds You in Romeo, Colorado
by Gwen Ford Faulkenberry
ISBN: 978-1-934770-46-7

*Love Finds You in Valentine,
Nebraska*
by Irene Brand
ISBN: 978-1-934770-38-2

Love Finds You in Humble, Texas
by Anita Higman
ISBN: 978-1-934770-61-0

*Love Finds You
in Last Chance, California*
by Miralee Ferrell
ISBN: 978-1-934770-39-9

*Love Finds You in
Maiden, North Carolina*
by Tamela Hancock Murray
ISBN: 978-1-934770-65-8

*Love Finds You
in Paradise, Pennsylvania*
by Loree Lough
ISBN: 978-1-934770-66-5

*Love Finds You in
Treasure Island, Florida*
by Debby Mayne
ISBN: 978-1-934770-80-1

*Love Finds You
in Liberty, Indiana*
by Melanie Dobson
ISBN: 978-1-934770-74-0

*Love Finds You in
Revenge, Ohio*
by Lisa Harris
ISBN: 978-1-934770-81-8

Love Finds You in
Tombstone, Arizona
by Miralee Ferrell
ISBN: 978-1-60936-104-4

Love Finds You in
Martha's Vineyard, Massachusetts
by Melody Carlson
ISBN: 978-1-60936-110-5

Love Finds You in
Prince Edward Island, Canada
by Susan Page Davis
ISBN: 978-1-60936-109-9

Love Finds You in Groom, Texas
by Janice Hanna
ISBN: 978-1-60936-006-1

Love Finds You in Amana, Iowa
by Melanie Dobson
ISBN: 978-1-60936-135-8

Love Finds You in
Lancaster County, Pennsylvania
by Annalisa Daughety
ISBN: 978-1-60936-212-6

Love Finds You in Branson, Missouri
by Gwen Ford Faulkenberry
ISBN: 978-1-60936-191-4

Love Finds You in
Sundance, Wyoming
by Miralee Ferrell
ISBN: 978-1-60936-277-5

Love Finds You in
Sunset Beach, Hawaii
by Robin Jones Gunn
ISBN: 978-1-60936-028-3

Coming Soon

Love Finds You in
Annapolis, Maryland
by Roseanna M. White
ISBN: 978-1-60936-313-0

Love Finds You in
Folly Beach, South Carolina
by Loree Lough
ISBN: 97-8-160936-214-0

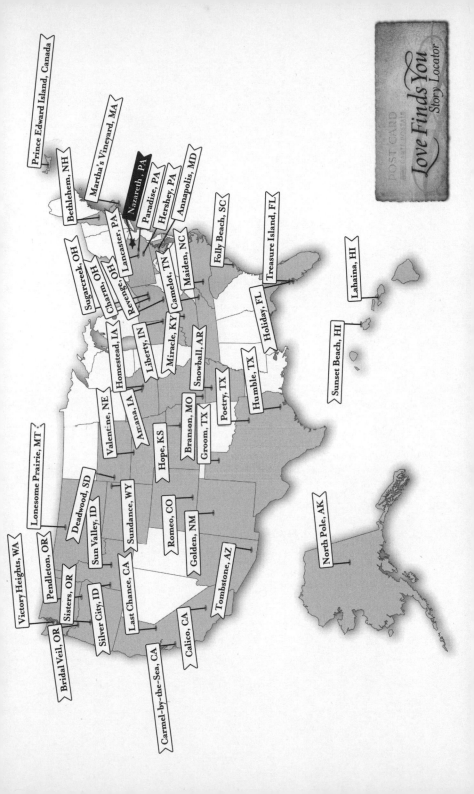